Forbi

Kim—

Thank you so much as always for being there for me to vent to, talk ish to & give me support. I'm so happy for your promotion, but so sad you're leaving me. I can't have a new front desk boo. Lol — Hope you enjoy — though I know you will.

Tiff

Forbidden Distractions

T.C. Flenoid

Forbidden Distractions ©2018

All rights reserved. No part of this book may be reproduced in any form or by any means without prior consent of the owner, excepting brief quotes used in interviews.

This is a work of fiction. Any references or similarities to actual events or real people, living or dead, is entirely coincidental.

First in print: February 2018
Cover Design: BHill

ISBN-13: 978-1983999369

If you can relate to Erykah Badu,
Next Lifetime, this is for you.

Acknowledgements

Lord I first thank You for your blessings, for the people who love me, and the gift you've given me and allowed me to share. My heartbeats, my babies, Keion, Elijah, and Trinity, you are who I work so hard for each and every day. I pray, above all else, that I make you proud. Karon and my mama, thank you both for your continuing love and support. I can't express what it means to have you two in my corner. Bria, thank you for the DOPE cover. It's exactly what I envisioned. And my family, no matter how far away we are, I LOVE Y'ALL! I gotta thank my girls, Shonda, Farren, Jeek, Jessica and Kim for the conversations, the laughs, and the friendship. Love y'all! Special thanks to my proofreaders, Shonda, Farren and my mama. No yes men over here, y'all definitely didn't let ANYTHING slide! This past year definitely had some horrible moments and I wanna thank everyone who prayed for me and my family. As always, to anyone I left out, anyone who believes in me and supports me, I appreciate it! THANK YOU! Four down, countless more to go!!

2 Chronicles 15:7- But as for you, be strong and do not give up, for your work will be rewarded.

NO ONE EVER MADE IT BY GIVING UP! GRIND, WORK HARD, STAY PRAYED UP, AND YOU'LL SEE YOUR DREAMS BECOME REALITY!

forbidden distractions   *t.c.flenoid*

Ch. 1

Jewell worked feverishly to cover the old bruise on her face. It had been six years since she had seen or talked to Xavier, and she wanted to make a good impression, not scare him away. She knew when she saw the friend request on Facebook that she was in trouble. Even though it had been so many years, her heart skipped a beat when she saw his face- that same sexy, dimpled face.

    She had scrolled down his page and grunted to herself when she read his profile: RELATIONSHIP STATUS- MARRIED. She knew his wife, *Deena*. They had all gone to high school together. Deena was quiet, shy, reserved... Not Xavier's type at all, or so Jewell had thought. She also saw that he'd opened the car shop he had always talked about. She smiled, remembering how he was always messing around with his and everybody else's cars. The number to the shop was listed on his page and Jewell drummed her fingers until she finally made up her mind to call. She bit her lip nervously, listening to the phone ring, contemplating hanging up.

"Black's Auto Body and Detail," a young guy answered. Jewell took a deep breath and went for it.

"Is Xavier Black available?" she asked, halfway hoping that he wasn't.

"Just a minute," the guy replied. Jewell was kicking herself as she waited. She had absolutely no idea what she was going to say to Xavier after ditching him all those years back. How would she explain herself? What would she-

"Xavier Black speaking." The authority in his voice caught Jewell off guard and she temporarily lost her train of thought. "This is Xavier?" he spoke again.

"How are you, Zay?" There was a pause on the other end that made her nervous.

"Jewell?" he asked, making her heart nearly jump out of her chest. Was that hope she heard, or was she trippin'? Did he recognize her voice? Did no one else call him Zay? Did he just put two and two together since he had just sent her a friend request?

"Yea, it's me." She tried, unsuccessfully, to sound nonchalant.

"Hey! How have you been?" he asked.

"I've been good," she lied. "What about you?"

"I'm blessed. Can't complain." Jewell sighed softly. It wasn't that she necessarily *wanted* his marriage to be in shambles, she just still couldn't get past the idea of him with *Deena*. He was outgoing, spontaneous, hood when he needed to be, outspoken, funny... and Deena just... wasn't. Sure she'd heard the cliche', opposites attract, but *damn*.

"I know I'm late, but congratulations on the wedding and the baby and the business." She rolled her eyes as soon as the words came out, feeling like she sounded stupid. "Looks like you're doing well for yourself."

"Thank you. A *lot* has happened since we last talked." Jewell thought she sensed a hint of irritation in his voice, but she pushed it away. It must've been in her head. He couldn't possibly still be holding that against her, could he? "As a matter of fact, I'm free if you wanna stop by and see the shop today." Maybe Jewell was overanalyzing things as she had a tendency to do, but she could've sworn it sounded like he was flirting. It didn't take much coaxing for her to agree. She was nervous as hell to see him after so long. She tried to calm herself while she got ready by reminiscing almost ten years back to high school.

By senior year, everybody about knew everybody at Parkway North High School. Jewell and Xavier had been hanging with the same group of kids for the past couple of years, but had never really spoken one on one. To Jewell,

Xavier had the prettiest eyes and smile and there was some mystery about him that was intriguing to her. Her shyness around guys wouldn't dare allow her to approach him, though. On top of that, females were drawn to his charisma like a magnet, and Jewell didn't feel like dealing with the competition and drama.

    Over Christmas break that year, Jewell and some friends were at The Palace skating rink. They'd had a few coolers and Jewell was feeling herself. That was the only reason she had the courage to speak to Xavier when she spotted him. He had on a green Polo shirt with khaki's and Timberland boots and was looking good as hell. She waited until he was by himself getting a drink before she sauntered over to him like he was already her man.

    "Hey, Xavier." She tried to sound sexy. He turned around and she could tell that he was impressed. He looked her up and down and grinned. She tried not to blush because she knew she was on point. She was thick in all the right places with her red, Aeropostale sweater fitting snugly over her 34D's, and jeans that hugged her healthy waist and hips with no mercy. She had curled her micros and pinned them up, letting a few fall around her deep, caramel face.

    "Wassup, Jewell?" he asked.

    "Nothin'. Saw you over here and decided to come speak." Xavier nodded and they both stood in awkward silence, waiting. The coolers had gone to Jewell's underaged head, and she figured she and Xavier had been a long time coming. "You gon' give me your number so we can talk, you know, outside of school?"

"Naw," he answered flat out. Jewell was about to giggle, before she noticed the serious look on his face.

"Are you for real?" she asked.

"Yea, I'm for real. You see me every day at school and don't say nothin' to me." Jewell stood there dumbfounded as she watched Xavier walk away. She was beyond embarrassed, even though no one was paying enough attention to see her jaw hit the floor. Back with his friends, Xavier seemed to act like nothing had happened. He had his damn nerve, cocky ass! Instead of storming over to him and giving him a piece of her mind like she wanted to, Jewell chucked it up as a loss. Close to the end of the night, she felt a tap on her shoulder. She turned away from her cousins and couldn't help but smile. There was Xavier, smiling in her face.

"Had to make you sweat a lil' bit," he said as he handed her his number.

"Sweat? Boy please." Jewell rolled her eyes, even though she was doing summersaults on the inside.

"You better hold on to that. That's gold," he joked before he winked and walked away.

Jewell shook her head and laughed to herself as she headed towards the door. That had been the beginning of one of the best friendships she'd ever had. Her heart was beating double time as she pulled up to the car shop. It was only a fifteen minute drive from her house and it dawned on her that she'd seen it a couple of times before. The sign gave her a warm smile, *Black's Auto Body and Detail Shop*. Never in a million years would she have assumed that it was *Xavier* Black's shop.

    She exhaled as she parked and checked her makeup, making sure the bruise above her eye couldn't be seen. She braced herself as she walked in. The door buzzed when she entered, causing the workers to glance up. She noticed the way their eyes bugged out at her in her skinny jeans and thigh high boots. She unzipped her coat and straightened her burnt orange, cowl neck sweater, trying to get rid of the butterflies in her stomach. Pushing her shoulder length curls out of her face, she scanned the room. A handsome young man approached her with a mischievous grin on his face.

    "How can I help you today?" She gave him a half smile. He was working man dirty, which was actually kinda cute, but she was looking for one man in particular.

    "Is Xavier Black in?" It came out almost as a whisper.

    "Aw man," he joked. "Just a minute, I'll get him for you." He turned away from her and Jewell felt like she was about to start sweating. She grabbed at her sweater and pulled it away from her neck, trying not to pass out. What the hell was wrong with her?! It was just *Xavier*! *Xavier* who she had fallen for years ago. *Xavier* who should've been her man. *Xavier* who she had thought about so often over the years... It felt like it had been an eternity since she had gotten pregnant and ended their homie-lover-friend relationship by simply refusing his calls.

"Jewell?" She spun around at the sound of his voice and her heart almost stopped. It was Zay like she remembered him, only he'd matured, and had a grown man, boss swag about him that was hard to ignore. His midnight blue button down and grey slacks would've looked nice on another man, but on *Zay*... they looked like they were made to be peeled off.

Jewell tried her best to clear her mind as he descended the steps from his second floor office. Once he made it to the main level, they didn't hesitate, they didn't speak, they simply embraced. The ancient fire between them ignited automatically, and for a moment, Jewell thought she'd never let him go. He smelled so good and his body was so hard and warm against hers. Only the whispers around them broke their concentration, causing Xavier to lead Jewell up the stairs.

"Sorry about my nosy employees," he said after they were behind his office doors. "Has it really been *six* years?" he asked. Jewell nodded her head, unable to look at him.

"A little longer than that. My daughter just turned six." She remembered being heartbroken when she'd found out she was pregnant. She and Xavier had never had sex so there was no way it could possibly be his baby, and he didn't act any differently towards her. He still treated her like he always had, but that was the problem. She wanted him to treat her like his one and only, not his best friend. After four years of tiptoeing over, under and around their feelings, Jewell was devastated to call it quits. It hurt so bad to have to let go of him. He had crossed her mind plenty of times, but she never thought that seeing him would stir up so much emotion in her.

"I tried calling your mom's a couple years back, just on a whim," he told her.

"You know what, I remember her telling me you called. I was real close to getting your number from her, but that woulda started something." As soon as it came out, Jewell wished she could take it back. When she looked over at Xavier, he was nodding his head. "Don't laugh, but I actually called your old job looking for you," Jewell admitted. Instead of laughing, Xavier leaned against his desk beside Jewell and put his arm around her.

"Aww, you been lookin' for me?" he asked. Their closeness, his hand on her shoulder, the contact, it all made Jewell's heart race. She opened her mouth to talk, but nervous excitement stopped her. Finally, Xavier moved his hand. When he did, he cleared his throat. Jewell sensed a little nervousness on his end too, and laughed.

"What?" he asked.

"It's just weird sitting here talking to you after all this time."

"Just a little." The two of them laughed, joked, and caught up on old times. It was like the years that they weren't in touch had simply dissipated.

"It's almost time for me to pick up Alicia from school." Jewell said, glancing at her watch. She couldn't hide her disappointment. It had been forever since she'd laid eyes on Xavier, and all she had gotten was a few measly minutes of his time.

"Yea, and I guess I need to get back to this paperwork," Xavier replied. He pulled Jewell close to him and she felt the heat again, though she tried to ignore it. She wanted to rub her hands across his back and brush her lips on his neck. Then she remembered the ring on his finger, and backed away abruptly.

"We have each other's numbers now so we're gonna keep in touch, right?" Xavier asked. Jewell nodded.

"Definitely." She smiled at Xavier and he walked her down to the front door, hugging her one last time before she left. He turned back into the shop and all eyes were on him.

"What?!" he laughed. "Y'all fools get back to work!!"

Ch. 2

Xavier could barely focus as he climbed the stairs to his office. *Jewell*. Her eyes, her smile, her skin, the way she hugged him... he hadn't wanted her to leave. If it wasn't for the fact that she was married, he would've at least held her a little longer, caressed her back, tasted her full lips...

He sighed as he twirled his own wedding band and shook his head- job number two, he called it. As he sat there at his desk, he thought about the look on Jewell's face when they locked eyes. She was still so gorgeous, and her smile was beautiful as ever. He picked up his phone and dialed her number.

"Hello?" she answered. Her voice made him grin.

"Fifteen minutes," he told her.

"What happened?" she asked, sounding concerned.

"Fifteen minutes with you made my day. Hell, it

made my week."

"Whatever, Zay," Jewell sighed, even though she was smiling from ear to ear.

"I'm serious. I do so much in one day. It was refreshing to be able to relax with you. I miss that." There was a pause and Jewell almost started stuttering trying to figure out what to say. "What happened to us?" he asked. Jewell took a deep breath before answering.

"You know we talked about any and everything under the sun, right? You knew everything about me and Brian and I knew everything about you and all the girls you talked to-"

"Aw wait a minute," he cut her off. "I'm not even gonna get on Brian because that's your husband now, but I was only talkin' to maybe two or three-"

"Maybe four or five," she laughed, avoiding his comment about Brian. "Honestly, I had really started feelin' you. You know we messed around a lil' bit, but we basically just hung out. I started to want more than that. Then I ended up getting pregnant." She absolutely loved her daughter, but at that time, that was the last thing she needed. Xavier nodded his head, remembering how crushed he'd been when Jewell broke the news to him. He had assumed that eventually she'd have to get tired of Brian and he'd just slide on in. He didn't bet on Jewell getting pregnant.

"Why didn't you tell me how you felt?" he asked,

realizing they'd talked about everything except their feelings for each other. It was sort of unspoken knowledge. *Hell why didn't I tell her how I felt?* Xavier shook his head at himself.

"I didn't expect you to drop those other girls for me."

"Why not? They didn't mean shit." Xavier tried to push the what-ifs from his mind, but they weren't going anywhere anytime soon. Back then, he'd tried to respect Jewell's relationship, even though the dude was 100% asshole. Between Brian's name calling and disappearing acts, Xavier became Jewell's shoulder to cry on. Sure, there'd been a few times they had slipped up, a little kiss here and there, but it was always made painfully clear that she was with Brian. She tried her best to be faithful, and he tried his best to honor that. They had never had sex, but they'd been close. If Xavier had known for a fact that Jewell wanted him as bad as he wanted her, she would've been his.

"I don't know why I didn't speak on it, Zay." They were both quiet, not knowing where to take the conversation, until he broke the silence.

"Well, I guess you gotta go, huh?" he sighed. He didn't want to get off the phone, but he knew she had to pick up her daughter and get home. Plus, he had a mountain of paperwork.

"Yea I guess." Jewell heard the sadness in Xavier's

voice and felt the tug at her heart too as they reluctantly disconnected.

~~~

"What's wrong wit'chu?" Brian asked Jewell.

"Nothing," she answered. She was on cloud nine, quietly reminiscing. Seeing Xavier had lifted her spirits, and she wouldn't let Brian ruin her high.

"Well why the fuck you not speakin' to me then?" On that note, Jewell perked up a little.

"I'm sorry, Brian. I'm just trying to finish cooking."

"You better be puttin' some carrots and broccoli over in that roast too." Jewell rolled her eyes. Brian knew damn well she made roast the same way every time. He did whatever he could just to start an argument.

"Okay," she replied, trying her best to avoid a blow up. She held her breath for what seemed like a full minute as she cut the carrots before Brian finally turned and left the kitchen. She exhaled, trying not to think about it, but her mind wandered to the first time Brian had put his hands on her, four years earlier.

Jewell and her cousins, Daisha and Neeka, had been everywhere that day. They'd been shopping at Northwest Plaza where Jewell had picked out a pair of sexy red and white, lace panties with a matching bustier that made her D's sit up pretty. They went to Blackberries and Jewell got her then short hair laid out. By the time they made it to

Sun Nails, they were beat.

"So you tryin' to put it on him tonight, huh?" Neeka asked Jewell.

"Girl like he never had it before!" The three of them laughed as they were getting their pedicures.

"Y'all need this," Daisha told her. "Especially with Alicia lil' bitty bad ass runnin' around."

"You better quit talkin' about my baby!" Jewell scolded her. "Me and Brian do need something special though. My mama said she'd watch Alicia this weekend. I still got two hours before my man get home from work, and both of us are off for the next two days so don't neither one of y'all heffas call me!"

"Don't nobody wanna call you!" Neeka yelled.

"Horny ass..." Daisha added. They broke out laughing again, irritating the women working on them. When they finished, Jewell admired the French tips on her hands and feet. She couldn't wait to get back to her and Brian's little two-bedroom apartment to show off for him.

She said bye to her cousins and stopped at the grocery store to pick up a fruit tray and some whipped cream. Once she made it home, she hopped in the shower to wash off the funk of the day. When she got out, she sprayed herself with her Victoria Secret Pear Glace body spray that she knew Brian loved, and slid into her sexy outfit. She lit candles to illuminate the living room wanting to make sure the mood was set before Brian walked in. She knew any minute it would be on and poppin'.

Eight unanswered calls, countless texts, and almost four hours later, Brian stumbled through the front door drunk off his ass. Jewell had not too long fallen asleep on the couch and the candles were burning weakly. Brian took one look at her half naked body and flipped out.

"Wake the fuck up!" He snatched her up by her arm and her eyes shot open.

"Brian!" she yelled, startled.

"Brian nothin'! Who the fuck you have up in my house, Jewell?"

"What? Nobody! I was just-"

"Shut yo' ass up if you gon' lie!" He let her arm go and came across her face with a quick backhand that sent her sprawling into the couch. Jewell grabbed her cheek, moaning in pain. "Yo' muthafuckin' ass done went and got yo' hair done, got on lil' bitty clothes and shit. You lightin' candles and shit. Who you fuckin' cause I know you ain't do all this for me!"

"It was for you," she whispered between small sobs.

"What the fuck you say?" Brian stormed across the living room and Jewell scrambled over the side of the couch to get away from him.

"What is wrong with you?!" she asked. "I did all this for you and you don't answer my calls, you get home hours late and you wanna curse at me and hit me?! You never put your hands on me Brian-"

"Some bitches need a dose of act right, and you turnin' into one of them bitches."

"Oh, and you callin' me a bitch now?!"

"Jewell shut the fuck up, you givin' me a headache."

"You had a headache before you got home. Yo' drunk ass is trippin' comin' home actin' like you the head nigga in-" Brian's hand cut off her windpipe before she could finish her thought. He had come across the couch so quickly she didn't have a chance to dodge him.

"You need to watch who the fuck you talkin' to like that," he growled, blowing his alcohol breath in her face. "This shit right here," he said, grabbing between her legs like it was his own crotch. "This pussy belongs to me. Next time you try and give my shit away, I'mma break yo' ass in half." He threw Jewell down to the floor and went to bed like nothing had happened.

Jewell balled up into a fetal position. Her cheek stung, her throat was on fire, and her side was throbbing from hitting the hardwood floor. She cried silently to herself, praying that Brian wouldn't come back for round two. He didn't...at least not that night.

Tears sprang to Jewell's eyes as she thought about her situation. She had reasoned away the first incident because Brian was drunk, the second because she was late from work, the third because she had gone off on him, and so on. Eventually, she ran out of excuses for him, and for why she kept forgiving him. There had been a time when Jewell told herself that she was just sticking it out for Alicia. She wanted their daughter to have both parents in the house, but Brian had started spending more and more time away from home. Jewell suspected he was cheating, but could never prove it. She was too terrified to go through his phone or throw around accusations without having evidence.

    To cheer herself up, she thought about Xavier. She didn't want to read too much into his phone call. *Fifteen minutes with you made my day.* She figured he was talkin' crap. Had to be. Either way, Jewell was humming a happy tune for the rest of the night.

Ch. 3

Xavier looked out onto the shop from his second floor office. Everyone had gone home for the night and he was still there, pretending to do paperwork. He dreaded going home sometimes, knowing his house would be dirty, his daughter would be hungry, and his wife would bum rush him with an irritating round of twenty questions. There was no denying the fact that he loved his wife, but that wasn't the reason they were married.

    He and Deena had been teenagers when they hooked up. To him, it was just one of those things teenagers did. He ran into her after high school graduation and, even though he never considered her as his girlfriend, she felt otherwise. She was always around, always popping up, determined to drive every other female out of his life until she was the only one left standing. Then she got pregnant, and even though he felt she'd tricked him somehow, he took the adult route and stuck it out. Four years later, he found himself at the alter under duress. Deena and her mother had practically bugged the hell out of him until he broke. They were still newlyweds with less than a year under their belt, but Xavier felt like he'd been tied to her for an eternity.

    As he sorted aimlessly through papers on his desk, his thoughts wandered to the one person he had tried unsuccessfully to avoid thinking about all day, Jewell. He hadn't been lying about the impact of those few minutes with her. He was beyond excited when he saw her on Facebook, and he'd been anxious when he realized it was her on the phone, but the moment he saw that smile, he was bombarded with memories.

    Xavier's family had moved during senior year, but he still made it his business to pick Jewell up from school almost every day. It drove so many females crazy, but that wasn't the point. Whether they sat on each other's porch, in his car, or went to some lil' spot he had found, they spent an enormous amount of time together. He was instantly comfortable with her. It was easy for Xavier to get along with most people simply because of his own personality, but Jewell was different. There was a vibe with her that he just couldn't get with any other female. He knew she was with Brian, even though the fair-weather boyfriend obviously didn't make her happy, or deserve her. Xavier tried to respect that, but the kisses became unavoidable. They could kiss forever. The attraction was too strong to deny, but they never let themselves go any further than that. He couldn't help but wonder if he and Jewell had hooked up, maybe it would've been his baby instead-

"What the hell?!" Xavier said aloud, shaking the thought from his head. "Jewell is a *friend*. An old, *married* friend from years ago. That's it." He tried to reassure himself as he locked up for the night. He knew in his heart though, that no matter how many years had gone by, his feelings went much deeper than friendship.

~~~

Jewell tried to focus on the computer screen at her desk at work. She had read and reread her emails, but nothing was registering. On any given day, she'd rather be home baking or spending time with Alicia, but today her mind was preoccupied with the chills she still felt from Xavier's touch.

to Zay:
GOOD MORNING MR. BLACK

She tried to convince herself that she was just bored at work and saying hello, but a wave of excitement swept over her when her phone vibrated.

from Zay:
AND JUST LIKE THAT, MY DAY GOT BRIGHTER

Jewell immediately broke out grinning.

> to Zay:
> **WELL ARENT YOU SWEET**
> from Zay:
> **NO LIE. JUST THINKING ABOUT THAT SMILE. I NEVER FORGOT**
> to Zay:
> **I WANNA APOLOGIZE FOR HOW WE LOST TOUCH.**
> **I JUST STOPPED ANSWERING THE PHONE.**
> from Zay:
> **IT'S GOOD. IT WAS A LONG TIME AGO. I WISH YOU WOULD'VE SAID SOMETHING. THINGS COULD'VE BEEN DIFFERENT**

Jewell swallowed hard. *Things could've been different.* Was he hinting at wanting something more with her? She tried not to read too much into what he had said. Then her phone vibrated again.

> from Zay:
> **WHAT TIME DO YOU GET A BREAK?**
> **CAN I COME SEE YOU?**
> to Zay:
> **1:30**

Jewell didn't hesitate with her answer. She didn't care that the females in her office were nosy as hell. Xavier wanted to see her and damnit she wasn't gonna disappoint him.

    It was exactly 1:30 when Xavier pulled his black Audi A5 onto the parking lot of Jewell's job. He got out wondering why he was so nervous. It was *Jewell*, his home girl. Then he saw her heading towards the car and she was the epitome of beauty. He'd always been extremely attracted to her, but it seemed like that day the winter sun rays were following her. Her purple skirt swayed in the cool breeze as she jogged to him. Her brown, leather jacket fit snugly and Xavier bit his bottom lip and shook his head as he watched her.

"Hey," Jewell said with a smile that melted Xavier's heart. He opened his arms and pulled her to him. She smelled sensuous. He wanted to stand there with her in his embrace for the rest of her break, but he went ahead and opened the car door to let her get in.

Small talk may have been just that to anyone else, but to Jewell and Xavier, it was fifteen minutes of bliss. It was as though they'd been in touch the whole time. They were more comfortable and at ease with each other than they were with their significant others. Much to their anguish, Jewell's break flew by. Before they knew it, it was over. Xavier got out and walked around to open Jewell's door. When she got out, they held each other, letting the silent intensity seep into their pores. Finally, Xavier let go, afraid of what he might do if he held her any longer. He watched her walk away and had to fight the urge to run after her. Instead, he eased into his car and drove far under the speed limit to job number two.

He treasured his daughter and the relationship they had. He had a gorgeous wife and a beautiful three bedroom home with his own space in the basement for times when he flat out didn't wanna be bothered. He finally had his business and Deena was thriving in accounting. They were materialistically comfortable, financially blessed ten-fold, but Xavier's heart wasn't fully in the situation. After being stalked, tricked into a baby, then punked into marriage, he couldn't always be so happy-go-lucky about his accomplishments. Before long, he was pulling up in front of his house. As soon as he opened the door, he was bumrushed,

"Hi, daddy!" He loved Miranda's high pitched, four-year-old voice. "I'm hungry," she whined.

"Deena!" Xavier groaned, calling through the house. "Did Miranda eat?" He hung his coat up and his daughter tagged along behind him to the kitchen.

"Well hello to you, too. She ate breakfast and some chips!" Deena yelled from the living room. Xavier backtracked.

"Breakfast and *chips*?!" He had wanted her to say 'of course she ate, but he knew better. He turned the corner to the front room where his wife was lounging on the couch while their daughter was walking around hungry. "Deena it's almost three o'clock! You couldn't have made her a *sandwich* wit' her chips or somethin'?"

"You know what, it *is* almost three, which

forbidden distractions   *t.c.flenoid*

means *you* are late from work." Xavier huffed and headed back into the kitchen, knowing he normally left the office at one on Fridays. He had waited around so he could see Jewell. "Naw, don't walk away." Deena hopped up after him. "If you had been here earlier she wouldn't be so hungry now would she?" Xavier ignored her as he pulled out the lunchmeat. "Why are you so late?"

    "I told you plenty of times that I can't always leave the shop at the exact time I want-"

    "Yes you can! It's *your* shop!" Xavier took a deep breath and kept doing what he was doing. "Xavier!" Deena yelled.

    "I'm not about to argue with you," he said calmly. "I was at work. And even if I wasn't, Miranda should've had lunch by now." Deena stomped back into the living room, fuming. Xavier finished Miranda's sandwich and joked with her like nothing had happened.

    "Thank you, daddy," Miranda chimed as she took her lunch and ran off. Just like most other days, Xavier retreated to the basement where he could be alone with his thoughts.

Ch. 4

Jewell had been sitting at her computer in a daze. Work was the last thing on her mind. The night before, Brian had supposedly been at a late work meeting, which had given her a couple of free hours to talk to Xavier. She had started to feel inferior to him. He'd graduated from college, started his own business, and was doing very good for himself. She, on the other hand, had a handful of college credits which didn't really amount to anything, and was stuck working at Enterprise. It was decent money, but it wasn't where she had envisioned herself ten years out of high school.

"Tell me what you wanna do and I can help you do it," Xavier had told her. Jewell grunted and switched ears. "What? I'm serious. I know some people, and I kinda know how to get a business up and runnin'."

She laughed a little, unable to get his voice out of her head as she sat at her desk doing relatively nothing. Xavier had amped her up so much about starting her own bakery, something Brian hadn't done in years. A lot of their conversation was a blur though, much as it had been when they were younger. They'd be on the phone for hours, just enjoying each other's conversation, and the next day neither of them would have the slightest idea how they'd talked for so long. While Jewell was daydreaming, her phone vibrated her back into reality.

from Zay:
I WANNA SEE YOU
to Zay:
1:30?
from Zay:
THAT'S GOOD

Jewell closed her eyes and smiled. Her break couldn't come fast enough.

<center>~~~</center>

Xavier was pulling up as soon as Jewell walked out of the door. Like before, he got out of the car and waited. Just the sight of him made her whole body smile. His haircut was fresh, his eyes twinkled behind his glasses, his grin was sexy as hell, and she never thought a man could look so fine in jeans and a button down shirt.

"Red looks good on you," was all she could think to

say as she pressed her body against his. His scent almost paralyzed her, and his hands on her back made her eyes roll. His touch felt so good it was hard to let go.

"Did I tell you I was happy I found you?"

"Happy you found me?" Jewell asked.

"Yea, you! When you get your business off the ground you gon' blow up! I want a piece of that."

"Whatever!" Jewell laughed and gave Xavier a playful punch. As he talked, she thought about all that he claimed he was willing to do for her. In the three days they'd been talking, he'd offered to fix the hole in her rear window that she had patched with duct tape. She told him that some kids were playing around and broke it, when it was really Brian in one of his fits of rage. Xavier was adamant about helping Jewell, looking up classes that would benefit her and researching government grants. He even offered to kick the janitor's ass who couldn't keep his nasty comments to himself.

Jewell looked at him and anxiety built up in her chest as she felt her heart rate double. *I love him*, she thought to herself, then shook the thought away as soon as it came. *What the hell?! That's not possible!*

Just like the previous day, fifteen minutes passed way before they expected them to. Xavier got out and walked to the other side of the car. He exhaled and braced himself for the hug. Jewell's hands slid across his back as he pulled her to him. When they backed away from each other, her temple slowly brushed against his cheek and they froze. When the heavy breathing started, Jewell turned away abruptly.

"I gotta get back," she said.

"Yea, okay," Xavier reluctantly let her go. She only got about six steps away. "One more." Jewell turned around and grinned from ear to ear. She walked right up on him and wrapped her arms around his neck. She wanted so badly to feel his lips against hers, but she told herself to behave, and instead lay her head against his shoulder. His hands caressed her back and she shivered at his touch. She held on to him like she was saying goodbye forever. His lips were so close she could feel his breath pass between them and brush across her ear teasingly. *Kiss me*, she begged silently. But he didn't. She didn't even know how she'd react if he did.

Jewell had to force herself not to turn and look back at Xavier on the way to her building. She was sure if she looked at him for any longer, there was a possibility she wouldn't go back to work. No soon as she stepped foot in the door, her phone vibrated.

from Zay:
I KNOW

She bit her bottom lip and smiled.

to Zay:
YOU KNOW WHAT?

from Zay:
I KNOW HOW YOU FEEL. I FEEL IT TOO

Almost out of reflex, Jewell pulled the phone to her chest and exhaled. *Xavier*...

~~~

"Are you even listenin' to me?!" Deena yelled at Xavier and he blinked at her a couple of times.

"Huh? Uh, naw, I'm sorry. What did you say?"

"Ugh! You get on my nerves!" Deena stormed out of Xavier's basement office and he turned back to his computer unfazed.

"Must not have been that important," he mumbled to himself. He'd been staring blankly at the computer screen, undoubtedly thinking about Jewell. He tried to push her from his mind, besides, he had a whole wife and child at home. Well, maybe not a *whole* wife. Nonetheless, he *was* married. He logged onto his Facebook page and noticed he had a new message. The sight of Jewell's name and the subject of the note, *Inappropriate*, made something in him stir. He got up and closed the door to his office, just in case his wife decided to bring her nosey ass back downstairs. Then he opened his message.

**Simple conversation, a few hugs and I'm trippin.
Wondering what you did to me, I mean damn we were kids then.**

forbidden distractions   *t.c.flenoid*

Memories migrate, inhabiting my heart.
I wanna know you, touch you, feel every part.
Inappropriate, I know...
I'm trying to redirect but that shit won't take effect.
My mind is wandering.
What ifs driving me crazy, the past is no longer hazy.
You came back and stormed your way into my heart,
But damn I been tryin to shake you.
Inappropriate, I know...
This connection is so deep I feel you in my sleep.
Waking up in a sweat wondering when our lips will meet.
Wrong on so many levels I know.
I try to stop but my thoughts just flow.
So inappropriate...
But I can't let go.

Xavier clasped his hands behind his head and sat back in his chair, letting a calm wash over him as he soaked in Jewell's words.

    "Xavier!" Deena called, breaking his trance. He huffed and closed his message, dreading the night ahead of him. At that point, all he wanted to do was find Jewell and hold her in his arms again.

    "You too busy for me tonight, Daddy?" Deena purred as Xavier entered their bedroom. He tried not to groan out loud when he saw her sprawled across the bed in her bra and panties. He didn't feel like any overtime. Nine times out of ten, that's exactly what sex was with her... *overtime*. Xavier bent over backwards to please Deena. After she got her fill, she'd fall fast asleep, leaving him hard and frustrated. He had already used 'tired' and 'don't feel good' in the past week, so he felt obligated to put it down real quick so she'd go to sleep and leave him alone.

"Well, what are you waitin' for?" Deena asked. "Don't let it go to waste." She traced the pink lace of her panties teasingly and bit her bottom lip. Her full, jet black hair was spread across the pillow below her, and her silky, light brown thighs were inviting him in. Xavier stood there feeling crazy. There was his wife- sexy, horny, damn near naked, and practically glowing- and he wasn't the least bit hard. Was Jewell turning him off of Deena, or was he just plain bored with her? *Fuck it*. He was married and had to do what he had to do.

Even though Xavier felt scandalous as hell, Deena didn't seem to notice. He was trying so hard not to think about Jewell that he couldn't get his stroke quite right. Deena was enjoying herself though, so he kept up the charade until she screamed his name. He knew she was satisfied, as always. Once she had passed out, he retreated to the bathroom to get his own release. There he could think about Jewell all he wanted.

Ch. 5

Jewell parked behind the cafe where Xavier had asked her to meet him for lunch. She was nervous as hell and had no idea why. The first three days they'd been in touch, they'd also seen each other. Jewell had gotten spoiled. One day had gone past and she was trippin'. It was her off day and she'd spent the morning perfecting herself for him. She had pinned her hair up and kept her face natural since her bruise was gone. She was sure her deep blue jumper would grab his attention.

When Jewell made it to the front door, she spotted Xavier walking from his shop. He wasn't very far up the block, and she started to get antsy at the sight of him. He had on black slacks and a deep purple button down under his leather coat. He stood out from the rest of the lunch rush crowd, and when he smiled at her, she wanted to melt right there on the sidewalk.

"You look real good in that blue," Xavier said once

they entered and Jewell had taken off her coat.

"Thank you," she replied. Xavier was glad she wasn't looking at him or she would've caught him drooling over her like a dog in heat. He couldn't help but stare. The fabric clung to her in places he had kissed in his dreams. "You lookin' nice yourself, Zay." She smiled and he automatically smiled back. Her eyes were captivating. He almost blushed in her presence. Then he felt it. Her smile was tugging at his heart. Her eyes, her laugh, her hand on his arm, her hugs, her intelligence, her sincerity... he loved her. He always had. He wanted to listen to her talk forever and a day. Somewhere in the back of his mind, he knew he had gotten himself into a hell of a situation, but, at that point, he was enjoying Jewell so much that he wasn't willing to lose touch again.

~~~

"Mom-mee," Alicia whined. Jewell was trying to clean the kitchen, but her mini-me was clinging to her. "Can I go outsiiiide? Pleeease," she begged.

"Brian!" she called, irritated. "Can you take Alicia outside please?" Since she had been home from work, Jewell had been busy cleaning the kitchen and trying to get ready to make dinner.

"I'll take her out in a lil' bit," Brian answered as he walked past the kitchen into the bathroom. Jewell rolled her eyes and went to knock on the bathroom door.

"It'll be time to eat in a *lil' bit*," she yelled

sarcastically. She had a serious attitude since she hadn't heard from Xavier all weekend. It was pissing her off how he was getting under her skin. So what she didn't talk to him for a couple of days? So what he hadn't bothered to answer her text messages?

"I'll be back," Brian said once he got out of the bathroom. Jewell spun around in disbelief and Brian was standing in the doorway to the kitchen latching his belt. She groaned and cut her dish water off, not surprised at all.

"What'chu say?" Brian raised his voice and stepped into the kitchen.

"Nothin'," Jewell commented, keeping her head turned away.

"Thought so," he said. Then he kissed Alicia on the forehead and was gone.

"Mommy, can I go outside?" Alicia asked almost in a whisper. Jewell took a break and put their coats on. She figured dinner could wait, especially since there was no telling when Brian would be home. Just as frustration was starting to get the best of her, her phone vibrated.

from Zay:
LET ME SHOW YOU THINGS YOU HAVEN'T EXPERIENCED. THE INTRICATE WAYS OF MY TOUCH. I WANT TO EXPLORE YOUR DEEPEST DESIRES AND MAKE YOU MOAN…

"Why is this man playin' wit' me?" Jewell said out loud. After not hearing from him all weekend, *that* was what he was gonna hit her with? She looked up to check on Alicia, then decided to play along.

to Zay:
I HAVE AN UNCONTROLLABLE DESIRE TO MAKE YOU WANT ME. MAKE YOU SWEAT IN THE MIDDLE OF THE NIGHT

She bit her lip, concentrating, trying to figure out what to say next. It had been so long since she'd even attempted to talk nasty to anybody, it felt like she had forgotten how. She shook her head as she typed.

to Zay:
IF YOU CAME HOME TO ME, I'D MASSAGE EVERY PART OF YOUR BODY TO ERASE THE TENSION OF A LONG DAY. MY TONGUE WOULD FOLLOW MY FINGERS TIL YOU COULDN'T TAKE IT ANYMORE. NOW YOU MOAN...

Xavier was at his shop, holed up in his office. He had been thinking about Jewell on and off all weekend, but he'd been with his family. He was missing her and needed her to know nothing had changed, but he wasn't expecting the response he got. He replied with the first thing that came to his mind.

to Jewell:
YOU CAN GET IT

Jewell laughed out loud as she watched Alicia jump rope.

to Zay:
WHATEVER LOL, DON'T PLAY GAMES WIT ME.
from Zay:
ANYTIME YOU WANT IT TELL ME AND I'LL GIVE IT TO YOU. ANY WAY YOU WANT IT. WITH A FLICK OF MY TONGUE AND A KISS OF MY LIPS. NO REGRETS.
to Zay:
YOU GOT ME SPEECHLESS. YOU MADE ME WANT YOU SO BAD I CAN'T THINK ABOUT ANYTHING ELSE RIGHT NOW.
from Zay:
CAN I SEE YOU JEWELL?

Even though it was nippy outside, Jewell was *hot*. Her heart was pumping overtime. She was nervous to see Xavier after that conversation. Sure, there had been some flirting, but they had turned it up a notch. Her phone rang making her jump.

"Hello," she answered with a smile.

"Can I see you?" Xavier asked with no hesitation. He normally wouldn't call without asking if she could talk first, but he needed to hear her voice.

"Of course you can," she said teasingly, even though the anxiety was killing her. Once she got off with him, she called Neeka.

"Hey, can you watch Alicia for a couple of hours?" she asked,

"I'm busy. Where you goin'?" Neeka snapped.

"Heffa, don't worry about it," Jewell snapped right back. "And what'chu doin? You never do anything!"

"Nun'ya. Where yo' husband at anyway?"

"I don't know, cousin. But that's ok. I'll call Daisha."

"Alright." Neeka clicked her phone off and jumped at the slap on her ass. She spun around and smiled.

"Who was that on the phone?" Brian asked.

"Nobody," she answered. She pulled his face to hers and kissed him like only she could. He stretched his hands over her bare butt cheeks and squeezed until it hurt. Neeka wasted no time positioning herself just right to be tasted. *While she scramblin' to find a babysitter, her baby daddy over here wit' his tongue in my pussy.* The thought gave her a rush and she pushed Brian's face deeper between her legs.

~~~

"Mommy will be right back in a little bit," Jewell said and kissed Alicia on the forehead. "Thank you," she told her cousin. I should only be gone a couple hours, if that long."

"No problem," Daisha said as they left Alicia in front of the t.v. with her happy meal. "Where you goin' anyway?" she asked.

"Just makin' a couple runs. I have no idea where Brian's ass is, and I didn't feel like taking Alicia with me." Daisha studied Jewell's face and deduced that she was lying.

"Bullshit," she almost yelled, making Jewell jump.

"What?!"

"I known you almost thirty years heffa, I know when you lyin'. Makin' runs my ass. You all jittery. What the hell you goin' to do?"

"Nothin! I'm goin' to the grocery store and wanted to look at some shoes. Damn I gotta get the third degree because I asked you to watch Alicia? I'll take her with me," Jewell said, mentally crossing her fingers. She had told Xavier to give her an hour and she didn't want to stand him up.

"Oooh, and defensive too. Naw, she cool," Daisha told her. "You go ahead and make yo' *runs*," she said sarcastically.

"Whatever," Jewell quipped. She jogged to her car, eager to get to Xavier. He had given her directions to a secluded park area about twenty minutes from the shop. When she pulled up and parked, all she saw were bare trees. Xavier had told her to follow the path so she walked until she finally saw him sitting on one of the benches under a park heater. He stood up to greet her and they hugged. It was so comfortable that they had to tear themselves away from each other to sit down.

"It's nice out here," Jewell finally said.

"Yea I come out here sometimes, just to be alone and take in the scenery."

"How do you find these places?" Jewell asked, remembering the spots he used to take her to years before.

"I was thinking about moving to this neighborhood," he said, focusing on her angelic face. Her hair was pulled up into a high bun giving him a clear view. "Can I kiss you?" he asked.

"Yes." Jewell tried not to scream, but she had been waiting impatiently for him to ask. He leaned towards her anxiously. Their lips parted, sending fireworks through them both. Jewell moaned and wrapped her arms around Xavier's neck as he sucked her bottom lip. He pressed himself closer to her to kiss her deeper, and she felt herself getting wet. After a few moments, they slowly pulled away from each other and Jewell could do nothing but stare at him. It had been years since she'd been kissed like that. She had forgotten what his kisses could do to her.

"You remember the first time we kissed?" she asked him. "We went to eat at this lil' place you had found downtown and I wasn't ready to go home so you took me all the way out to some lake and started playin'-"

"R. Kelly, T.P.2," he cut her off and they started laughing.

"You stayed playin' R. Kelly," she said. "But we went out on the gazebo on the lake and the stars were out. It was so nice, I guess you just couldn't help yourself."

"Oh I couldn't help myself?" he asked.

"That's what I said." She cocked her head at him and he smiled at her.

"Well I can't help myself now either." Xavier grabbed Jewell and pulled her to him again. Her lips tasted so good and her perfume was driving him crazy. He let his hands roam up and down her back. His dick was throbbing, wanting to feel her. He got up from the bench and motioned for Jewell to follow. She thought she was about to pass out from her heart beating so fast. Over the years, Xavier had almost seemed to become a figment of her imagination, but there he was, in the flesh, licking her neck, roaming her body with his hands, making her dripping wet.

"I want you so bad," he whispered in her ear. "Can I have you?"

"Yes-" Jewell moaned automatically. She could barely get the word out before Xavier was tugging at her pants. "*Zay*! What are you doin?!"

"What you think?" he smiled in her face and she had to laugh at him. He was so damn sexy when he was horny. Almost irresistible. *Almost...*

"I didn't mean yes right now! It's too cold out here for all that!"

"Too cold?" he asked, like he didn't know it was February.

"Yes, Zay," she laughed.

"You sure about that?" he whispered. He was so close to her face. His lips were barely an inch away from hers. "Because I will lay you out in the middle of this park and give you the business."

"Oh the *business*? It's that good?"

"Actions speak louder than words." He winked at her.

"Mmmhmm. I'mma hold you to that, Mr. Black."

Ch. 6

*J*ewell tried to ignore the chills running circles around her spine. She had to calm herself down before she picked Alicia up, or Daisha would be all in her face. She couldn't help it though. Xavier had her mind racing. He was intellectual, he was sexy, business oriented, funny, generous, and he could kiss his ass off. Jewell laughed at both of them. They'd acted like junior high school kids, practically clothes-burning in the park.

It wasn't weird to her at all that she didn't pause to consider her husband's feelings. She could count on her hands the number of times Brian had been remotely nice to her in recent years, but had lost count of the number of times he'd hit her. She didn't even know her husband.

They never talked anymore. Whatever he enjoyed doing, he did without her. If he wasn't at home or work, Jewell had no idea where Brian was. It was always, "I gotta make a run," or "I'll be back," or "I got a meeting." Jewell had just stopped caring. She enjoyed time alone or with her daughter. Besides, the more time Brian spent away from home, the less reasons he found to hit her. Jewell pulled up to Daisha's house and parked, checking her hair and clothes before she got out. The last thing she needed was to look like she had been doing things she had no business doing.

"Hey girl," Daisha greeted her. "You just missed Brian. He came to get Alicia." Jewell groaned and slapped her forehead.

"What did he say?" she asked.

"He called and asked if she was here and if I knew where you were. I told him she was here because you had runs to make and he said he was comin' to get her-"

"Did he sound mad?"

"No. Jewell, *what's wrong*!? Was I supposed to lie? Was I not supposed to let him take her?"

"I'm sorry, Daisha. It's fine. Don't worry."

"No it's not, Jewell. You're *shaking*." Daisha grabbed her arms. Jewell hadn't even noticed. She knew she was dreading going home to Brian though. He would want to know why she left Alicia with Daisha, where she went, how long she'd been gone, what it was that Alicia couldn't see that she had to be dropped off somewhere... She knew that if she didn't come with the answers fast enough, or if it wasn't what Brian wanted to hear, then there'd be hell to pay. She wanted so badly to confide in Daisha, but she couldn't bring herself to say anything. It was slowly killing her, keeping the abuse to herself, but what were her cousins supposed to do, beat Brian's ass and force him to stay away? They'd probably end up talking about her to each other. The idea of anybody knowing her business simply for the sake of just *knowing* had never been appealing to her.

"I'm fine," she said. Daisha threw her head back and decided to leave it alone. She figured that when or if Jewell wanted to talk, she would. No use trying to drag it out of her.

Paranoid, Jewell stopped at QuikTrip on her way home. She wanted to do her best to scrub off any scent Xavier may have left on her. Daisha hadn't mentioned smelling anything, but Brian was sure to notice if a hair was out of place. She wanted to drive two miles an hour, but she knew that she was only prolonging the inevitable. She couldn't spend the night at anybody's because it would only make her look guilty and piss Brian off more. She also didn't want to leave Alicia with him. The only thing that kept her calm on her way home was the lingering feeling of Xavier's hands caressing her. The tingles kept a grin on her face until she parked. Just looking at the house knowing Brian was waiting for her had her scared. As soon as her foot hit the steps, the front door flew open.

"Where the *fuck* you been?!" Brian yelled, paying no attention to the nosy neighbors on the porch next door.

"You left, so I decided to go window shopping-"

"Well why couldn't Alicia go wit'chu? Why the fuck you droppin' my daughter off places and not lettin' me know?"

"Daisha is family-"

"Fuck Daisha! If you leavin' this house and my baby ain't goin' wit'chu, then you need to call and ask me first." Jewell wanted to roll her eyes, but she kept them trained on the step between her and Brian. "Get'cho ass in this house!" Brian snatched her by the collar of her coat and yanked her inside. "What y'all lookin' at?" he yelled to the neighbors. "Nosy muthafuckas."

Jewell flew to the bathroom and slammed the door. Brian was right on her heels. "Let me in, Jewell." He sounded calm enough, until he followed with three hard pounds on the door.

"Brian, *please*!" Jewell begged.

"Please my ass! Get out the damn bathroom!"

"Brian I just went to get some time to myself!" she whined, wondering if her secret rendezvous had even been worth it.

"Time to yourself? I thought you said you went to look at clothes! Which the fuck is it?!"

"I went to the mall and looked at clothes to get some time to myself." It irritated her to have to make up lies to explain herself to a man who didn't give a damn about her and did what he wanted when he wanted.

"Bullshit!" Brian yelled as he pounded again with his huge fists. Jewell sat rocking back and forth on the edge of the tub, praying that Brian's fists would get sore, or that he'd get tired of yelling.

"Daddy, stop!" The little voice was full of power and anger. Brian turned around and there was Alicia, all puffed up with her little fists balled up.

"Hey, princess." Brian softened his voice and scooped his daughter up, trying to win her over.

"Why are you being mean to Mommy? Are you fighting again?" she asked.

"No, sweetheart, we're not fighting," Brian cooed as he carried Alicia to her room. Jewell pressed her ear against the door but couldn't hear much. She knew Brian had walked away after Alicia yelled at him. It was a damn shame that her daughter had more heart than she did. On the other hand, her daughter hadn't been getting abused for the past four years. Either way, she was supposed to protect Alicia, not the other way around.

After waiting another ten minutes just to be safe, Jewell eased slowly out of the bathroom. Her heart was racing and her palms were sweaty. She bypassed her own bedroom and crept into Alicia's. There was no way she was going anywhere near Brian. She'd made that mistake before, thinking it was over. Jewell knew from experience that he'd get her. Maybe not that particular night, but he'd get her.

~~~

    Brian had been gone almost two hours and Neeka was still laying naked on her plush living room carpet in a daze. The air hung heavy with the vapors from her second strawberry blunt. Good dick plus some good loud always got her right real quick. Over analyzing her relationship with Brian was getting old. It was painfully obvious that, after years of fuckin' around, she was still just that- a *fuck*. She made sure that she was the best fuck she could be though. She did any and everything Brian asked, all three holes, bent over backwards, hands tied behind her back, hanging from shit, legs cranked behind her head... Neeka was the baddest bitch he had *ever* had, and they both knew it.

    It had been a little over three years since she got carried away at a New Year's party at Jewell and Brian's. Neeka could smoke like a barbeque grill, but she only drank occasionally. Two jello shots, a glass of 1800, and three shots of Patron had her horny as hell.

    "Look at her, Jewell," Brian had whispered while pointing at Neeka who was sprawled out on the couch giggling. "She can't drive home like that, and she sure in the hell can't stay here wit' her drunk ass. You gon' help her get up her steps and to her apartment." Jewell scrunched up her nose and Brian smiled to himself. "Fine then, I'll take her home," he said with a fake attitude. "Wit'cho lazy ass. This is yo' people," he mumbled as he scooped Neeka up off the couch. "At least open the door, damn!" he yelled. Jewell hurried out to the car, eager to get Brian and Neeka away from the rest of their guests.

    Brian sped through the city with a ready dick. Neeka had been making goo-goo eyes and side comments for far too long, and it was high time for her to back that shit up. He looked over at her and she was staring dead at him.

    "I coulda walked to the car myself," Neeka told him.

    "I didn't want yo' fine ass to fall." Brian licked his lips thinking about when Neeka had walked in and he saw her in those heels with her thighs glistening under a black, skin-tight dress that barely covered her thick, round ass cheeks. Oh yea, he was gettin' up in that. No doubt.

    "I'm sure you woulda caught me if I did." She leaned over and ran her hand up his inner thigh, grabbing his dick with so much force that he almost ran the red light.

    "Damn, Neeka!"

    "Damn, Neeka nothin'. I seen how you was lookin' at me. I know what you want." She continued to massage his dick through his pants, thinking about how Jewell said he put it down. And he had, thoroughly. He got her in the house and had her screaming through tears of pleasure and pain.

It hadn't been Neeka's intentions to fall for Brian. He was an easy target. She already knew he had that fire because of Jewell's big mouth. Even though she hadn't talked about their sex life in a while, Neeka knew he could've only gotten better. And any fool could see that Jewell wasn't happy. Neeka was sexy, thick, and chocolate, and knew she could get any man of her own if she wanted, but she hated the hassles of a 'relationship'. She figured Brian would be a good, quick fuck who couldn't want much because he was her cousin's man. She hadn't expected him to have that once-you-pop-you-can't-stop dick. She hadn't expected it to last as long as it had. She hadn't expected to be at their wedding. She certainly hadn't expected to be at his beck and call. Whenever he wanted it, she made herself available to him, to the point where she couldn't even have a man of her own. Shit, Brian *was* her man. Now she was stuck on stupid and straight in love with her *cousin's* husband.

She forced herself to get up from the floor, almost plummeting right back down. The high hit her like a semi truck, and she groaned softly. She loved her cousin, but Jewell didn't deserve Brian if she couldn't make him happy, and the man definitely was not happy. At least not where he was. He needed to be where he was content and could be himself. To Neeka, that was only with her.

Ch. 7

"Mama, can you watch Alicia for me for a while?"

Jewell crossed her fingers. It had been a week since her rendezvous with Xavier. Not seeing him and only being able to hear his voice for the past few days wasn't doing anything but frustrating her. Xavier was the one on a crazy schedule, so whenever he could see her, she was game. Brian supposedly had a *business meeting* that night. Even though she'd always wondered what the hell type of business meeting construction workers could be having late at night, she had stopped asking. First it was, "Why you trippin'? You and Enterprise ain't keepin' a roof over our heads." Then it was, "Don't worry about when and where we got our damn business meetings." When he got tired of explaining himself, he used his fists to shut Jewell up. So now, when Brian said he had a business meeting, he had a business meeting.

"Yea, sweetie, she's fine," her mother answered. Jewell grinned from ear to ear. She had been nervous at first when Xavier texted her to see if she was free. She and Alicia had been lounging at her parent's house, so Jewell wasn't dressed to impress. Xavier didn't care. He wanted to see her anyway.

He had left his office and was sitting at the ground desk. He hadn't been able to concentrate all week after meeting Jewell at the park, and was anxious to get his hands on her again. She had felt so good in his arms... so natural. He was going to be tied up in meetings for the next few days. Between that and home, he probably wouldn't even be able to hear her voice. He made it his business to try and see her.

The soft rapping at the door snapped him out of his trance and he grinned from ear to ear. When he opened the door though, the smile disappeared.

"Dang, were you expecting somebody else, or something?" Deena asked, walking right past him.

"Naw, baby. Just trippin' 'cause I gotta be here late." Xavier stole a nervous glance up and down the street before closing the door.

"Mmmhmm..." Deena rolled her eyes and glanced around the shop. "I was goin' to pick up Miranda from my mama's and thought I'd stop by and pay my hardworking husband a visit since he had to *stay late*." She walked up to Xavier who was guarding the front door. "You're here by yourself, right?" she asked, leaning her chest against him suggestively.

"Yea, but I got a lot of loose ends to tie up before the conference, baby."

"Aww... not just a little bit?" Deena begged, reaching between her husband's legs.

"Now you know it's not goin' down in my shop," Xavier said, grabbing her hand. "Besides, I *gotta* finish this paperwork."

"Okaaay," Deena whined. She knew Xavier had built that shop from the ground up and would never have sex in it, but there was an uneasy feeling in her gut that made her stop. Defeated, and with nothing to bitch about, Deena opened the front door to leave. She tried to stall, but she could tell that Xavier wasn't having it, so she leaned in and kissed him deeply. Xavier gave in, knowing it would ease Deena's mind. She moaned as he slid his hands over her cheeks and gave them a little squeeze. With that, she was satisfied. She practically bounced out to her car, scolding herself for doubting her man.

Xavier choked out a sigh of relief. He was feeling Jewell big time, but he hadn't figured out exactly what that meant yet. Thoughts of the two of them being together had frequently crossed his mind. What would his life be like if either of them had expressed their feelings for each other? He knew that back then Jewell could've easily knocked Deena out of the box if she wanted, but she tried to keep it kosher because of Brian. Times had changed though. Simply because he had feelings for Jewell didn't mean he was ready to break up his family. It definitely didn't mean he wanted the two women to run into each other.

~~~

    Jewell had turned onto the shop's street about a block away, but pulled over to the curb when she saw a woman walking to the door. She held her breath when she realized who it was. Deena looked the same as she had in high school, from what Jewell could tell, just older and much prettier. Xavier's *wife*. It was in that instance that Jewell felt the guilt build up inside her. What right did she have meeting up with another woman's husband? The fact that somebody was probably riding her own husband at that very moment meant nothing. Two wrongs didn't make a right, but it would sure feel good as hell to be in Xavier's presence again...which lead her to jealousy. In the back of her mind, she kept kicking herself for not speaking up all those years ago. She sat there in her car wondering why the hell she was still sitting there, and trying not to imagine what was going on inside. She tried to keep from getting angry, telling herself that he wouldn't have asked her to come if he'd been expecting Deena. She had to have just stopped by.

    Jewell contemplated where she would go to at least

keep her mind off of Xavier and Brian. As soon as she was about to turn the key to leave, Deena was coming out of the shop. She figured Xavier had probably tried to keep the surprise visit short because he knew she was on her way. She had never thought about him having to lie to his wife to be with her. She knew Deena *existed*, but it didn't seem real until she saw her in the flesh. Her conscience was nagging at her. Let Xavier tell it, she was an apathetic wife and mother, and he was beyond tired and bored with her. Did that mean she deserved to be cheated on, though? Brian deserved whatever his abusive ass got as far as she was concerned. Either way, she and Xavier may have had a past together, but that was then. They were both grown and married, and knew they were playing with fire.

"I have self-control," Jewell reassured herself as she pulled up a little closer. She had no idea when Brian would be home. At the mere thought of him at another one of his *business meetings*, Jewell thought fuck it. She got out and walked the half block up the street, making sure she kept her head down. The last thing she needed was somebody to see her. Nobody had any business at a car shop in the middle of the night. She glanced at her watch. 9:20 p.m.

Xavier had been pacing back and forth, grateful that Jewell hadn't shown up while Deena was there, and wondering if she had seen Deena coming or going. He wasn't focused on guilt at all, he was focused on the fact that if Jewell saw Deena, then she may have gone home. She had already let him know that she didn't want to cause problems where she assumed there were none. He had eased her mind each and every time. Then the soft knock at the door eased his. He looked out the blinds and his heart flipped at the sight of her. When he opened the door, she walked through timidly as if someone else was waiting in the shadows.

"It looks so different in the dark," she broke the ice. "Almost scary,"

"You think it's scary?" Xavier asked, locking the door behind her. "I think it's sexy," he commented, peering through the semi-darkness at the columns of steel, the walls full of tools, and the jet black steps leading up to his office... his dream in the flesh. He walked up behind Jewell and guided his hands around her waist until he was cradling her against him.

"I almost didn't come," Jewell informed him.

"Why not?" he asked, inhaling her scent. As soon as the words came out, he wished he could take them back. He already knew why. He was sure she'd seen Deena, and that was the last person he wanted to talk about.

"You had a visitor and I didn't wanna interrupt. It only lasted a couple of minutes though." She attempted to put on a sarcastic front, while trying to shake the image of Deena from her mind.

"But you're here now and that's all that matters. This moment right here." Xavier kissed Jewell's neck and she peeled herself away and turned to face him. They stared at each other for a few moments making Xavier nervous. Was she about to leave? Was she about to curse him out? He had to act quickly to ease the tension. "Come on," he grabbed her hand, pulling her to the steps. "It's not as scary upstairs." Jewell let herself be led upstairs as a wave of nervous excitement rushed over her.

"I'm glad you called me," Jewell said, watching Xavier close the door. He didn't answer. Instead, he walked over to the C.D. player and clicked it on. None other than R. Kelly, T.P.2. "Oh you are *real* slick." She shook her head waved her finger at him. If there were to be a soundtrack to their relationship, that C.D. would be it. No matter how much time had passed, whenever she heard any of the songs on the radio, she was reminded of Xavier.

"Slick?" He shrugged his shoulders and lowered the music a little bit. "I don't know what'chu talkin' about."

"Mmmhmm," Jewell smiled, rolling her eyes.

"I missed you," Xavier leaned in and whispered in her ear. She closed her eyes as his lips brushed against her cheek and moved down to her neck. He turned her around so they were facing each other. He could read her arousal as he slowly unbuttoned her coat. The tension built up with each button as they locked eyes. Jewell thought her chest was going to explode. When her coat fell to the floor, she flung her arms around him and kissed him with so much emotion that she almost knocked him down. He held on to her as she worked him over, returning the kiss with his own rugged passion.

"I missed you too," Jewell panted between breaths.

"Yea, I can tell," Xavier joked. She laughed and let her head fall back as Xavier's hands caressed her hips. He moaned into her neck as he played with the waistline of her jogging pants. Her mind was focused on his tongue easing dangerously closer to her cleavage, and his hands gently tugging her pants down.

"What are you doing to me?" Jewell asked. Xavier was the only other man since Brian that she had let get close to her. There had only been a couple before Brian, but he had captured her heart. So had Xavier. Even through the mental and physical abuse, she had never let another man in. And here comes Xavier, back in her life, and in less than a month, she was half-naked in his car shop.

"I'm showing you how much I want you." He kissed her and guided her slowly backwards until she was up against the wall. He pulled her shirt up over her head and admired her.

"What?" Jewell asked shyly.

"You're beautiful," he replied. The black bra held her 34DD's just right, and the black panties hugged the sexy curve of her thick, deep caramel hips. He traced the outline of her bra with his tongue and slid his fingers inside her, surprised at how wet she was.

"Oooh," Jewell moaned, rubbing the back of Xavier's head. His fingers were hitting her g-spot at a mile a minute. He kissed her lips again before stooping down in front of her and kissing her belly button. He teased her stomach with his tongue as he slid her panties down. He took one of her legs and lifted it to plant kisses on her inner thigh. Jewell couldn't control her heartbeat. Her mind was working overtime. She wanted so bad to give in to temptation, but that damn conscience of hers was cock-blockin' to the extreme. She ignored the aching need that was brewing between her legs, and put her hand on Xavier's head to stop him. He grabbed her hand and kept kissing her inner thigh. Jewell leaned her head back against the wall but the closer he got to her wetness, the more paranoid she got. Her heart was way too attached to Xavier already. If they had sex, she'd lose every inch of sanity she had left when it came to him. "We gotta stop," she whispered, not sure if she meant it. He stroked his fingers in and out, massaging her inner walls with expertise. When he blew softly on her clit, Jewell screamed out and jerked along the wall away from him.

"You runnin'?" Xavier grinned and stood up to follow her. "I ain't done nothin' yet." He pressed her against the wall and kissed her like she belonged to him.

He made her weak, in the knees, in the head, and everywhere else. He slid his hands down her side and stopped at her bare hips. "Can I taste you?" He flicked his tongue across her lips while he stared in her eyes. Every part of her body was screaming *YES*!!

"We gotta stop," Jewell whispered again, unable to believe that she was actually telling him no. He dropped down to the floor and, for a minute, Jewell thought he was about to disregard what she said. Instead, he grabbed her panties and began to slide them up her legs. He moved painstakingly slow, like he was waiting for her to change her mind. Once they were on her hips, Xavier leaned in and rested his head against her stomach. Jewell placed a hand on his head, speechless, mentally kicking herself. She could tell he was about to put in work. All of a sudden, he popped up and they were face to face again.

"You wanna know something," Xavier sighed, rubbing Jewell's arms. She didn't say anything, just waited. He smiled, showing off his dimples. "I'm sure it's happened more than just with you, but every actual memory I have of blue balls is connected to you." Jewell's mouth dropped and Xavier started cracking up. "That just means I want you," he explained, grabbing her hands and holding them out so he could admire her. "I really," he roamed the length of her body with his eyes, "Really, want you." He shook his head and turned away, picking up her clothes. She watched, unable to do much else. What the hell was she thinking?! What was she about to pass up?! "Please," he handed her the pile of clothes and licked his lips. "Before I take it." He winked at her and she almost told him to go ahead. He drove her crazy, watching her and rubbing himself through his pants as she put her clothes on. She never knew putting clothes on could be so sensual, but she felt like the most desirable woman he had ever seen in his life.

    Once she was fully dressed, Xavier sat in his chair and pulled Jewell down on his lap. There was a silent understanding between them. When or if they ever had sex, it wouldn't be in a car shop. They had waited years on top of years for each other, and if it was meant to happen then it would happen. They sat there, clinging to each other, letting T.P.2 soothe them.

Ch. 8

By the time Jewell got back to her parent's, everyone was sound asleep. It was almost midnight and Brian hadn't called or texted her once. She really didn't give a damn. It was actually better that he hadn't. If she would've seen his name on her phone, it would've blown the high that Xavier had given her. He was the only man to ever hold her and just let the music wash over them. The first time he'd done it was that night at the lake, their first kiss. She had felt her heart do the same cartwheels they were doing as she crept past her parent's bedroom like she was back in high school. Alicia was sprawled out in the bed like she owned it. Jewell laughed at her in her old bed and kissed her on the cheek. She thought years back to the late nights Xavier would text her saying that he was up bored. She'd slip something on and climb out of her window to go riding with him. They wouldn't go anywhere in particular, just cruise through the streets without a care in the world. She missed that with every fiber of her being.

~~~

Xavier woke up bright and early the next morning. His good mood had carried over from the night before and it was irritating the hell out of Deena.

"What are you so damn happy for?" she asked, still frustrated that he hadn't made it home until close to midnight.

"Today is my first meeting, baby. I gotta pump myself up. Gotta get ready. I'm tryin' to expand and get some extra paper. I'm tryin'a be like Jiffy Lube!" He bounced around the kitchen while Deena watched on in mild disgust.

"So what took you so long getting home last night?" she asked. "I rolled over when you came in and it was midnight."

"You know I'm a perfectionist. I needed to make sure everything was on point. I gotta meet with these sharks today and one mistake could blow this."

"Yea, but you coulda worked in your office in the basement and we coulda avoided this argument."

"This is an argument?" Xavier asked, looking up from his breakfast. "Because if it is, you can save it. I got a lot on my plate today Deena, and I don't feel like arguing wit' you this morning." His phone went off just as Deena was opening her mouth to reply.

from Jewell:
WISHING YOU GOOD LUCK TODAY! I BELIEVE IN YOU! NO WAY CAN THEY TURN YOU DOWN!

He suppressed his smile and put his phone back in its case with a straight face. "I gotta go open up today," he told Deena as he wrapped up his bagel and grabbed his coffee. He stroked her face and gave her a dry, cheek kiss before heading out.

"Love you too," Deena whispered to herself as she watched him kiss Miranda and leave. "*Workin' late*," she mumbled.

Once Xavier made it safe inside the car, he pulled his phone out.

to Jewell:
THANKS BABY, I NEEDED THAT

He wanted to talk to Jewell, but he wasn't sure if Brian was around, so he just clicked on Rickey Smiley and laughed all the way to the shop. When he got there, he opened up and tried not to get nervous. He had talked five of the most talented guys into letting him help them get their mechanic's license, he'd applied for numerous grants, he'd workshopped like crazy, cruising neighborhood after neighborhood, passing out fliers. He'd smooth talked his way onto the local radio stations and the news, and even saved up enough for his own commercial. The hard work had paid off more than he had dreamed. He'd only been in business a few months, but the workload had become overwhelming. He needed more workers, more space, and more money. He was ready to for the challenge.

He climbed the steps to his office and was met immediately with vivid images from the night before. It was as if Jewell's presence was still lingering there, beckoning him. He felt his dick getting hard at the thought of her. He had wanted so bad to go further with her, but that would have to be saved for later when the time was right.

He sat down at his desk to check his email. He wasn't expecting much, but it was routine. His heart skipped a beat when he saw Jewell's name. He hesitated before opening it, wondering if she'd throw him off his game. He didn't need any distractions, but he wouldn't be able to focus wondering what it said.

IT'S HARD AS HELL TO PUT INTO WORDS HOW I FEEL. JUST LIKE YOU I'M WONDERING WHY? HOW? XAVIER I WANNA WAKE UP AND KISS YOU, GO TO SLEEP IN YOUR ARMS, AND EVERYTHING IN BETWEEN. I TRY TO STOP THINKING ABOUT YOU CONSTANTLY BECAUSE YOU DONT BELONG TO ME. BUT UR TAKING OVER MY EVERY THOUGHT. IF I COULD GIVE MYSELF TO YOU IN EVERY WAY THERE'D BE NO HESITATION. BACK THEN, YOU WERE ZAY WHO I KICKED IT WITH. REMEMBER WE'D STAY ON THE PHONE TIL 3AM TALKIN ABOUT ANY AND EVERYTHING?

YOU GOT UNDER MY SKIN AND I REALIZE YOU NEVER LEFT. ONLY NOW UR XAVIER. STILL SILLY AND FUNNY AS HELL, BUT A GROWN MAN ABOUT HIS BUSINESS. YOU TAKE CARE OF UR DAUGHTER AND YOU GOT A WAY OF THINKING THAT'S AS SEXY AS YOU ARE... STILL. YOU GOT WORDS THAT MAKE ME SWEAT AND I KNOW YOU TAKE PRIDE IN TAKING CARE OF YOUR WOMAN IN MORE WAYS THAN ONE. HOW COULD ANYBODY NOT WANNA MAKE YOU HAPPY? I WANNA DO JUST THAT... BUT I KNOW WHAT'S UP. I WANNA RESPECT THAT, BUT YOU MAKE IT HARD. OK, I WON'T PUT IT ALL ON YOU- WE MAKE IT HARD. I KNOW WHAT I DESERVE AS A WOMAN AND YOU HAVE THE POWER TO GIVE IT TO ME. I HAD MY CHANCE AND I DIDN'T TAKE IT. NOW TIME SPENT WITH YOU IS LIKE A DREAM WHERE I ONLY GET A SMALL PIECE OF YOU, NOT NEARLY ENOUGH TO HOLD ME OVER UNTIL I CAN STEAL YOU AWAY AGAIN. THEN I WAKE UP THINKING... DAMN...

Xavier had to keep himself from blushing. He felt that Jewell didn't realize how much of an amazing woman she was. She had already made him smile with her wish of good luck, and the way she expressed herself made him have to pause. She had made his day. He had so much to do, but for Jewell, he had a few minutes.

SOMEHOW YOU HAVE A HOLD ON ME. LIKE YOU POURED YOURSELF INTO A CUP TO NURTURE ME. I CAN BARELY SLEEP BC ALL I DO IS THINK OF

YOU- DAY IN AND DAY OUT. EVERYTHING ABOUT YOU... I DON'T HAVE ENOUGH WORDS TO EXPRESS MYSELF. TRUST ME, IM RARELY FOUND SPEECHLESS, BUT I'M AMAZED BY YOU. YOUR SMILE IS PRICELESS AND YOUR VOICE IS MUSIC TO MY EARS. YOU INSPIRE ME TO PUSH MYSELF TO THE LIMITS. EVEN THOUGH WE HAVEN'T TALKED IN YEARS YOU ARE STILL THE SAME JEWELL. ZAY'S JEWELL.

~~~

"What the fuck you trippin' off of?" Brian asked as he watched Jewell grinning at her phone. She resisted the urge to roll her eyes and tried to calm herself by thinking about her email from Xavier.

"Nothing," she told Brian.

"Well stop doin' all that damn cheesin'," he said, and threw the mail on the table before leaving the living room. Jewell suppressed her giggle and flipped through the mail. A purple envelope stuck out like a sore thumb, a save the date for her ten year class reunion. She jerked around to make sure Brian wasn't near her. The last thing she needed was him all in her face about it. He wasn't going to ruin her good mood, and he definitely wasn't going to her reunion to embarrass her. Jewell couldn't remember the last time she had been out in public with Brian, and she certainly wasn't interested in showing him off to former classmates.

Then the thought hit her, *Xavier and Deena*. No doubt Deena would wanna throw Xavier's fine, successful ass in everybody's face. When they were in high school, most of the females were trying their best to throw it at him. There was a number of people who knew that he and Jewell had started hanging out the end of senior year, but if they didn't know yet, everyone would know that the underdog, Deena, had snatched him up, latched on, and had that ball and chain on tight. Jewell's mind started racing. Would she be able to stand seeing them together? Would she even be able to look Deena in the face? Then she wondered what would be worse, showing up with Brian and trying not to stare at Xavier and Deena all night, or showing up alone and trying not to stare. Looking over the invitation, she saw that the reunion had the nerve to be a three-day event. There was a meet and greet on Friday, a formal dinner on Saturday, and a picnic on Sunday.

"Ughh," she groaned out loud as she stuffed the invitation back in its envelope, folded it up, and shoved it in her pocket.

~~~

"So since when you start ignoring me?" Neeka asked Brian as he tore open his chips. It had been over a week since she'd even spoken to him and he was acting like it was all good. She was livid.

"Since my wife started doin' shit she ain't got no business doin'," he said, not turning an inch from the t.v. All the years he'd been with Jewell, he knew when something was up. Talkin' shit to him, leaving Alicia with people, not calling, happy all the damn time. he could sense a change in her demeanor and he didn't like it at all. *He* was the man! He did what he wanted, no questions asked. But his woman, his wife? Naw, she was supposed to keep her ass in line.

"Why all of a sudden do you care what she does?" Neeka was trying not to get agitated. Brian giving a damn about Jewell was a step in the wrong direction.

"Don't fuckin' question me about my marriage. That ain't got nothin' to do wit'chu!" he yelled, still looking at the t.v.

"Nothin' to do wit' me?!" Neeka was outraged. She moved between Brian and the television. "Four years and now you tellin' me it has nothing to do wit' me?"

"Get from in front of the t.v., Neeka," Brian said calmly.

"After four years what the fuck am I to you, Brian?" Neeka put her hands on her hips and leaned forward, on the verge of tears.

"I thought I told you to get yo' ass from in front of the t.v."

"Understand this, this is *my* t.v. in *my* house. And if I wanna stand between you and this muthafucka, I will." Brian rose from the couch, irritated as hell. Neeka had some good, tight pussy, fire ass face, and she didn't ask questions- until now. He wasn't having that.

"Let me get up outta here before you get yo'self hurt." Brian tried to turn and leave, but Neeka practically jumped over the table and grabbed his arm.

"Where you goin'!?" she yelled and Brian yanked away.

"Get the fuck off me," he growled at her, completely turned off. If he wanted to be stressed out, he could've stayed home with Jewell.

"You ain't leavin'!" Neeka grabbed Brian's shoulder and tried to turn him around to her. He turned like she wanted, but he brought a backhand with him. The slap resonated through Neeka's eardrums and sent her stumbling over the table and into the entertainment system. She dropped to the carpet and the t.v. teetered in its place. Brian watched to see if it would fall or not. Once it stopped rocking, he turned and left, leaving Neeka groaning.

Ch. 9

"Are y'all going to the class reunion?" Jewell asked Xavier over lunch. It had been almost a week since she got her invite, so she knew Deena had to have gotten hers.

"I don't know." Xavier was busy with his sandwich. "Mine is that next weekend, so we're trying to see what we're gonna do." Jewell tried to swallow the lump of jealousy, but it wasn't working. Whenever the conversation involved Deena, Jewell tried to suppress the green-eyed monster, but that bitch was strong.

"Are you scared to go to my class reunion?" she asked.

"Scared? Why?" He looked up from his food.

"I'mma be lookin' real good, Zay. Are you gonna be able to keep your hands off?" she teased, trying to shake off the nervousness of seeing him with Deena.

"You come up in there lookin' too good, we gon' have to dip off somewhere."

"Mmmhmm-" Jewell paid him no mind.

"Seriously. I wanna trace every hidden part of your body. I wanna know every intimate thought in that sexy mind and make it reality." Jewell's breathing had become heavy and she couldn't blink.

"You need to stop playin' wit' me before I yank you up under this table."

"I *dare* you," Xavier teased. He leaned across the table and planted a kiss on her lips.

"Aren't you ever scared somebody will see?" Jewell asked. As long as Xavier wanted to meet her, she wouldn't turn him down. It was just weird that they were right up the street from the shop and not once did he ever seem paranoid.

"If somebody sees us, they just see us," he replied.

"So you're not worried at all?"

"I mean, not really." Xavier bit into his sandwich. "I'm not trying to shove anything down her throat, but if we get caught, we get caught. It is what it is." Jewell watched him eat for a moment, thinking about what she was going to say.

"And exactly what *is* it?" she asked. That made him pause. Jewell knew they cared for each other, but what the hell were they *doing*? Xavier finished chewing, wiped his mouth, and leaned back into the booth, leaving Jewell

71

on the edge of her seat.

"To be honest with you, I don't really have an answer to that. I know how I feel about you, but I can't put into words what I actually want. I know I never felt like this before, thinking I lost somebody then they come back and it's like they never left. It's like *you* never left. And my feelings... this is something I can't even explain to anybody because they wouldn't understand." Jewell nodded her head in agreeance, even though she was hurting. True enough, she hadn't confided in anyone, but she didn't discredit the idea. Xavier flat out told her he wouldn't let anyone know about her. While being someone's little secret could be fun for a minute, they weren't twenty anymore.

"I agree with you," she lied. "It's not like your family will condone you messing with somebody after they grew to love Deena." Jewell wanted to slap herself on the forehead. She had let herself fall into a trap. What could she possibly expect, for Xavier to leave his wife and daughter and run to her simply because they had rekindled a friendship they had years back? She had to get it through her head that, to him, she could never be more than an old friend. They may hook up, they may not, but she couldn't possibly get anything other than that from him. She knew he cared about her, but she also knew he had a family, no matter how much he complained about Deena. No matter how much he expressed what could have been, that time had come and gone. He was married with a family, and that wasn't going to change.

She, on the other hand, was entirely willing to get rid of Brian's no good ass. It was almost as if she had been waiting for a push, and Xavier was shoving the hell outta her. For years she had let Brian belittle her, abuse her mentally and physically, and poison their daughter's young mind with his bullshit. In such a short time, Xavier had become her knight in shining armor, her savior. She knew she was a good woman. He had given her a glimpse of what a good woman deserved and what a good man was capable of. He'd shown her happiness that she hadn't felt since... hell since she'd spent time with him before. She felt the tears begin to form in her eyes and panicked. He was *not* about to see her cry!

"I gotta run to the bathroom real quick," Jewell blurted out.

"Okay." Xavier could see her demeanor change, but he had no idea of the storm that was brewing.

Safe inside a bathroom stall, Jewell leaned against the wall and cried silently to herself. Even if Xavier hadn't expressed any feelings for her, she knew her own heart. It always should've been him. The fact that they had connected again on so many levels made it even more painful that she couldn't have him, that she wasn't the one he came home to, that she had kept her mouth shut about her feelings, even that she had been stupid enough to fall into the trap. There was no doubt in her mind that Xavier cared about her, but was she just another female to him? It was easy to care about somebody, but the way she felt after all that time seemed almost impossible. It didn't help that it had been years since she felt like she loved her own husband. Now she had a thirst for Xavier again that she felt would never be quenched. It almost physically hurt. She made up her mind before she left the stall that she had to let him go or she'd drive herself nuts.

Xavier smiled when he saw Jewell coming back from the bathroom. He stood to greet her and sat down once she had taken her seat. "You feelin' alright? Is your salad ok?" he asked.

"Yea, it's- it's good," she stuttered, trying to choose her words before she spoke. Xavier was beginning to get antsy. He knew something was up. Jewell's face was stuck in her plate staring at her food. She refused to look at him.

"Talk to me, babe," Xavier whispered as he reached out and grabbed her hand. Jewell almost broke down. He made her feel nineteen again, cruising the night streets, windows down, looking for something to get into. What she wouldn't give to go back to those days and dodge the pain that her marriage had turned into. The only blessing she had was Alicia, and that little girl kept her sane without even trying. Then she found Xavier, or rather he had found her. With all the drama Brian put her through, those were her two lights... and she had to let one go.

"Xavier, this is getting to be a little much for me."

"What'chu mean?" Xavier tightened his grip on her hand, hoping she wasn't about to say what he thought she was about to say.

"I didn't expect it, but I'm in way too deep with you. *Way* too deep."

"What are you sayin'?" Xavier asked, squinting at her.

"I'm sayin' I can't keep doin' this, meeting you here, talking like we do. I'm falling for you all over again. I don't even know if I ever got over you-"

"I'm trippin' too, Jewell, but you tellin' me you just not gon' see me no more? You ain't even gon' *talk* to me?" He was hurt, frustrated, and confused. One minute, they were laughing and joking, then he blinked and she was telling him it was all over. He understood the situation was far from ideal, but he knew he couldn't build up the courage to end it. He loved their conversations and the time they spent together, and didn't wanna give that up. He didn't know where things were going with them and, even though it was selfish, he didn't want to have to let her go.

"I'mma end up getting' hurt."

"You know I would *never* do anything to hurt you, Jewell."

"Not intentionally, no." She didn't wanna tell him that it hurt every time she heard Deena's name, especially since she didn't talk about Brian. It hurt every time she had to lay beside Brian and think about him, every time she had to leave him, every time she couldn't talk to him when she needed to. She wanted to blurt out that his wife didn't deserve him. She wanted to plead her case and lay down every reason why she should be his woman, but she knew she'd be wasting her time. It wasn't like years ago where she'd be going against random chicks that he was on-again, off-again with. Deena was his *wife* and the mother of his *child*. "I had my chance with you and I didn't take it. That was a long time ago and now I'm just wishing we could go back but we can't." Xavier hung his head. He was feeling every word. Reminiscing was fun, but longing for what he couldn't have was depressing. It was painfully clear that after all those years Brian wasn't going anywhere. Even if Jewell did leave Brian, Xavier wasn't sure he had the balls to end his own marriage. He'd never want to leave his daughter and he wasn't sure how hard Deena would fight him for her if they separated. He loved her, but he'd never been truly happily married to Deena. His happiness was staring him in the face, saying goodbye.

"So you don't wanna see me- ever again?" He was hoping to coax her into changing her mind.

"I'm not saying I don't *want* to, I'm saying I can't." Xavier met her eyes and could see the hurt in them. He hated that he was the cause of it. So if not talking to him would save her some pain, then he had to let her go. He reluctantly moved his hand from hers and they both felt the warmth disappear. It was like they took their coats off in the freezing cold. Jewell, unable to take it anymore, simply got up from the table. "Bye, Xavier," she said. He wasn't able to look at her. He was trying to be more understanding and less upset, but he couldn't do anything but stare at the spot she had gotten up from. Jewell had walked out of his life- again.

Ch. 10

When Neeka called off work Friday, her eye was still swollen from Brian smacking the shit out of her. Over the weekend, her phone rang off the hook, co-workers, Daisha, Jewell, friends wanting to go out, everybody but Brian calling to apologize. There were even a couple of knocks on the door. Neeka wasn't in the mood.

By Monday, the bruise was clearing, but her spirit was broken. She was in love with a man who had made it clearly obvious that he wasn't interested in her. Interested in gettin' some ass maybe, but nothing else. She now assumed, after putting years of pieces together, that Brian had been beating Jewell's ass too. She still couldn't bring herself to feel any guilt. Brian was a good man, just unhappy at home. Neeka knew she provided the release that he needed, or else he wouldn't have continued to see her. She had mouthed off to him. She'd pissed him off and he had to put her in her place. That was what a man was supposed to do. She knew Jewell couldn't handle the type of man that Brian was. She was weak and uninteresting. She didn't even *smoke*! Being high was some of the best sex, and Jewell was depriving him of that. Neeka knew she was a gutta chick. She would have Brian's back through whatever, while Jewell played Susie Homemaker to their little brat.

What Brian needed, was what Neeka was willing to provide, an obedient woman to tend to his needs, give him his space when needed, and fuck him silly on the regular. She had messed around and driven him away, and she desperately needed to get back in his good graces. The easiest way to do that was to get his mind off Jewell.

~~~

After almost a week of not talking to Xavier, Jewell was feeling down and out. It was as if she had been on vacation and now she was back home, trying not to let the mediocracy depress her. It was the life she'd chosen and she had to deal with it.

"What I'm eatin' tonight?" Brian's gruff voice made her groan. She missed Xavier's smooth tone. It soothed her when she needed it, made her laugh, and when the time had presented itself, his voice turned up the heat.

"Baked pork chops, scalloped potatoes, and green beans," she said, just above a whisper.

"I want fried pork chops," he barked.

"They're already in the oven, Brian."

"Why didn't you ask me what I wanted before you put them bitches in there?! You gon' need to fry me one. And I want a baked potato." Jewell swung around to face him.

"*All* the pork chops are in the oven. Now if you wanna thaw one out and fry it yourself, then be my guest." Brian gave her a who-the-fuck-you-talkin'-to look, but Jewell didn't let up. "And if you want a baked potato, the potatoes are on the table and the foil is in the closet."

"You fall and bump yo' head or somethin'?" Brian asked. "I said I want a gotdamn *fried* pork chop and a baked potato. What the fuck wrong witchu?"

"Ain't nothin' wrong wit' me. I'm tired of arguing over fuckin' food! If you don't like what I cook take yo' ass to McDonald's." Jewell stood there waiting for the hell she knew was coming. Alicia was at her parent's house, she already had an attitude brewing, and Brian was getting in her face yet again. He was pushing all the right buttons.

"Oh, you tryin' to get fucked up?" He grinned and walked up on her. He was so focused, he didn't see her grab the skillet handle. She waited until he had cocked his fist back, then she swung the skillet up off the stove, scalloped potatoes and all, and clunked him square on the side of his head. He stumbled back into the table, groaning and cursing. For a split second, Jewell glanced down at the food on the floor, but the adrenaline kicked in and she swung again, this time, catching his knee.

"Oooh, you stupid bitch!" He slurred in pain and slid down to the floor grabbing his knee. The room was spinning and he thought he could grab Jewell, but there were about four of her.

"I got'cho bitch!" Jewell held the skillet up over her head. She knew after this she'd have to kill Brian, or it was her ass. She stared at him as he tried unsuccessfully to get up. He was dizzy and had a massive headache. His whole left leg was throbbing, and every time he tried to get a little leverage, the potatoes on the floor caused him to slip right back down. Jewell had never had the upper hand and it felt good- damn good! She could easily get him one more good time in the head and finish him off, but she didn't have it in her.

"You ain't shit," he taunted her. She ignored him and returned the skillet to the stove. "I can barely fuckin' move and you ain't gon' do shit!" He laughed a bone chilling laugh as Jewell ran out of the kitchen. She wanted more than anything to crack him over the head and shut him up for good, but she couldn't have that on her conscience.

~~~

Jewell swooped by her parents' house to pick Alicia up. She knew once Brian got himself together that would be his first stop. She drove around and around letting Alicia's precious, high pitched voice erase her mind with question after endless question.

"Mommy, where are we going? Can we go to McDonald's? Is it too cold to jump rope? Can we stop and get some toys and juice?" Jewell wore her happy disguise perfectly. If it weren't for her daughter, she probably would've been sitting in a corner somewhere crying and scared shitless.

She ran through a list of family and friends. Most of her family, she wouldn't feel right imposing on, especially without being able to divulge the truth. It occurred to her that she was putting her pride and secrecy ahead of her well-being. For the life of her, she couldn't bring herself to tell anyone what she had been going through. She had a handful of friends who she talked to every now and then just to catch up. Her closest friends were her cousins, Neeka and Daisha. Jewell knew Brian would just bombard his way in looking for her. It finally dawned on her that she'd have to get a hotel. She wanted desperately to call Xavier. She knew he'd have a solution or two. On top of that, just hearing his voice would ease her mind. But she had made a decision and she had to stick to it. Maybe they'd cross paths in another six years. That thought had her close to tears, so she quickly tried to shake it away as she stopped at the ATM. She withdrew everything she could, just in case Brian was able to sweet talk some bank teller into giving up her information. Not likely, but she knew Brian would stop at nothing to find her.

Paranoid and desperate, Jewell checked into the first Motel 6 she thought Brian wouldn't suspect. The hotel room was typical. There was a queen-sized bed with a hideous, floral comforter, blue carpet, basic cable, bone white bathroom, and a nightstand with a Bible in the drawer. Alicia was bouncing wildly on the bed, but Jewell paid her no mind. She took the Bible out of the drawer and clutched it to her chest.

"Lord, what am I doing?" she whispered. She had just up and left. Emptied her bank account like she was in a position to move herself and her daughter away from Brian for good. The reality was that she had no next move. She and her baby were in a hotel with $856 and no plan B. Was she fully ready to leave Brian? She knew that despite what he said she could financially hold her own, but where would she go? What would she tell people? More importantly, how would she steer clear of Brian, especially since she had their daughter with her?

"Mommy, I'm hungry." Alicia scooted up to Jewell on the bed, comforting her without even knowing it.

"Hey, you wanna go to Wal-Mart?" Jewell asked. Alicia broke out giggling and clapping. Wal-Mart was *everything* to her. She could get toys, shoes, clothes, food and ride on a toy train! "I'm guessing that's a yes," Jewell laughed.

Wal-Mart was packed, as usual. They'd been

window shopping about half an hour when Jewell heard someone call her name. She recognized the voice and turned quickly down an isle.

"Jewell!" There it was again.

"Mommy look!" Alicia pointed and yelled. "It's Daisha!" Jewell rolled her eyes and turned around trying to play it off.

"Hey girl," she said calmly. Daisha was almost out of breath as she jogged up behind Jewell.

"You didn't hear me callin' you? Got my fat ass chasin' you through this store!" They both laughed. Daisha had a beautiful face, but she still felt like it couldn't hurt to lose about 60 pounds.

"Uh uh," Jewell answered, wanting to pop Alicia upside her head. "I guess I'm just in a daze."

"You ok? I ain't heard from you in a minute."

"Yea, I'm good. Me and Alicia are having some mother-daughter time." She hoped Daisha would get the hint and back off, but she just tagged along with them through the store. Jewell picked up a few personal hygiene items and a couple of outfits for she and Alicia, checked out, sat down, ate, and Daisha was *still* rambling on. By that time, she was going on about some guy she met, but Jewell wasn't trying to hear her. She just wanted to get back to the hotel.

"So what else y'all been doin' today?" Daisha asked.

"Nothin', why?" Now Jewell was skeptical.

Whenever Brian wanted to get in touch with her and she didn't answer the phone, he started calling Neeka and Daisha. If she didn't answer his text quick enough, he called Neeka or Daisha. She wondered what condition he was in, or if he was just that pissed, surprised, or embarrassed that he hadn't called anyone. Maybe he was out looking for her.

"I'm just used to talking to you every day. At least every other day."

"I know, I just been busy," Jewell lied. She hadn't felt like dealing with anyone lately. Distancing herself from Xavier had her feeling a loss she couldn't explain. It irritated her to her core. Why couldn't she just let go and not trip?!

"Well call me if you need me," Daisha told her.

"You know I will," Jewell forced a fake smile. She turned and wheeled her cart away, eager to dodge Daisha's suspicions.

Ch. 11

Jewell felt like a complete hypocrite sitting among the congregation Sunday morning. She had beaten her husband with a skillet of smothered potatoes and was asking for forgiveness. She had lied to Daisha, pushed her away and shut her out, knowing she and Neeka were her only real friends. She had made a conscious decision to call her parents and Neeka to let them know she was ok and just needed some time to herself, just in case Brian tried to reach out to them with questions. She had tucked her daughter in the night before like she hadn't knocked the girl's father upside the head. Then she had settled in next to her and stared at the ceiling where she was haunted by Brian's pained face all night. Even as she sat in the pew of the random church with her arm around Alicia, she could smell smothered potatoes. It felt as if everybody was looking at her and whispering, like they knew something.

The guilt was eating away at her.

"Come on, sweetie. Time to go." Jewell already didn't go to church like she should, and there she was creeping out in the middle of service. If people weren't looking at her before, they were surely watching her then.

"Mommy, why did we leave?" Alicia finally asked as they walked down the hall to the room in the hotel. Jewell was pondering her answer as she swiped the key card. As soon as she opened the door, Alicia hollered out.

"Daddy!" Alicia yelled and ran to Brian who was lounging comfortably on the bed. Jewell couldn't believe her eyes. How the hell did he know where to find them? And how did he get in.

"Hey, sweetie!" He scooped Alicia up in his arms and glared at Jewell with such evil and hatred that she was paralyzed right where she stood. "Did you and mommy have fun on your little vacation?" he asked.

"Yes! We went shopping, and to Wal-Mart, and to church!" Alicia yelled.

"That's nice, baby." Brian put her down and began walking towards Jewell. He was walking with a limp and she could clearly see the nasty bruise on his face from where she'd hit him. She was breathing so hard she could hear herself. Everything in her soul was telling her to run, but she refused to leave her daughter with him. He stood right in front of her and they stared each other dead in the eyes. Then the unimaginable happened. Brian leaned in, kissed Jewell on the forehead, and wrapped his arms around her...*lovingly*.

"Wha- what are you doing?" Jewell recoiled in his embrace, but he didn't pay her any attention.

"We gon' go home, and we gon' work this out." His tone was calm, and that scared the shit outta Jewell. He didn't sound like a man who'd been attacked with a skillet. She didn't know if by 'work it out' he meant sort out their problems rationally, or that he was gonna beat the brakes off her ass as soon as he got the chance. Either way, he had her in his grip and she didn't know how she was going to get away. She returned his hug, though it was half-assed. She didn't want her daughter to get an inkling that things were any worse off than normal. "Come on, baby," Brian called to Alicia. "You get to ride home with daddy." He grabbed his daughter's hand and walked past Jewell. She quickly gathered up their belongings and followed. She had no other choice but to. He had Alicia, and Jewell wasn't the type to make a scene.

Following Brian and thinking too hard had Jewell in a daze. She turned when he turned and stopped when he stopped. Then he turned onto a street that triggered precious memories. Xavier's shop was in the next block. Visions of the two of them together, his breath on her neck, his hands all over her, the taste of him, made her clit jump. He seemed to know her body as well as her mind, when to be forceful and when to be gentle with her. He knew exactly how to handle her, how to speak to her when she needed encouragement, when she needed entertainment, when she felt that longing that couldn't be fulfilled by anyone else. No one was perfect, but Xavier was as close to it as she had ever experienced.

BEEP!! BEEP!!

The light had turned green while Jewell was sitting there daydreaming. She eased onto the gas slowly, knowing she was about to pass by the shop and that Xavier was more than likely inside. Instead of creeping past, she pushed harder on the gas and stared straight ahead. She had told Xavier they were done, and there was no use dwelling on the past. With tears in her eyes, she caught up with Brian and began wondering again how he knew where to find her anyway. She had told Neeka and her parents that she needed time away, and she hadn't told Daisha anything.

Surprisingly, the night was without incident. Brian wasn't all lovey-dovey, but he wasn't his normal asshole self. He had cleaned the kitchen, which made Jewell pause. She was almost positive that he would've left potatoes all over the floor just to spite her. The rest of the house was spotless also, and it smelled amazing. Jewell walked around in awe, like she was seeing everything for the first time. Brian normally dropped whatever was in his hands wherever he was. It didn't matter if it was clothes, shoes, food, or trash. He got a kick out of being petty, but it seemed like he had spent a considerable amount of time trying to impress her.

They didn't speak much, and that was just fine with her. The silence was a little scary, but it was definitely a step up from the shouting and cursing matches. She wasn't expecting Brian to clean every day, automatically be sweet as hell, or even compliment her on a regular basis. If he was serious about changing, Jewell reasoned that she could only expect baby steps. In any case, she was still watching her back. Knowing Brian, it could all be a trick and he'd wait until she was good and comfortable, then the beatings would begin again. At that point, she was thankful for some peace and quiet. She just hoped he wouldn't try and get any.

~~~

Neeka was beyond furious. She didn't know what she was planning on doing when she went over to Brian and Jewell's house. Jewell's ass was proving more and more that she didn't want or deserve Brian. She needed *time to herself*? What the fuck was that? Neeka had decided to go over and lick Brian's wounds, only to find him pulling up with Jewell right behind him. While Neeka was begging for his time, calling him like crazy, and getting ignored, Jewell was neglecting him and trying to leave and take his kid with her, but he was all up her ass, tracking her down to bring her back home. She wanted so bad to run up, knock on the door, and tell Jewell the whole truth. She needed to know that it was really Neeka that Brian wanted, not her. He just felt some type of obligation to Jewell and Alicia, and that was pissing her off.

With tears burning her eyes, Neeka made a u-turn and slammed on the gas. She had convinced herself and she knew that his heart was with her, but he was just being stupid. Why couldn't he see what was right the fuck in front of him?! She asked herself that over and over again as she sped home. After all she had done for Brian, all the time she had given him, all the other dick she had passed up, he was still shacked up with Jewell's ass! She had listened to Jewell complain about petty shit for far too long. Now she knew the deep, dark secret her precious cousin had been hiding. She couldn't deal with it, but Neeka could. If she didn't want Brian, she needed to set him free so Neeka could scoop him up. Jewell would eventually get over it. She had to... they were family.

Ch. 12

It was after ten when Xavier finished the last of his paperwork. He had impressed the contractors, and they had approved his proposal to expand, awarding him the grant he'd applied for. He flipped on his radio as he had done many times, stalling before he had to go home. His Pandora was set to 90s R&B and it had him in a reminiscing mood. He closed his eyes and he and Jewell were riding in his red Corsica with the windows all the way down. The night-time summer air blew through while they talked, and quiet storm played softly in the background. He said something funny, which he tried to do all the time just to see her smile. Her whole face began to glow with that one gesture.

Xavier couldn't take it anymore. For years, he had wondered where Jewell had disappeared to and how she was doing. Then, like a quick rain, she was in and out again. Things had moved so fast in the few short weeks they'd been back in touch that it scared him a little. Not enough to give up though. It had been two weeks since she had walked out of the cafe with his heart in her fist. He couldn't let it end like that. Not again. He sat up from his lounging position and clicked his computer on.

YOU'VE BEEN ON MY MIND JEWELL. I MISS YOUR VOICE, YOUR SMILE, YOUR HUGS... I WANT YOU TO KNOW THAT I WOULD NEVER INTENTIONALLY HURT YOU AND I'M SINCERELY SORRY FOR WHATEVER PAIN YOU WERE IN. I FIND MYSELF WANTING TO SEE AND HOLD YOU AGAIN. BELIEVE ME, I HEARD EVERY WORD YOU SAID BEFORE YOU LEFT THAT DAY AND I DON'T WANT TO DISRESPECT YOUR WISHES, I JUST NEEDED YOU TO KNOW THAT NOT A DAY HAS GONE BY WHERE I HAVEN'T THOUGHT ABOUT YOU.

He tried to clear his mind on the way home. Even though he missed Jewell like crazy, he was tired of comparing Deena to her. He had made the decision to settle down and have a family. It wasn't fair that he kept trying to make his wife live up to a fantasy- which was exactly what Jewell felt like to him. His head was all mixed up. He cared about Jewell more than he should, more that he wanted to. He didn't want her on his mind, especially since she had walked out on him. He wanted to say fuck her and go on with his life. It was evident to him that she had been able to do just that. He knew he couldn't do it. He knew how to find her now. He knew her cell phone number,

Facebook page, email address, and where she worked. Even if she never answered his inbox, he was confident that they'd bump into each other again.

~~~

Jewell stared out the window as Brian pulled off. The clock on the living room mantle read 9:32 p.m. She couldn't remember the last time Brian had lied about a supposed *business meeting*, but that time she actually cared. It had been almost a month since he had forced her to leave the hotel. Since then, he'd been decent to her, cooking on occasion, he'd cleaned and washed clothes, and even said some kind words to her. He hadn't cursed her out or hit her, and they'd actually had sex a couple of times and it had been surprisingly good! Things had been looking up, or so Jewell thought.

Brian was taking a shower so she got it in her head that it was about to go down. That was, until he got out claiming he had a meeting. Jewell's heart dropped. She definitely wasn't expecting that. She stared at him quietly as he got dressed, and almost laughed at herself as he gave her a peck on the cheek and headed out. He had played her real good. She kept telling herself that the day was coming when the bubble would burst. He was starting off slowly. First, it was this business meeting, then he'd start ignoring her again, only talking to her to curse her out or call her out of her name. Eventually, the beatings would start again.

Jewell had to read three Berenstain Bears books before Alicia finally stopped fighting her sleep. She couldn't help but smile at her, so innocent. Her daughter was the perfect combination of both she and Brian. She had Brian's dark complexion, and thick lips, and Jewell's deep brown eyes and dimples. She wondered how something so beautiful could come from something so twisted. That's exactly what she felt her relationship with Brian was- twisted. She made a vow that she would teach her daughter better. She'd teach her to value herself enough to walk away from any situation that was hurtful or any man who degraded her and treated her like anything less than a queen. Her daughter wouldn't follow in her footsteps. She'd do everything in her power to make sure of that.

    Jewell popped a bag of popcorn, poured herself a glass of wine, and settled on the couch with her laptop. She figured a little retail therapy might do her some good. She began browsing through her inbox looking for coupons. She groaned at the hundreds of emails that had piled up while she'd been on her social hiatus. Between breaking things off with Xavier, getting caught up with Brian again, and going back and forth in her head wondering how stupid she was being, she hadn't really had time for anything at all. There were so many random emails to delete that she almost clicked Xavier's too. Her breath caught as she looked at his name. It was over a week old, and she knew he was probably cursing her out to himself. She had walked out on him again and didn't even answer him when he did reach back out to her.

She erased every piece of mail she didn't need before she let herself read Xavier's. It almost brought tears to her eyes. Why was he doing that to her?! He just needed her to know he was thinking about her?! A month had passed since she had seen him, but she could still *feel* him. She could hear his voice as she reread the email. *That* was what Xavier Black did to her. She longed for him in a way that was indescribable. Maybe knowing that she couldn't have him made her want him more. Maybe the fact that her own husband walked all over her made her want him more. Maybe it was just... *him*... No matter what, she had it bad.

It was after eleven, so Jewell knew Xavier more than likely wasn't still at the shop. She wouldn't dare call or text him, even though she was tempted to anyway. She wanted to write him, but there was so much she wanted to say that she couldn't think of where to start. Besides, she wouldn't be able to sleep wondering what his response would be. Instead of writing back, she decided to hold off until she was sure she knew he could respond.

The next morning, Jewell's heart was beating out of her chest thinking about Xavier. She kissed Brian before he headed out to take Alicia to school. Neither of them brought up the fact that he had crept into the house in the wee hours of the morning. It was funny to Jewell how she had been hurt when Brian left, but one email from Xavier and she could act like she didn't feel her husband slither his snake ass under the covers at 2 a.m.

By the time Jewell went on her first break, she was itching to text Xavier. She had thought all night about what she wanted to say, yet she was still unsure. Her finger hovered over the button for a few seconds before she finally pushed send.

to Zay:
I JUST GOT UR EMAIL, DIDN'T KNOW YOU MISSED ME SO MUCH

What she wanted to send was "Xavier I missed you like hell, I almost cried when I got your email, I feel like I need you. This shit is CRAZY!" But she just sat in the breakroom and waited for her phone to vibrate.

from Zay:
HOW HAVE YOU BEEN?
to Zay:
I'M DOING OK. YOU?
from Zay:
GOOD, WORKIN...

Jewell tried not to be too hurt that Xavier wasn't talking to her like he normally did. He always had a joke to make her smile or sweet words to make her blush. He'd at least call her baby or something. She got none of that from him, even after the email. It was understandable, but disappointing all the same. She figured he was either highly pissed at her, trying not to start anything up, or both.

to Zay:
DID YOU GET NEWS ABOUT EXPANDING?

She couldn't think of anything else to say. She wanted to talk to him, but she didn't want to start a conversation about missing him.

from Zay:
YEP, THEY APPROVED ME

Jewell didn't know what she really expected, but she was getting upset. She wasn't about to beg him or kiss his ass, no matter how badly she wanted to talk to him. She said forget it, and put her phone up. He was the one who wrote her. He couldn't be mad if she didn't reply as quickly as he wanted her to.

    Thirty minutes later, Xavier checked his phone again. No new messages. By that time, he was kicking himself. His heart and dick started jumping when he got her first text, but he tried to play it cool and not scare her away again. *Great job, Zay,* he scolded himself.

to Jewell:
AM I EVER GONNA SEE YOU AGAIN?

He desperately wanted, no, needed to see her. They weren't kids anymore. He was a grown ass man, so there was no reason to play games and beat around the bush. Yes, there was a lot at stake, but that was only if they tried to be more than just friends. He could handle just being her friend, right? All it would take was self control... and a lot of cold showers at the office. What he couldn't handle was not having her in his life.

Jewell sat staring at her phone so hard she almost forgot it was her lunch time. *Would he ever see her again?* How should she respond? Should she respond at all? Could she handle seeing him without falling into his arms? Just because he wanted to see her didn't mean she had to give in. She had given him his answer a month before in the cafe when she walked out.

from Zay:
I MISS YOU SO MUCH JEWELL

Jewell huffed and rolled her eyes. Fuck it.

to Zay:
OF COURSE UR GONNA SEE ME AGAIN

Ch. 13

"Hurry up, damn!" Brian yelled. Neeka was always stingy with the blunt. She took another quick puff then passed it obediently. She watched him as he lay in her lap blowing smoke rings in the air. She admired his naked body, glistening from the hour of hurting he had just finished putting on her. His deep, bronze skin was perfect. She rubbed his waves and traced his thick eyebrows. She placed her hand on his bulging arm and slid her fingers across his chest and down between the abs on his stomach. His rod was semi-hard and still had a drop of cum sitting at the tip. Neeka licked her lips at the sight.

"You lookin' real sexy right now," she moaned as she traced the vein alongside his manhood.

"Come on now baby, a nigga dick need a rest." Brian gently brushed Neeka's hand away, trying to ignore the slight jump her touch gave him. On a scale from one to ten, she was a twelve, but she was starting to get needy as hell. As good as she was, he wasn't about to give that ass up. He needed good pussy, and she was there to provide it. He knew she had feelings for him, but so what? Didn't they all? She was just gon' need to get it through her head that they fucked on *his* terms.

"I'm glad you started comin' back around," Neeka said, taking the blunt and putting it to her lips. Brian looked at her, uneasy as to where she was going with the conversation. She took a long drag, held her breath, and threw her head back before she let smoke seep out between her lips. He had to admit, she was sexy as hell. Dark chocolate, thick, suckable lips, with hips, thighs and ass to match, and dreads half way down her back. She looked like she was in ecstasy, letting the weed take full effect. Then she looked back down at him. "Finally tired of playin' the perfect husband, huh?" She had to go and fuck it up.

"What the hell you talkin' about now, Neeka?" he asked, annoyed.

"I'm just sayin', you call me complainin', this heffa tryin' her best to get away, and you drag her back and start ignorin' me." Brian huffed and got up from the bed to get his boxers. "Where you goin'?" She hopped up after him in a panic.

"I didn't come over here for this." He pulled on his pants and Neeka searched for something to say to make him stay.

"You know you want some more of this." She grabbed his hand and guided one finger inside her.

"Damn right." He grinned and sucked the wetness off his finger. "Just not right now." Neeka was fuming.

"Then when, Brian? How long am I gon' have to wait this time? While you suck up to your precious *Jewell*! What makes her ass so fuckin' special?!" He shook his head as he pulled his shirt on. If her sex wasn't so damn good, he would've left her ass in the dust a long time ago. It just so happened, he couldn't find a better fuck than her. She wasn't his only, but she was his best. That made her smart mouth ass very lucky.

Brian's silence was driving Neeka crazy. She absolutely hated being ignored! "You standin' there like I ain't shit. I bet yo' ass will talk up if I call Jewell and tell her you just got done suckin' my pussy." He spun around and glared at her. She stared him down, silently begging him to give in and stay. He reached out instead, and gripped her tiny neck. Surprised, her hands flew up to his arms, scratching, trying to pull away.

"You open yo' mouth, I'm breakin' this bitch," He gave her neck a quick, tight squeeze and pushed her back onto the bed. Then he walked out, leaving Neeka gasping for air.

~~~

Jewell sat at the cafe table with butterflies in her

stomach. Xavier had sent her a text saying he was running late for their lunch date. That gave her some time to pull herself together. Even though she was trying not to think about the last time they were in the cafe, she was overly excited to lay eyes on him again. They'd talked and been decent with each other, making sure to shy away from feelings and shoulda-coulda-woulda's, and avoiding late night conversations that would undoubtedly turn x-rated. She was risking every ounce of sanity to see him, knowing damn well she didn't wanna just be that man's friend. Every time she'd thought about Xavier over the years, it had been accompanied by a 'what if.' What if she had told him how she felt? What if she hadn't gotten pregnant? What if she hadn't stopped answering his phone calls? What if they had actually gone as far as having sex?

"Jewell?" Her thoughts were cut short and she turned to see Daisha grinning at her. "I thought I saw your car outside!" She squeezed into the booth seat right across from Jewell. "Girl I don't know why they make these things so doggone small! Big girls gotta eat too." She laughed and began unbuttoning her jacket. Only then did she notice the pained look on her cousin's face. "Oh, I'm sorry, were you meeting somebody?" Jewell wanted so bad to tell her damn right and to have her ass get up outta that seat. She wanted to confide in her cousin so bad, but she couldn't bring herself to let anybody taint her relationship with

forbidden distractions   *t.c.flenoid*

Xavier. Of course Daisha and Neeka had known about him back then, and heard about him over the years, but that was then. Now, he was married with a child, as was she. She didn't need anybody to tell her that her feelings were wrong. She was fully aware of that herself.

"Hey, Daisha! Naw I ain't meetin' nobody. Just out." She tried to sound as upbeat as she could, even though she wanted to cry. Of all the days she could run into her, it just had to be the day she was meeting Xavier. After a couple of minutes of Daisha rattling on about her boyfriend, Jewell eased her phone out to text Xavier.

to Zay:
MY COUSIN POPPED UP AND I DON'T THINK I CAN GET RID OF HER. WHEN ARE YOU FREE AGAIN?

Not five seconds after she pushed send, the cafe door opened and in he walked. Jewell immediately felt a rush. A wave of emotion swept over her as she stared at him. He wore jeans and fresh Jordan's with a crisp white tee, a black jacket and a Cardinals cap down low over his eyes. That man looked good in *anything*. She watched as he fished his phone out of his pocket and checked his message. His brow crinkled and he swiveled his head until he found her. Their eyes locked and the familiar warmth filled the space between them.

"Earth to Jewell," Daisha waved her hand in front of Jewell's face and turned to see what she was staring at.

"Oooh he is *fine*," she whispered and giggled. Jewell tore her gaze away. "Girl, you know him?"

"Naw, I don't know him." Jewell answered quickly, relieved she wasn't with Neeka. They had all gone to school together, but Daisha had graduated a couple of years after them, which was why she hadn't recognized Xavier. It probably would've taken Neeka a minute, but eventually it would've hit her exactly who he was. There was no telling what her wild ass would've done.

"Coulda fooled me," Daisha chimed. "Dang, where the waitress at?" Jewell suppressed the urge to roll her eyes. She could look directly at Daisha and clearly see Xavier take a seat at the counter. Two women at the table behind him seemed to be admiring him. One got up and approached him. She looked like a fake Barbie to Jewell, although that could've just been the jealousy talking. Her weave was long and silky, her eyebrows were drawn to perfection, titties sitting up high, almost in her neck, and her waist was damn near invisible. She couldn't tell what the female was saying, but she knew what it was regarding. Xavier flashed his ring and the woman smiled and said something else then took her seat. Jewell didn't know why she was so frustrated. Xavier was an attractive man. Women were bound to hit on him just like men hit on her.

To say Xavier was disappointed would be an understatement. Even after Jewell agreed to see him again, it had taken a couple of weeks to butter her up. Having to just look at her and not be able to sit and talk with her irritated him to his soul. Had it been a couple of months ago, he would've texted her and told her exactly what was on his mind, that he needed to be closer to her. Fuck Brian. He had never been good enough for Jewell. Xavier understood she wasn't ready for him, but he didn't like it. And instead of staring at her wishing he was in her cousin's seat, he got up and left. He purposely didn't make eye contact with her. He was determined to make it hard as hell for her until he broke her down.

~~~

"Where the hell you been today? Because yo' ass shole wasn't at work." Jewell huffed and walked past Brian, escorting Alicia to her room. *Nigga can't even speak to his daughter before he start in on me.* Jewell ignored him and slipped into their bedroom. Brian followed. "So you deaf now?" he demanded. Jewell yanked off her shoes and turned to face him.

"I was off today Brian, so no, I wasn't at work. I laid around. I had lunch with Daisha. I made some runs. I scratched my ass. I went to pick up my daughter. What did *you* do today?" She put her hands on her hips and waited. Her chest heaved from anger and anticipation. She didn't know what was coming, but she was tired of being Brian's prisoner. Add that to the fact that Daisha had crashed her lunch date, and her attitude was on ten.

"I want another baby." Jewell paused and blinked at him.

"Say what?" She was waiting to get swung on or cursed out. That, she did *not* expect.

"I said I want another baby." Brian closed and locked the bedroom door.

"I don't feel like playin' wit'chu." Jewell tried to walk to the door and Brian grabbed her shoulders. "You know I'm on birth control," Jewell blurted out, trying to calm the fear that was bubbling.

"Don't make me say it again. I'm not asking you, I'm telling you. Alicia wants a lil' sister or brother." Jewell tried to yank away, but Brian pushed her and she flew back into the side of the bed and dropped to the floor. "If it's a girl, we can let Alicia name her." He yanked her up from the floor and dropped her on the bed. She instinctively grabbed her belt, thinking that would keep Brian away. Negative. He grabbed her hands and pinned them over head while he pulled her belt off.

"Brian *please*!!" Jewell begged quietly, not wanting Alicia to hear. She kicked at him, trying to break free, but he was determined.

"I dont know what you fightin' me for." Brian grinned at her.

"Get off of me," Jewell growled. Brian stopped pulling at her pants and punched her in her side. She winced in pain, and immediately gave up. Brian was twice her size, horny, and determined. She felt like it was her own fault. She couldn't help but think what the hell did she even come back for? She could have found somewhere else, *anywhere else to go*. She had ample time and opportunity to get away. But there she was, dealing with Brian's bullshit again. He had never gone that far though.

    Jewell closed her eyes and went limp. She wouldn't give him the satisfaction, though she tried not to flinch when he forced his way inside of her. Brian's dick was far from small, and he was acting like he didn't know it. She tried her best to go numb and stick it out until it was over. He seemed to be enjoying himself, and she figured the pain from the friction of his dick was better than the bruises she'd have to hide if she tried to fight him off again. With every dry, excruciating thrust, Jewell drifted further off into her head. She thought about the feeling she had the first time she held Alicia and the joy that had come to her watching her grow. She thought about her own childhood and how blessed she was that her parents were married and raised her in a loving home. She tried to let every wonderful thought she had in her head wash over her in an attempt to dull the pain.

    When she finally felt Brian stiffen and begin to shake, Jewell was relieved. He pulled out and she quickly balled up and turned on her side, even though it hurt like hell to move. Brian hopped up and jumped into his pants like he hadn't just got done raping her.

"Guess what, baby," he said, sounding way too happy. Jewell kept her eyes closed, listening to him shuffle around a little, hoping he would just leave. "Now when we go to your reunion in a few weeks, we can say we're havin' a baby. That's way more exciting than you just tellin' people you work in customer service don't you think?" He slapped her on her butt and she flinched a little. When he left, he closed the door behind himself. Thankful, Jewell grabbed the sheets to cover up her nakedness.

So many thoughts ran through her mind. If she hadn't thought her husband was crazy before, he had pushed her there. She figured he had found out about her reunion on Facebook, which was of course where everybody got their information. She flat out did not want to go with him. She wasn't sure if she wanted to go at all. There was definitely no way she was having another baby with that man. She was on the pill and he knew that. He just wanted to do some ignorant shit, and there was no reasoning with him. He was gonna do what he wanted, and Jewell didn't know why she hadn't been expecting it before. There was no way she was going to stop taking her pills and give him another baby, and there was no way in hell she was letting him touch her again!

Ch. 14

"Do you have anything for me?" Deena didn't even bother to say hi when she saw who was calling her.

"Well damn, *hello* to you too," the woman on the other end snapped.

"Hi, Tori," Deena huffed.

"I still don't have anything. I stepped it up like you asked and approached him. He didn't take the bait, and I'm Puerto Rican and fine as hell." Tori admired herself in the mirror. "It's been over a month. How long you want me to do this?"

"As long as I'm paying you!" Deena yelled and hung up. She could've slapped herself for being so desperate. Tori dug up so much shit on both of her baby daddies she made herself look like Sherlock Holmes. And for $100 a week, Deena was sure her co-worker would've been able to dig up some dirt on Xavier by now. She brought her nothing but disappointment. Deena felt like her husband had to be up to something. Her marriage was far from perfect and she knew that. But she loved Xavier and refused to look like boo-boo the fool. She couldn't shell out for a professional without Xavier finding out, so her bootleg investigator was just gonna have to work harder.

~~~

Tori pulled her hair out of her ponytail holder and let it hang freely down her back. She grabbed a Bud Light out of the refrigerator and plopped down at her desk, hooking her camera up to her printer. She took a swig and grinned as she printed out the pictures she'd snapped. Tori had a weakness for a black man, and Xavier was chocolate, successful and sexy in whatever he wore. She had pictures of him in a suit and tie with glasses looking distinguished, and then there were pictures of him at the gym all sweaty and muscular playing basketball. She loved them camouflage niggas. Them Jay Z, 50 Cent type of dudes that could eat with kings and talk that boss language then turn around laughing, cursing and playing spades with his people in his Timbs and sweats.

Tori could tell Xavier was a go-getter. His business swag was so sexy, she started to enjoy following him around. She could tell he knew how to have a good time. He had just been so stressed and wound up between expanding his business and Deena being on his case day in and day out. Tori had been hesitant at first when Deena came to her, but if she could earn $100 every Monday just by being nosey then so be it. Nosey was her middle name anyway, so it was easy money. She was excited when Deena decided to have her approach Xavier. She had never met a chick so dead set on having her man cheat. She could see why Deena was so nervous, though. The man was a rare find. And now she knew he had a smooth ass voice to match. She'd taken her friend to the cafe near Xavier's shop just to keep a watch out for him, and it was just her luck that he walked in. Yea, he flashed his ring in her face, but she also saw that all too familiar look in his eye. She could tell he liked what he saw, and that heffa, Deena, had gotten one too many attitudes with her. Tori figured she'd just have to accidentally run into her husband again.

~~~

    Xavier pulled into his driveway and let his seat back as far as it would go. Jewell was on his mind, as always. He'd sent her a text a couple of hours after he left the cafe jokingly asking her if she had enjoyed her lunch. A little later he told her that he had wanted to stay, but it didn't look like her company was leaving any time soon. No answer either time. He had tried to concentrate on work, but his thoughts kept drifting to why she hadn't been answering him. Finally, he swallowed his anguish and headed home, only to sit in his driveway thinking about her again. He huffed and clicked on the radio.

We can't be friends...cause I'm still in love with you...

Deborah Cox and R.L.'s crooning voices practically slapped him in the face."Oh you gotta be kidding me," Xavier laughed and cut the radio off. He could see that the light was on in the living room. There was no doubt in his mind that Deena's butt would fuse to the couch one day. Whenever she wasn't at work, that was her favorite place to be. Only the thought of his daughter's smile motivated him out of the car.

"Daddy!" Sure enough, Miranda's little voice greeted him, and he swung her up on his side. "Mommy's cooking!" she told him. Xavier's eyes widened.

"Oh, is she?" He put Miranda down and headed towards the kitchen. The closer he got, the stronger the smell of shrimp scampi became. He stood in the doorway admiring Deena as she scurried around the stove. He wasn't one to say a woman's place was in the kitchen, but it was a nice sight every now and then. After a couple of minutes, she finally realized that he was standing there watching her.

"Oh, hey," she was a little nervous, praying her impromptu dinner was a step in the right direction of fixing whatever was wrong with her marriage, since Tori couldn't find any evidence of another woman.

"Hey yourself," he smiled at her. She had her hair

pulled up in a messy ponytail with a tank top and jogging capris on. There was no denying his wife was fine. Sometimes it was just hard to see it through her ignorance, childishness and selfishness. Watching her in the kitchen cooking for him, seeming like she actually wanted to impress him and make him happy, made him cock his head and lick his lips. He hadn't done that in a while. Later on when he gave her the business, he might not even have to fake it.

~~~

"Thanks for letting us stay here for a lil' bit," Jewell said, sitting her and Alicia's bags down. Neeka stared at the back of Jewell's head with her lip turned up. Her house wasn't a fuckin' hotel, but having *her* there meant she could get closer to Brian.

"You good, cuz," she lied through her teeth. She was growing more and more bitter towards Jewell every day. The bitch had to be crazy to throw her husband and family away, and for what this time? Neeka played the concerned family member perfectly, wanting to know what happened and extending prayers, but of course, Jewell didn't feel like talking about it. She never told the whole story. Neeka figured whatever it was, it was too stupid to even speak on.

"It's only for a few days. A week at the most." Once that week was up, Jewell had no idea what she was going to do. No plan at all. That scared the shit out of her.

After three days, Neeka was *tired*. Tired of seeing cartoons on her damn t.v. Tired of waiting in line to use her own bathroom. Tired of sharing her space with the same woman she had to share her man with, especially when she didn't even know why she was there in the first place. Jewell still thought they were thick as thieves like they used to be, but she was dead wrong. The moment Neeka had to fight for attention that used to be given to her with no question, Jewell had become the enemy.

"I'm leavin' for a lil' bit," she shouted from the front door. Without waiting for a response, she jetted to her car. Her heart was racing as she drove with her mind on one thing. In less than twenty minutes, she was sitting in front of Brian and Jewell's house. The yard was neat, the walkway was clean, the front porch was welcoming, the damn swing was swaying a lil' bit in the breeze. Neeka wanted to throw up. Everything was so fuckin' perfect lookin'. Jewell didn't deserve any of it. That was supposed to be *her* swing on *her* porch. She got out and walked up to ring the bell before she lost her nerve. She hadn't heard from Brian in a few days so she was really taking a risk.

"Neeka?" he answered the door half sleep and seemingly confused, even though it was two in the afternoon.

"Hey, baby," she pushed past him before he had a chance to turn her away. "Close the door, I wanna show you somethin'."

"What'chu doin' here, Neeka?" he asked, rubbing his eyes. She watched him with a devious smile on her face. He didn't have an attitude with her. He didn't argue. He simply closed the door like she asked.

"I'm here for you, baby." She took off her jacket and let it drop to the floor. He just stared at her. She turned away from him and headed up the hallway, pulling her dress up over her head. By the time she made it to the bedroom door, she only had on heels. She turned around to see Brian walking after her like a puppy. *Checkmate, bitch.*

"You gotta get up." Neeka woke to Brian shaking her. She was groggy, but she could clearly make out that sexy face staring down at her. His lips, his hands, his stroke, his bed... "Come on, Neeka, you gotta go." He dropped her clothes in a pile on top of her. That's when she noticed he was fully dressed.

"What's wrong?" she asked.

"What'chu mean what's wrong? You in my bed. Get up and put yo' shit back on." Neeka scrunched her nose up at him, but got up and started getting dressed. She wasn't really sure what she expected, showing up at his house unannounced. She got him to give in to her, but the moment was over, and he was pushing her through the hall to get out.

"Okay, Brian, damn! I'm goin'!"

"Well go. I got stuff to do." She was barely able to snatch her jacket up off the floor before she was out on the porch and the door was closing behind her. She rolled her eyes and stomped to her car like a kid. At least she made it into the bedroom. It wouldn't take much time for her to claim Jewell's spot.

Brian watched out of the living room window, making sure Neeka left. He shook his head at himself, and his weak dick. Did he really need it that bad? No bullshit, that ass was good, but damn. Did he have to have her in the bed? Oh well. What was done was done. And Jewell had had enough days to think. It was time for her to bring her ass home.

Jewell turned her phone over in her hand. She hadn't heard from Xavier since the day Brian raped her. She hadn't been up for conversation or jokes. She knew Xavier would be able to tell something was wrong, and she wasn't ready to tell him what was going on. Brian hadn't tried to text or call with any apologies. She had the nerve to be a tad disappointed in him. Her phone had been pretty quiet, outside of her mama and a couple of people from work she talked to on and off. She had been tossing and turning every night, begging God to help her come up with a solution. Having her daughter sleeping on a pallet on her cousin's living room floor was not a high point in her life. Neeka had offered numerous times to teach her the ins and outs of being a booster, which, along with welfare, kept her living decent. It was tempting, but Jewell was too paranoid. If Neeka got caught up it would only affect her. Jewell had Alicia to look after. She knew all she had to do was say the word and Xavier would help her with whatever she needed. She wouldn't dare go to him though. She couldn't ask her parents. They would hit her with a hundred questions, and she really didn't feel like a lecture. She couldn't go to Daisha. She loved her cousin, but she was nosier than anybody she knew.

With Neeka gone doing whatever Neeka did, Alicia at school, and Jewell at the apartment alone, the knock at the door scared the crap out of her. She was filled with mixed emotions when she saw Brian through the peep hole. She exhaled and tried her best to compose herself before she opened the door. They locked eyes and Brian had one of the saddest looks on his face she had ever seen.

"Hi, baby," he said with tears welling up. Jewell's heart almost broke. She couldn't remember the last time she'd seen him like that. Probably before she had Alicia. "I'm *so* sorry, Jewell. I miss you," he told her. He moved forward and she instinctively moved back. She wasn't sure how to react. His tears looked genuine. So much so, that she wanted to pull him to her. Instead, she stood still and he came to her. He slid his arms around her waist and up her back as he pulled her closer. He rested his chin lightly on her head and let out a sigh of relief when she finally wrapped her arms around him. She began to sink into him, but the feeling was short-lived.

"*Brian*?!" They both jumped at Neeka's voice. "What the hell are you doin' here?"

"I came to take my wife home," he growled. His nostrils flared up as he stared at her. He was so close, and if she fucked it up for him, he was gonna have to fuck *her* up.

"Oh, so now you wanna come and take her home?" Neeka was kicking herself for stopping at the store. Maybe she would've caught him before he did the ignorant shit. What the hell was he thinking?!

"It's okay, cousin." Jewell put her arm around Neeka, naively thinking that she was coming to her defense. Neeka and Brian both knew what was really up.

"Babe," Brian grabbed Jewell's free hand. "These past few days have been hell for me-"

"What makes you think you can just stroll on over here talkin' that shit-"

"The house is lonely without you," he cut Neeka off. "*I'm* lonely without you." She couldn't believe what she was hearing! Not three hours earlier, he was ramming into her like no one else in the world existed. Just as she pictured her legs propped up on his shoulders, she felt Jewell's arm slip from around her own. She couldn't hide her disbelief.

"Cousin, what the fuck?" Neeka slammed the front door behind her and grabbed Jewell's arm. Brian quickly pulled her back to him.

"Neeka, you really need to mind your business. This is between me and my *wife*. Babe, you wanna get your stuff?" Jewell avoided eye contact with Neeka as she went to the hall closet to get her and Alicia's things together. Brian made sure Jewell was busy before he grabbed Neeka under her arm and yanked her out of the apartment.

"What the hell are you doing, Brian?" Neeka whispered.

"Don't ask stupid questions. I'm here for her."

"What about earlier?"

"What about it? We fucked," he whispered, irritated.

"*Briiian-*" she reached out for him and he smacked her hand away.

"Stop whining. That shit ain't cute." She turned away from him and stared up the hall at the other apartment doors, trying to keep herself from crying. Who the hell did he think he was anyway? She had the power to blow his shit clean out of the water and fuck his life all the way up, but she didn't want him upset with her. She shook her head at herself. She didn't have the balls to make him mad. Jewell would *have* to forgive her because she was family, but she couldn't risk it with Brian. He may never speak to her again. That would kill her.

Jewell pulled the door open and handed Brian her and Alicia's bags. "I'll meet you at the car, ok." Brian nodded and kissed her on the forehead, then headed to the car without giving Neeka so much as a glance. Jewell waited until Brian was on the elevator before she turned to Neeka. "I know what you're thinkin'."

"You couldn't *possibly* know," Neeka huffed.

"I took vows. Brian is my husband." She watched Neeka roll her eyes and sighed. She didn't have any other choice. She couldn't stay on Neeka's couch forever and she didn't have any other options at that point. She'd rather take her chances at her own house. She couldn't trip off of her cousin's feelings about the situation. It wasn't Neeka's life to live.

Ch. 15

Tori sat in the parking garage gripping her steering wheel, trying to build up the guts to do what she had planned. Her heart was beating double time as she said a quick prayer and put her Jeep Cherokee in reverse. She took a deep breath, slammed on the gas, and flew backwards into the column behind her. Even though she knew it was coming, the impact shook the hell out of her. She pulled back into her parking spot and got out to check the damage to her back end. She wasn't trying to put her baby outta commission, she just wanted it dented a little. Grinning and pleased with herself, Tori hopped back in the car. "Guess I'mma have to get that fixed," she mumbled.

    Ten minutes later, she pulled into Black's Auto Body and Detail Shop. She checked her hair and makeup and made sure the girls were sittin' pretty. "Let's see him turn me away this time." She blew herself a kiss in the mirror and smiled.

The bell over the door sounded out when Tori walked through. All eyes were on her and she loved it. She was used to it of course, but it was always a rush to command the room. She swayed her ass and long legs across the floor and leaned over to give the young man at the counter a face full of cleavage.

"Hello," she glanced at the name stitched on his shirt. "*Mason.*" She smiled and licked her lips. "I need my bumper worked on."

"Oh, I can definitely handle that," Mason replied. He was trying desperately to stay focused on her eyes and not her chest, but she was in his face like she wanted to breastfeed him. He flirted a little as he took down her information. She handed him her key like she was handing him her panties. He nodded his head at her, thinking she didn't have to lay it on so thick. He was planning on asking for her number anyway. But she burst his bubble real quick.

"Is Xavier here?" Mason's jaw dropped and he grabbed his chest. Just as he was about to tell her how much she was hurting his feelings, the bell chimed over the door again. Tori stood straight up when she saw Deena step through the door with Miranda. The women locked eyes throwing daggers at each other. The workers gawked at the two of them, eager to see a girl fight. Having finished giving her information, Tori walked past Deena and clean out the door.

"Miranda, sit here baby." Deena looked up. "Y'all, watch her," she told the workers. She spun around and marched out after Tori.

"Aye, Black!" Mason called out and Xavier appeared on the second floor.

"Wassup?" he asked hurrying down the steps when he saw Miranda.

"Some fine ass chick dropped her car off and was lookin' for you," he whispered, not wanting Miranda to hear. "Boss Lady came in and she ran her off, though. They might be about to throw them hands on the sidewalk." Mason and a few of the other men laughed as Xavier walked over to look out the window. He caught the tail end of what looked like an intense conversation Deena was having with a woman who looked vaguely familiar to him. As soon as he turned away, it hit him. It was the woman who had approached him in the cafe. He had no idea what was going on, but he knew Deena wouldn't voluntarily tell him. He'd have to find out himself.

"So I decided we should go to all of my reunion events," Deena announced.

"Oh, *you* decided?" Xavier replied with a frown. His wife had a sneaky way of making him feel like he wasn't a man, like he didn't make any decisions, like even though he worked his ass off, nothing he did was good enough. On top of that, he was already frustrated that she had decided to drop her car off to get serviced without letting him know. He'd have to cut time out of his day to drop her off and pick her up. It wouldn't have been a problem if he had planned for it, but he was positive she had something up her sleeve.

"*Yes*, honey, I decided!" she answered with a smile. "You know how it was in high school. I bet nobody expected me to be married, successful *and* beautiful." She reached over and rubbed Xavier's bicep. "I snatched you from all them hoes and I wanna show you off."

"They've seen me before." Xavier muttered. He wasn't nearly as excited as Deena was. Thinking about the time he spent at Parkway for high school made him think about Jewell. That was something he didn't want to do, especially since she had done her infamous disappearing act again.

"They saw you like *eleven* years ago though, baby." Deena went on and on, but Xavier had stopped listening. Who was the woman Deena had been arguing with? What did she have up her sleeve? Why had Jewell stopped answering his messages? Was she ok? Was Brian still mistreating her? He huffed at the thought. "What?" Deena asked.

"Nothin'. Go ahead." She kept talking, not even realizing that he wasn't listening. She wasn't perceptive at all, always in her own world. The new Deena was so short-lived, he had almost forgotten about her. There was that one shrimp scampi dinner, he actually got some decent head that night, and she made sure the house was clean for a couple of days. He figured maybe she got bored with actually *being* a wife. Cooking and cleaning must've drained her.

"Xavier!" she yelled!

"What?" he yelled back with an attitude.

"You're about to pass my building!"

"Oh, my bad." Xavier put his blinker on and got over so he could turn onto the lot.

"4:30, don't forget!" She hopped out of the car without a thank you or a kiss goodbye. She didn't even tell her daughter she loved her. He shook his head, watching her walk inside.

"Are you ready for school, sweetie?" he asked Miranda. She started clapping and laughing, so he took that as a yes. He couldn't wait to get back to work to look at the mystery woman's paperwork and find out who the hell she was.

~~~

"Fuck you too you bitch ass nigga!" Brian deleted the latest voicemail from Neeka. He was tempted to go over to her house and give her ass a dose of act right, but he had to be on his best behavior again. Jewell had the nerve to be acting like she was still mad. She hadn't spoken a full five sentences to him in the two weeks she'd been back home from Neeka's. She cooked and didn't make his plate, she didn't wash his clothes, and she slept in their daughter's room which meant he wasn't getting any. He hadn't even tried to get ass from anybody else, which was a big deal for him. Brian barely went three days without a nut, and not by his own hand. Let him tell it, as long as pussy was available, then a man was supposed to be able to get his nut off. Just because he had married Jewell didn't mean it had to be her all the time. It just meant she was supposed to be willing and available whenever he decided he wanted her. And her ass hasn't been willing to do a damn thing, even when she was off work. Fuck her. Fuck Neeka too, for now. She needed to calm down some, then he'd bless her with the D again. But he needed some ass quick, before he lost his mind. He peeked into the kitchen where she was making cupcakes. He laughed to himself. If she paid more attention to her husband and less to tyring to be a damn pastry chef or whatever the hell she wanted to be, they wouldn't have half the problems they had. He turned around and left the house without saying a word.

    Jewell froze for a few seconds, just to make sure Brian was really gone, then she exhaled a sigh of relief. She had made the decision to go back home to keep some type of normalcy in her daughter's life. While she appreciated Neeka for letting them stay there, she hated seeing Alicia out of her comfort zone. Going back home *with* Brian was different from going back home *to* Brian. Sure, she followed him back that day, but she'd be damned if things would go his way. If he thought he was getting his obedient wife back, he had another thing coming. He had tried to make small talk, tried to flirt, even tried to kiss her, but she finally realized that she was better than the bullshit. She helped pay bills in that house so she wasn't leaving, and her daughter wasn't either. Just because Brian was there didn't mean she had to act like it. She hadn't given him the time of day, and ignoring him had her feeling empowered. After a couple of weeks, he finally seemed to give up. She stood her ground with him, not speaking, sleeping in Alicia's room, not giving in, but she walked around on eggshells. She knew Brian, and at any moment, she knew he was liable to snap. She finished whipping up her icing and was waiting for her cupcakes to cool when her phone rang. She almost dropped her bowl trying to get to it. When she realized it was only Neeka, her heart dropped.

    "Hello?" she answered, disappointed.

    "Dang, you could sound happier to hear from me!" Neeka yelled.

    "I'm sorry, cousin, I thought you might be somebody else." *Xavier*...

    "Oooh, a *man* somebody else?" Neeka listened intently, waiting for any ammunition she could use against her.

"No, not a *man*. I'm waiting to hear from a job," Jewell lied.

"Really, what job?" Neeka asked, uninterested.

"This place in the county, I don't think you've ever heard of it."

"Oh, well are my cupcakes done?"

"Yea, I'm just now finishing up."

"Ok, Brian ain't there, is he?" Neeka crossed her fingers, eager to get in his face as soon as Jewell turned her back.

"No, he just left." Jewell rolled her eyes. She knew Neeka wasn't the biggest supporter of her going home, but she didn't know the full story. She thought about telling Neeka the truth, even though it really wasn't her business. She was just tired of hearing her gripe about her going back home.

"Oh, ok, I'm on my way then." Neeka got off the phone and huffed. She hated wasting gas. She didn't even want any damn cupcakes.

Ch. 16

Tori made sure she was on point before she called her ride. Xavier had contacted her *personally* to let her know her car was ready. She figured Mason had told him that the sexiest woman he'd ever laid eyes on had asked to see him. She laughed to herself and pushed her breasts up in her shirt. Xavier had to see what she was about. During the uber ride, Tori was surprised to find herself nervous. It wasn't like she hadn't messed around with a married man before. What she hadn't done before was mess around with the husband of somebody she knew. Deena had decided to call the whole thing off when she saw her at the shop. Tori tried to explain that she was only doing what Deena asked, getting closer. The bitch had the nerve to call her crazy.

"Who the hell wrecks their car on purpose, Tori?" she had asked her.

"Oh please, Deena. I didn't *wreck* it! There's a *dent* in it."

"*Still!*" Deena yelled at her. Tori had wanted to deck her ass right there on the sidewalk, but she was sure it would be a bad look. She had been planning on using Deena's money to pay for her car, but she had the nerve to ask her to stop cold turkey. Just like that, her Monday payouts were over. Either way, she had accomplished what she wanted and gotten Xavier's attention, so oh well. She wasn't on a mission for Deena anymore. She was on a mission for herself.

The trip was short, and Tori couldn't wait to pay the driver and get inside to talk to Xavier. She primped herself a little, making sure everything was perfect before she walked in. Once that bell rang above the shop door, she knew it would be lights, camera, action.

"Hey there, miss lady. Nice to see you again," Mason made his way from a car he had jacked up to greet her.

"Hello, Mason." Tori gave him a huge smile. "I got a call from Mr. Black that my vehicle was ready to be picked up."

"Sure thing. Go ahead and have a seat and I'll get him for you." Xavier had already let his workers know that he was waiting for her to show up. He needed to find out what she wanted with him, and how she knew Deena. Mason walked over to the desk and called the office. After a few seconds, he escorted Tori up to the second floor. He winked and Xavier shook his head at him, letting him know it was nothing like that. Mason grinned and closed the door to leave. Tori took a deep breath and turned to face him.

"Well hello, Mr. Black," she put on her seductive voice. She was holed up in Xavier's office staring him dead in his face and he was so damn sexy she was trying to keep herself from getting wet.

"Miss Peloza." He gazed up at her from his seat at his desk. He wanted to get up and wait for her to sit, like a real gentleman should, but if he got any closer to her, he was sure she'd get the wrong idea. Plus, there was a vibe about this chick that he didn't like. She was fine as hell, but everything about her was setting off red flags in his head.

"I was surprised you called. I'm sure you have staff to make calls for you." She rubbed her finger across the desk as she walked, never breaking eye contact. Xavier was tired of the act.

"Why did you approach me at the cafe across the street?" Tori stopped and put her hands on her hips and smiled.

"So you *do* remember me?" Xavier crossed his arms and glared at her. "I was hoping you would."

"How did you hear about my shop?" he asked. "You stay clean across town."

"You know where I stay? Have you been checkin' on

me, Mr. Black?"

"Look," he got up from his desk and Tori scanned his body with hungry eyes. "I'm not for these games. What do you want with me and how do you know my wife?" Tori was surprised he'd asked about Deena. He must've seen them going at it outside the shop. She was pissed, but she recovered quickly.

"I work with Deena. We aren't the best of friends, but we do talk on occasion. I honestly didn't know she was married." Xavier lifted his eyebrow, waiting for more. Tori huffed playfully. "My friend that I was with that day asked me to lunch. She stays in the neighborhood and brought her car here before. She said y'all do good work, so when I had my fender bender, I decided to give you a little business."

"Why were you and Deena arguing?" Xavier asked, still not satisfied.

"She had the crazy notion that I knew you were her husband and that I was pushing up on you." Tori put her hand on her chest. "I had *no* idea. She doesn't even talk about you. There's a picture of a little girl on her desk, but I haven't seen any other ones," she lied. Deena couldn't help bragging about her fine, successful husband who bought her any and everything she could possibly want.

"Ok. You can go on down to pay and get your keys," Xavier replied. He kept a straight face. If that was all this woman had to say, then that was what he was gonna leave it at. He wasn't a detective, and he was much too busy for games.

    Tori didn't move for a few seconds. Was she being *dismissed*?! When Xavier walked past her and opened his office door, she got the memo loud and clear. She had never been so humiliated! How dare he treat her like that! She was Victoria fuckin' Peloza! She kept her composure and stuck her clutch under arm. He was *definitely* not about to see her sweat.

    "Hopefully we'll cross paths again some time," she smiled as she swept through the door like she wasn't bothered at all. The truth was, Xavier had her shook. She wasn't used to being brushed off like that. He had done it *twice*. She knew that there was no way he had asked his wife about her. He was coming to Tori because he figured Deena would lie. And she was proud that she had put the idea in Xavier's head that his wife didn't even claim him. She may have gotten shut down, but defeat was something she didn't accept.

    Xavier closed the door before Tori made it to the bottom of the steps. He knew for a fact that Tori was leaving out details, flat out lying, or both. He didn't know how to feel about her saying Deena didn't talk about him. That could just mean that she didn't go around telling all their business. It could also mean that she didn't think enough of him to mention him at all. He realized then that he didn't even know if she had friends at work who she'd confide in, or if she just talked to her sisters. He groaned at the thought as he plopped back down at his desk. When Deena and her three sisters got together, he wanted to cut his ears off with butter knives to escape the drunken cackling and man-bashing. He'd retreat to the basement, but he could still hear through the damn vents. He shook his head. He wouldn't be surprised if one of his crazy sisters-in-law had talked Deena into doing something stupid. He'd bet his check that Deena had Tori following him. He didn't know for how long, but it was just his luck that Jewell's cousin had shown up that day at the cafe. He closed his eyes and let out a long breath. Thinking about Jewell would almost definitely give him a headache, so he dove into his inventory, trying his best to shut her out.

~~~

"I'm hungry as hell," Neeka complained.

"Me too," Daisha chimed in. It had been forever since they all just sat up talking about nothing. Their lives seemed to have taken different turns that caused them not to see each other nearly as much as they had. They were lounging on Daisha's couch and she was enjoying the company. She missed her cousin's immensely.

Jewell liked being away from home, if it could be called that. She still hadn't given in to Brian, and she assumed he didn't care anymore. She walked around on edge a lot of days, wondering when he'd start in on her again. She tried her best not to think about what Xavier was up to, what he was thinking, if she'd ever see him again, and if he'd even give her the time of day if she did.

Neeka rolled her eyes and sucked her teeth, irritated with life. Jewell and Daisha didn't pay her any mind. She always looked like she had an attitude. The only reason she was there was so they wouldn't question why she wasn't. Daisha's ass was persistent, and she couldn't think of a lie quick enough to decline the invite, so she threw on the first pair of jeans and shirt she could find, pulled her dreads up and headed out. The last thing she wanted to do was have a heart-to-heart with Jewell. Things had been cool when she saw Brian on a regular basis, but Jewell had started fuckin' up. Brian was focusing more on why she had been actin' so crazy, and less on spending time with Neeka. Something was up with Jewell, and Neeka wanted to know what it was.

"Ooh, Jewell we should go to that cafe I saw you at that day-"

"No!" Jewell yelled.

"Damn, was the food that nasty?" Neeka laughed.

"Naw the food was so good!"

"Wait, y'all hoes went to lunch and didn't invite me?" Neeka sat up straight ready to go off. Jewell shook her head, but before she could speak, Daisha opened her big mouth.

"I was on my way to the store and I saw Jewell's car so I went in to see what she was doin'." Then she leaned over like she was whispering to Neeka. "I think she was supposed to be meetin' somebody."

"Oh shit, now we gettin' to the good stuff," Neeka scooted to the edge of the couch, a little too eager. Jewell shook her head, not knowing whether to laugh or be irritated. Daisha had a big ass mouth.

"Don't listen to her, Neeka." Jewell shook her head and rolled her eyes at Daisha.

"Oh but a nice piece of man did walk in there, and he was fine!" Daisha ignored Jewell.

"Naw, I wanna hear more about who she was supposed to be having lunch wit'!" Neeka crossed her arms, waiting.

"Girl I wasn't waitin' for anybody." Jewell waved Neeka off. "Can I have lunch by myself?"

"*No!*" Daisha and Neeka yelled in unison.

"You are such a goody two shoes," Neeka said, frustrated. "Like you never do anything wrong." She wanted to let her know that Brian had told her something was up. She could let it out though. The secret had been eating away at her forever, and she was tired of it. Brian was acting like a lil' bitch, staying in the house while his so-called wife was ignoring him to death. Why the hell couldn't the both of them just call it quits. It would be much easier for Neeka to keep her man if Jewell would just let him the fuck go!

"You got a attitude because I wasn't meetin' up with some man?" Jewell asked, confused.

"No, I got a attitude because you think you better than everybody!" Neeka yelled, jumping up from her seat.

"*Neeka!*" Daisha screamed, surprised. "Calm down!"

"Naw, Daisha. Apparently she got somethin' on her chest that's been there for a while. I wanna hear what she gotta say." Jewell glared at her cousin, and Neeka gave her a mean mug right back.

"Ever since you got married and got you a house you think yo' shit don't stink," Neeka commented, letting her emotions get the best of her. Jewell squinted her eyes.

"That doesn't even make sense!"

"*That doesn't even make sense,*" Neeka mocked.

"Oh my God, how old are we?" Jewell put her fingers to her temples.

"Old enough to know bullshit when we see it!" Neeka put her hands on her hips and Jewell huffed. She didn't know what the hell was going on in Neeka's head, but she didn't feel like sticking around to find out.

"Daisha, call me later." Jewell snatched her jacket and purse and marched to the door.
"Wait, cousin!" Daisha began to run after her, but she was too slow. Jewell was already damn near out the door by the time she made it out of the living room. She turned around to face Neeka. "What the hell was that about?" she

asked. Neeka shook her head, trying to slow her breathing. She didn't want Jewell to be upset with her, she was just tired of being second best. She knew she could be the better woman, and the need for more time with Brian was driving her nuts.

"You know you feel the same way sometimes," she tried to coax Daisha into being on her side.

"Ummm... *no*! I love my cousin. You must be jealous that she got a man and a house or somethin'!" Neeka cocked her head back. Her ass hit a nerve.

"Fuck you too, Daisha!" she yelled, deep in her feelings. She brushed past her and out the door, leaving Daisha almost in tears.

Ch. 17

"*I* got somethin' for you," Brian whispered. Jewell looked up from painting Alicia's nails to where he was standing in the doorway. He had been showering her with gifts for the last couple of weeks, hoping to keep her mind off her cousin. He hit the roof when Neeka told him what happened.

"What the hell were you thinkin', arguin' wit' her?" he had asked.

"I'm just tired of havin' to share-"

"*Share*?! Well how about this, yo' ass is cut off." He hung up before he could even begin to hear a reply. It had gone on long enough. He was positive there was other good pussy out there, he'd just have to find it. If he couldn't, he had no doubt that Neeka would welcome him back with open arms. She'd have to seriously get her shit together, though. Neeka was forgetting her place. He wouldn't have any side bitches arguing with his wife.

"Give me a couple of minutes," Jewell replied, uninterested. She finished with Alicia and kissed her forehead. "Don't touch 'em, okay," she reminded her. Alicia wasn't listening. She was too busy admiring her pink toes. Jewell got up, wondering what Brian had gotten for her this time. It started with flowers on the kitchen table when she got home, then an edible arrangement sent to her job. Next, there was a necklace. A few days after that, she found a pair of earrings had appeared in her front seat. When he started a conversation with her, she found herself answering him. He made a stupid joke and she'd actually *laughed* a little. While she appreciated the gestures, two weeks of gifts wasn't going to put a dent into making up for the years of bullshit she had put up with from him.

"I'm in the room," Brian called to Jewell. She hesitated. The last time she was in their bedroom, Brian had raped her. She stood in the doorway, timidly. The shame in Brian's eyes showed that he knew exactly what she was thinking. He lifted a bag off the bed and walked over to her. "Unzip it," he instructed. She started at the bottom of the bag and pulled the zipper up until she revealed the elegant, fire red dress underneath. Jewell was in awe as she pulled it out of the bag to admire it. The halter and chest were adorned with jewels, and the length of the dress fell to the floor with a small train in the back.

She looked at the tag, surprised that it was the right size.

"Thank you! This is really beautiful!" She moved to the mirror on the closet door and held the dress up to her body, smoothing it over her stomach.

"That's not all." She turned around and Brian had a shoebox in his hands. He opened it and revealed the silver stilettos. Jewell's jaw dropped at the sight of them. Brian took the dress from her and watched as she took her shoes off and tried on the heels he bought. It was nice to see a genuine smile on her face and know that he put it there.

"I love these, Brian." She walked back and forth, grinning, getting a feel for her new shoes.

"They're gonna be even sexier when you wear 'em wit' the dress this weekend." Jewell stopped at his words.

"This weekend?" she asked.

"Yea, your reunion dinner. I got our tickets for the weekend already. One less thing for you to worry about." Jewell immediately felt panic.

"I don't wanna go to the reunion," she said flatly.

"Whatchu mean you don't wanna go?" Brian sounded upset and Jewell quickly tried to judge the space between her and the door.

"I'm just... not interested in going." She took off her shoes slowly, not wanting to move too fast. It would be like setting off a hungry dog.

"I bought you a dress, *and* shoes, *and* jewelry. I

been buying you shit for the past two weeks." Brian was seeing red.

"I know, and I appreciate it, believe me I do." Jewell eased towards the door. "I can wear it somewhere else, anywhere else." The feeling Brian had from making Jewell smile had been replaced by anger at her complete dismissal of his efforts to be sweet to her.

"I bought the fuckin' tickets already. We goin'. Friday, Saturday, *and* Sunday."

"Okay, that's fine. We'll go," Jewell lied. She had no intentions of going, faking and parading with Brian around a bunch of people. She definitely didn't feel like seeing Deena and Xavier, but she needed to diffuse the situation.

"You a damn lie!" Brian yelled at her.

"Huh?" Jewell whispered, caught off guard.

"You just sayin' that shit! You think I'm stupid or somethin'?" Instead of answering, Jewell rushed towards the hallway. Brian took two steps and was there in time to slam the door before she made it. "What the hell you runnin' for?" Jewell started to back up. She knew it was coming, and she wanted to try to get to the closet and close herself in.

"You're upset," she said. "You do some things you shouldn't when you're upset." Jewell spoke as calmly as she possibly could through her fear.

"I ain't upset, I'm mad as *fuck*. I been bendin' over backwards to try and make up wit'chu, and you actin' like I ain't doin' shit."

"No, I appreciate-"

"You don't appreciate a damn thing but yo'self." Brian started closing the space between them and Jewell turned to run to the closet. Brian took off behind her. He grabbed her shirt and yanked her back to him. "Bring yo' ass here," he grunted. Jewell tried to pull away, but he wrapped his arms around her so tight she couldn't move. "I don't know what the fuck you think this is, but you are my *wife*. Maybe you forgot."

"No, Brian, I swear I didn't forget," Jewell panted through short breaths.

"Yea, I think you did. You need a reminder." He pushed Jewell on the bed and she tried not to panic.

"Please don't, Brian." Jewell grabbed a pillow and put it on top of her shorts. He snatched the pillow and flung it before she even realized what he had done.

"Get that shit outta here." Brian climbed on top of her and pinned her arms down.

"I don't need a reminder," Jewell whispered with tears rolling down into her ears. She had been so careful up until that point. So cautious. She hadn't kissed his ass by any means, she'd just avoided him, and any possible confrontation. She closed her eyes, unable to move under his weight, knowing what was coming, wondering if it was worth it, just so her daughter could be comfortable sleeping in her own bed. He let her hands go and, before she could try and move, the first blow had her side on fire.

"You thought you was gon' keep walkin' around here disrespectin' me like I'm not yo' husband. Fuck is wrong wit'chu?"

"I haven't-" The fist to Jewell's mouth shut her up.

"Did I ask you anything?" he growled at her. She moaned, grabbing her lip. She tried to fight her way from under him, but he was way too strong.

"Alicia's in the other room," she groaned, trying to play on Brian's love for his daughter. She was sure he wouldn't want her to walk in on the beating.

"Don't worry about her. I got her," Brian replied calmly. Then he punched Jewell square in the side of her head. She yelled out and he covered her mouth and nose to quiet her screams. She flailed her arms at him in a panic to breathe, and he leaned down to her ear. "Alicia don't need to hear that punk ass screamin'," he whispered. He got up and Jewell grabbed her head, trying to stop the ringing. He walked over to the door, turned back around to face her and smiled. "We goin' to that damn reunion."

~~~

"Hello, Mr. Black, this is Victoria Peloza. I was hoping to follow up with you on a couple of issues, both personal and professional. Please give me a call back at your earliest convenience." Xavier thumbed his fingers on his desk, wondering what this woman's angle was. There was no way she was calling to confess anything. She was much too slick for that. What the hell did she want? She couldn't possibly have a problem with anything that his guys did. He knew they always did excellent work. He went back and forth in his head before he finally picked up the phone and dialed her.

Tori was stuffing her face when her phone rang. She took one look at the number and grinned. She knew she had put out just enough to make Xavier curious, and that sooner or later, he'd reach back out to her. She looked around the breakroom to make sure no one was in earshot before she picked up.

"Hello?" she answered, like she didn't know exactly who it was. She knew he'd be calling, she just didn't expect it to be so soon. She left the message on her way in to work. She'd only had to wait half the day. She figured he might be easier than she thought.

"Hello, Ms. Peloza, this is Xavier Black," he answered her. "I understand you have a few things to discuss with me."

"Please, Xavier, call me Tori."

"I'd rather not," he replied plainly.

"Ok, I'm sorry *Mr. Black*," Tori purred into the phone.

"How can I help you?" Xavier was getting irritated after only a few seconds.

"Well, I was thinking, and I wanted to go ahead and discuss the situation with Deena with you." Tori knew she had him when she heard the silent pause.

"Go ahead. Discuss." If she had anything to say, she needed to just spit it out already.

"Not over the phone, Xa-, Mr. Black."

"I assume you want to come back to the shop?"

"The issue, I believe, would be best discussed at dinner." Xavier rolled his eyes. This chick was really something else.

"The issue, if there even is one, can be discussed right now, or not at all." Xavier was tired of the games.

"Oh come on, Xavier." Tori was borderline exasperated. Why the hell was he playing so hard to get?! She knew damn well she looked way better than Deena, and Xavier obviously wasn't very happy with her, so what was the problem?!

"Look, Ms. Peloza, is there anything else I can help you with?"

"Oh, there's a lot you can help me with," Tori commented, suggestively. She held the phone in anticipation, waiting for his response. "Hello?" she whispered, uncertainly. She pulled the phone away from her face and was looking at the home screen. This nigga had hung up on her! *Her*! *Victoria Peloza*! He had his damn nerve! She was through playing nice.

Ch. 18

Tropicana Bowl was packed wall to wall with food, drinks, purple and white decorations, and Parkway North alumni. Even though the music was blasting and the atmosphere was spirited, Jewell was not in a cheerful mood at all. The absolute *last* place she wanted to be was sitting in the middle of old classmates pretending like she was having a good time. She was doing a horrible job at it. She sat on the bench with her arms folded, almost in tears from the frustration she felt. Her side still hurt, though her face looked better than it had. She had become a pro at covering bruises, as long as nobody was all in her space. She glared at Brian as he strolled up the bowling lane and threw a strike.

"Ok, whateva now you can sit yo' ass down." Neeka snapped at him and a few people at the lane with them laughed. He shook his head at her and took his seat beside

Jewell. The slight brush of his thigh against hers disgusted her, and she scooted a couple of inches away. She looked up and Neeka was staring at them. She wanted to ask her what the hell she was staring at. If she was so jealous of her bullshit marriage then she should go out and find her a bullshit man. Then they'd be even.

"Now why you actin' like you don't wanna sit by me?" Brian scooted Jewell back over to him, daring her to make a scene. She looked at Neeka, now laughing with some of their old friends from high school, and found herself feeling a little jealous. Neeka went where she wanted, when she wanted, slept with who she wanted, and did whatever the hell she wanted. She was a free woman. Jewell hadn't been free in four years. The minute she promised herself to Brian in front of God, their family, and friends, she made herself a prisoner. She got up, needing some space. "Where you goin'?" Brian asked with an attitude.

"Can I pee?" Jewell rolled her eyes and walked off. It was the first thing that came out of her mouth. She knew Brian was leery of her being out of his sight since he knew he had messed up, yet again. He was right to feel the way he did though. The wheels in Jewell's mind had been turning non-stop, trying to figure out what her next move would be. Staying in that house much longer wasn't safe for her.

Neeka waited good until Jewell was out of her sight

before she marched over to Brian. "What are y'all even here for?" she demanded.

"What'chu in my face for?" Brian huffed. "And why you so damn loud? You want all yo' lil' school friends to know yo' business?"

"Fuck them," Neeka blurted out. Brian huffed and glanced behind them to see if Jewell was anywhere near.

"Naw yo' lil' wife ain't close enough to hear anything." Neeka was reaching her breaking point. How much more was she gonna take? How much longer was she gonna let Brian keep her from living while he ran up behind Jewell's high-sadity, goody two-shoes, wanna-be perfect ass? "You need to get'cho shit together," she warned him.

"No, *you* need to get *yo'* shit together," he whispered back. "I told you I was done wit'chu." Neeka glared at him, then shook her head.

"Naw, you ain't done. Fuck that-"

"Neeka it's yo' turn!" one of her classmates called. She mugged him one more good time before turning back to the lanes. Brian rubbed his forehead wondering what he had gotten himself into. Neeka was turning out to be crazy as hell, and he didn't need her in his face all in public so people could start running their mouths. It didn't matter that these people didn't know him. They knew Jewell, and could easily see that the conversation between him and Neeka was far from innocent. He turned in the direction of the bathroom again wondering what was taking his wife so long.

Jewell leaned against the inside of the stall door, shaking her head. She had half a mind to run clean out of the bowling alley, but she was sure Brian would be on his way to Alicia as soon as he realized she was gone. She wanted to leave so bad she was having a hard time breathing. She thought about throwing some water on her face to stop the panic attack she felt coming. For whatever reason, it seemed like it worked in the movies, but she wouldn't dare. She'd wash off the make-up she had applied so carefully to her bruise. She grabbed some tissue and dabbed at her tears before leaving the stall. She looked at her reflection and rolled her eyes. She didn't recognize herself. She looked the same physically, but her soul was vanishing. She was letting that man steal her, and had been doing so for years. She stood there for a moment, trying to get herself together. She had to at least make it look like she hadn't been crying. By the time she walked out of the bathroom, she looked perfectly fine. The walk back to where Brian was seemed so long. The closer Jewell got to him though, the more she felt like her chest was about to explode.

"Hey, wassup Xavier!" Jewell stopped dead in her tracks. Out of all the noise and commotion in the bowling alley, *that* was what she heard. The voice came from behind her and she had to fight to keep walking forward. If she turned around, she might not be able to move. Or it might be just the opposite. She might run to him, push Deena out of the way and jump in his arms. The sight of Xavier would send her over the edge, she was sure of it. Her shoes felt like they were full of concrete as she tried to walk away from where Xavier was. She figured he would be there, but she didn't think she'd feel the pain she felt knowing she was so close to him and couldn't talk to him or hug him.

"Hey, babe. What took you so long?" Brian stood up when Jewell finally made it back to their lane.

"There was a line," Jewell answered blankly.

"Don't sit down, we been waiting on you!" a classmate yelled at her. She walked up to grab her ball and noticed Neeka sneering at her. Maybe they just needed to fight it out. She was tired of Neeka's attitude. Their class reunion wasn't the time though. Thoughts were swimming through her mind as she walked up to the line. How could she get away from Brian? How could she *stay* away? How could she make sure he wouldn't come for her? She cranked her arm back in pain, and flung it forward with so much anger that it bounced twice and flew into the lane next to them.

"Damn, cousin. You stressed out or what?" Neeka joked. Jewell rolled her eyes, trying to ignore her. When she turned to get her ball from the person in the next lane, she locked eyes with Xavier a few lanes down. He was staring dead at her, just like a number of people were. She had brought attention to herself, flinging the ball the way she did. Of course, people would turn and see what was going on, but of all people to lock eyes with, she had to look dead into Xavier's. Her heart started beating double time, then he smiled at her, and the world seemed to slow down. The music dragged along and everyone else disappeared except for the two of them. A hand on her back brought everything back up to speed.

"You good, babe?" Brian asked her. Jewell closed her eyes and nodded her head, wondering if seeing Xavier had been a figment of her imagination.

"Aye, ain't that the dude you used to kick it wit'?" Neeka walked up to them.

"What dude you used to kick it wit?" Brian demanded.

"I don't know who you talkin' about." Jewell made sure to look confused, trying to pull off her lie. How the hell did Neeka recognize Xavier that quick and from that far away? Unless, like over half the females in their class, she had had her eye on him back then too. She shook her head.

"I can't remember his name," Neeka answered, straining her neck and squinting her eyes through the crowd. "I don't even see him anymore." Brian pulled Jewell to him in a fake hug.

"Who the hell is she talkin' about, Jewell?" he

demanded in her ear.

"I don't know, Brian. *She* don't even know." Jewell silently prayed that Neeka wouldn't remember anything else about Xavier. She knew Brian's ego though. Even if he didn't see anybody, or learn a name, Neeka had planted a bug in his ear, and she was sure it would bite her in the ass before the night was over.

~~~

Xavier was feeling conflicted. He knew there was a possibility that Jewell would be at Tropicana, but seeing her there had him on a natural high. He had only seen her for a brief moment, but he wanted so bad to go to her and wrap his arms around her. Seeing her with Brian had him on the verge of a jealous rage. He had hated Brian as a teenager, and never thought he'd feel like he was still in competition with him years later. Everything they were going through felt like deja'vu. Jewell was once again pushing him away for Brian. What the hell did Brian have that he didn't? She always claimed that she wasn't happy, so he wondered why she was still with him. He figured he could ask himself the same question though. He looked over at Deena mingling with old friends. She was beautiful, and successful, but that was about the extent of her good qualities. If he just wanted a trophy wife or a showpiece, she'd be perfect. But he needed more. He wanted somebody he could truly love, not just deal with because they had a child together. He wanted somebody he could laugh, joke, and be silly with, somebody he could have deep, meaningful conversations with, somebody he could enjoy spending time with without having to say a word, somebody who supported and believed in him, not just to spend his money, but because he had dreams. He wanted Jewell.

    Knowing she was in the building was ripping at his insides. He had spent so much time trying not to think about her that when he finally did see her, he almost gave himself away. He didn't even know how long he stood there staring at her before Brian walked up behind her. He knew how he felt, pained that he was so close to her but so damn far away. He was pissed off that she was with another man, husband or not, and irritated that he couldn't just walk over to her and tell her how much he missed her. He could see by the look on her face when she saw him that he wasn't crazy. They were on the same page. He saw that longing look in her eyes, and believed there was still hope. He wanted to steal her away, like he should've done years ago, but he wasn't the type to make a scene. He'd have his chance again. He was sure of it.

Ch. 19

*J*ewell dabbed perfume on her wrists and the notch of her neck. She admired herself in the mirror and had to admit that the dress Brian bought her was *bad*. It fit like a glove. She had her hair pinned up, showing off her shoulders and Angela Bassett cheek bones. She felt a slight pang of guilt, using Brian to get to Xavier. She was positive he and Deena would be at the formal dinner that night, and this time, she'd be ready.

"You look beautiful." When she heard Brian's voice, she froze. She'd been paranoid the night before, locking herself in Alicia's room and getting up bright and early to stay away from him. Brian had pounded on the door for about fifteen minutes demanding that Jewell come out and tell him who Neeka was talking about. She didn't have time for the bull. She climbed under the covers, closed her ears and eyes, and fell asleep on his ass. **She let her** dreams fill with thoughts of Xavier and what she would say if she saw him at the dinner. She still had no idea, but she knew she wouldn't be caught off guard. She was ready for him.

"Thank you," she answered Brian, ready to be out of his hair. She'd make sure to mingle and try her best to have more fun. That way, if she ran into Xavier, it would look like she was just talking to another classmate. She thought back to his face, the way he was looking at her. He looked shocked and surprised. She couldn't tell if he was happy to see her or pissed, since she had shut him out again. After Brian raped her, she felt like she was no good. What could she possibly bring to the table? She was a damaged woman. Why would he want her? That didn't matter anymore. She needed Xavier to make her feel alive, even if only for the time being. At least that was what she told herself in that moment. Once she laid her eyes on him again, it would more than likely be a different story.

"I knew you'd look good in that dress when I bought it, but I didn't know you'd look that good. And that's all me? *Damn*!" Jewell tried to hide her eye roll. *All him*? Bullshit. She was tired of promising herself that Brian would never put his hands on her again.

"I do look good, don't I?" She smiled at her reflection, turned, and walked out of the room.

~~~

"You're gonna open my door right?" Deena asked

with an attitude.

"Why wouldn't I?" Xavier asked as he put the car in park.

"I just wanna make sure whoever sees us knows my husband is a gentleman." *I am a gentleman*, he thought to himself.

"You want me to carry you in too?" Xavier mumbled sarcastically as he got out. He walked around to Deena's door and opened it, quietly dreading the night ahead. Sure, he knew a lot of people at the reunion, but he didn't feel like being Deena's pet. He felt like she was dragging him around by a leash letting everybody ooh and aah at him. *Look at my puppy! He obeys me so well! Ain't he cute?* She wanted people to know she had changed, understandable, but the way she was parading him around was enough to make him want to curse her clean out in front of everybody.

"Hold on. Let me fix your tie." He stuffed his hands in his pockets as Deena fiddled with his tie and suit. He felt like a child. She might as well lick her finger and spread her spit across his eyebrow. "Ok, people are coming. Kiss me." His head jerked back.

"Deena turn around and walk inside." He was tired, and the night hadn't even started yet. They were right on time and there were groups of couples walking in. Out of the corner of his eye, he caught sight of a bright, red dress. Nonchalantly, he turned in that direction. Once he realized who it was, he had to supress his smile. Jewell stood out from the rest. Then again, she always had. He couldn't wait to get a closer look at her. He could see from a distance that she had her shoulders out. He wanted so bad to kiss-

"I can't wait to take pictures. I know we lookin' *too* good right now! I mean, I always look good, but you killin' that suit tonight baby."

"Thanks," Xavier replied to the half compliment. He wondered why his wife couldn't be more like Jewell. Maybe his marriage would be easier if she were. Then again, Jewell was one of a kind. There would never be another like her.

~~~

Neeka sat at the bar looking like she stepped right off a magazine cover. Her black, off the shoulder dress complimented her small, chocolate frame perfectly. With her dreads pulled up in a high bun showing off her flawless make-up, she looked like a goddess, however, she was drinking like an alcoholic. She had made the conscious decision to go to the formal dinner alone, knowing Brian would be there with Jewell. She didn't have any loud on her, and even if she did, she wasn't too keen on walking around in her ball gown smelling like weed. She had to turn to another method of release, drinking her sorrows away.

"You good, miss lady?" the bartender asked her.

"Why the hell do you care?" Neeka asked, feeling buzzed and irritated.

"I hate to see a sexy woman alone on a night like this." Neeka looked up at the bartender and cocked her head. She had been with plenty of white men, but this one had a Channing Tatum thing goin' on; dark eyes and hair, and the sexiest lips. She had half decided to give him some before she caught a glimpse of red out of the corner of her eye. She snapped her head in that direction and when she saw them together, her heart sank. They looked like a damn JET couple. Irritated to the core, she pointed.

"You see that? *That* is my problem," she grumbled. The bartender squinted in the direction Neeka was pointing.

"The woman in the red dress? What did she do?" he asked.

"She fucked up my life," Neeka slurred, pouring another drink down her throat, as she watched Jewell walk over to the balcony. "I should go push her ass," she laughed.

"Okay then." The bartender reached over the bar and grabbed Neeka's glass from her. "No more of these."

"Whateva," Neeka rolled her eyes. "I know who *ain't* gettin none," she threw her head towards him and turned back to Jewell. She watched her movements, her mannerisms, wondering what she was missing, what the hell Jewell had that she didn't. Why was she constantly in competition with her? She watched as a man that she recognized walked up to her. She *knew* it was somebody Jewell used to talk to, but she couldn't put her finger on it. She looked around the room, excited, trying to find Brian. Where the hell was he? He needed to see this shit!

"Hello, beautiful." The corner of Jewell's lip tilted up. She didn't wanna be overly confident, but she figured when she finally broke away from Brian that Xavier would eventually find her. She had readied herself, or so she thought, to talk to him, but the sound of his voice had her scared to turn around. She did, slowly, taking in his eyes, his smile, his broad shoulders under that suit he was wearing the hell out of.

"Hey, stranger," she said in a whisper. She wanted so bad to wrap her arms around his neck and beg him to carry her far away. "How have you been?"

"Good. Missing you." Xavier stared deep into Jewell's soul, making her blush.

"I miss you too, Zay."

"You disappeared on me again." Xavier was hurt and disappointed and he needed her to know that. "I don't know if maybe you assume I don't give a damn or I don't have feelings, but I do." He was making Jewell weak. She wasn't expecting that.

"I was just goin' through so much-"

"Why won't you let me in?" Xavier pled with her. He

wanted to be her confidant. He wanted to be her shoulder to cry on like he used to be. They used to be best friends. He missed that.

"Why would I open up more? What more can you give me besides conversation?" Jewell wasn't angry at Xavier, she was angry with herself and her life decisions. She was frustrated feeling like she was stuck in the situation that she was in. She didn't want to take it out on Xavier, but she felt like he was a door of opportunity that was locked with a deadbolt.

"If you can just be patient with me-" Xavier stopped mid-sentence and really took a good look at Jewell. Her expression was full of pain, but there was something else, something he hadn't noticed before. He scooted in closer and she immediately backed away. "What happened to your face?" Jewell's expression changed and her hand flew to her forehead.

"What?" she asked, not knowing what else to say.

"What the hell happened to your *face*, Jewell?" She tried to think of a lie. *I fell*. A lie that made more sense... she couldn't. "Did he *hit* you?" She lowered her hand and looked away, not wanting to lie to him. But what truth did she wanna tell him? He lifted her chin so that she was looking directly at him. They locked eyes and he knew without her having to say anything. His heart dropped and tears formed in his eyes. "That bitch ass nigga," he mumbled. Immediately, he turned to find Brian. "What the fuck is wrong wit' him?!"

"Xavier, please." Jewell grabbed his arm.

"What?! You expect me to sit back while that nigga put his hands on you?!"

"If you embarrass him, you embarrass *me*."

"You can't go back with him." Jewell looked out onto downtown from the balcony. "You hear me, Jewell. I won't let you go back."

"There she is, Brian." Jewell jerked her head back towards the ballroom where Neeka's snitchin' ass was dragging Brian towards them.

"I been lookin' for you." Brian spoke to Jewell, but his eyes were on Xavier, who extended his hand to him.

"Xavier Black," he introduced himself. He bit the inside of his jaw when Brian grabbed his hand. He had to do what he could to keep from swinging on him.

"Brian Palmer." The two men shook for what seemed like forever. Jewell felt like she was about to pass out from the tension.

"Well, I'm Neeka." She slipped in and threw her hand out to Xavier. Only then did the men release their grip on each other. Xavier turned his attention to Neeka and shook her hand. "*Xavier*. Oh yea I definitely remember you." She looked at Jewell and winked, causing Brian's temperature to rise.

"Come on, Jewell, let's get to our table." He threw his hand around Jewell's shoulders and spun her around.

Xavier started popping his knuckles, trying to calm himself down.

"You were cute when we were younger, but you got real fine and *thick*." Neeka looked Xavier up and down, taking in the anger on his face. She grinned, knowing she had finally found that sweet spot.

"What the fuck was you and that nigga talkin' about? Yo' ass walkin' off talkin' about you goin' to the bathroom." Brian had a grip so tight on Jewell's shoulder, it felt like he'd break it. She refused to answer. "Sit'cho ass down." He damn near threw her into the seat. Neeka wasn't far behind them.

"So what are y'all doin' after this?" she asked. Jewell fought off tears. She wanted to beat Neeka's ass. She wanted to beat Brian's ass. She wanted to burn the damn place down. She felt her purse vibrate and knew it was Xavier. Ignoring Brian and Neeka, she pulled it out and checked the message.

from Zay:
MEET ME AT THE FRONT IN 2 MINUTES
to Zay:
OK

Two minutes felt like twenty. Jewell got up from the table and Brian grabbed her arm.

"Where you goin'?" he demanded. Neeka rolled her eyes, wishing he'd just let her go already.

"To the bathroom. I lied before, remember." She yanked away, knowing Brian was too much of a punk to put his hands on her in front of a room full of people. Jewell turned the corner and walked clean past the bathroom to the front door where Xavier was standing. He swiftly put his arm around her waist and they walked out of the building.

Jealousy set in as Tori watched Xavier walk to his car with a woman that was *not* his wife. "Who the *hell* is that?" she asked herself.

Ch. 20

*T*ori was *hot*. She snapped a couple of pictures then slid down in her front seat, like Xavier or the strange woman he was with were really paying attention. They were damn near jogging to the car, and it looked like they were way too familiar with each other. She shook her head, wanting to run up and ask Xavier exactly who the heffa was. The fact that he had turned her down proved he'd be a challenge. She was up for it, which was precisely the reason she was camped out at the class reunion. Deena's big-mouth ass had been treating Tori like a leper, but it was okay, because she was planning on stealing that sexy piece of man right from under her prissy ass nose. She was not expecting to see him with another woman though. Whoever the bitch was, she had thrown a wrench in her plans!

~~~

"I'mma hurt her ass!" Brian punched the women's bathroom door leaving a fist-sized dent and causing Neeka to jump back a couple of feet.

"Brian, *please* calm down," she pleaded.

"Calm down?!" he yelled. "Jewell said she was goin' to the bathroom *twenty-three* minutes ago! Did you see her shittin' in any one of those stalls? *Fuck* naw!" Neeka crossed her arms, wondering when the hissy fit would be over. She watched him pace for a few more seconds before she finally grabbed his face, forcing him to look at her.

"Jewell left you," she stated plainly. "She been tryin'a leave you for a long ass time. When are you gon' face it?" She stared at him, silently begging him to give in to her. Jewell was desperate to get away from him, but he had Neeka right in his face, ready and willing to give him everything he wanted. For a moment, she saw his face soften. Then, as quickly as it came, it was gone.

"Man, fuck this." Brian pulled Neeka's hands from his face and walked off, leaving her stunned outside the bathroom door.

~~~

"*Xavier... Dontez... Black*, I don't know where the hell you are or what the hell you are doing, but I suggest you get your ass back here, *right now*!" Deena stood outside the hall with her hands on her hips. She didn't know whether to be hurt, stunned, scared, or pissed. Over the past half hour, she had had small bouts of each. She couldn't believe Xavier had left her there! After he'd been gone fifteen minutes to get a drink, she went to the bar to give the bartender a piece of her mind. There was no reason it should take that long. But Xavier was nowhere near the bar, and he wasn't in the bathroom. She searched the dance floor in a panic, calling his phone all the while, constantly getting his voicemail. She rushed out to the car, only to be met by an empty spot. Maybe she was trippin'. Maybe they had parked somewhere else. She ran around the parking lot like a mad woman, ending up over and over again back at the same empty spot.

"I'm trying not to think that anything bad happened to you. I'm confused. I don't know what's going on. Just ...*please* call me back." Deena clicked her phone off and leaned against the wall of the hall in her beautiful, pale blue dress. She didn't even care about how good she looked anymore, she was ready to pop off. She knew nothing bad had happened to Xavier. He was on some bullshit. She just figured she had to make him think she was worried to get a call back. He had his damn nerve! Deena had plans to go the hell off!

~~~

"How long has he been doin' it?" Xavier asked. They had been riding for a few minutes. The only sound cutting through the silence had been the buzzing of their phones.

Jewell kept staring out the front window. "How long?" he asked again.

"Years," she confessed in a whisper. She had never told anyone what she'd been through with Brian, but Xavier had seen the bruise. There was really no way she could lie to him about it. She looked in his direction and saw a single tear drop down the side of his face. He wiped it away quickly and she saw his jaw tense up. He gripped the steering wheel over and over again.

"*Years*?" he repeated. Jewell looked back out the front window. She couldn't take watching Xavier cry for her. This man, who she wanted so bad to be with, was crying for her, while the man she had chosen over him was the root of so much of her pain.

"Where are we going?" she asked.

"I'm taking you to a hotel."

"My daughter-" Xavier slammed on the brakes and Jewell flew forward.

"He's hittin' her too?!" he yelled.

"*No*!" They stared at each other until Xavier was satisfied that Jewell was telling him the truth. Finally, he turned away and eased back on the gas. "I just don't wanna leave her." She slid her phone out of her pocket and called her parent's. "Hey, mama. I need a favor."

"What's wrong?" Jewell's mother asked.

"Nothing, but if Brian comes to get Alicia, don't answer the door." There was a pause on the other end.

"Mama?"

"What's wrong, Jewell?"

"*Mama*!"

"Just tell her," Xavier whispered. Jewell huffed like a kid, but did as she was told.

"I'm leaving him," she said plainly. Xavier squeezed her thigh in support.

"Oh, baby I am so sorry to hear that!" Jewell's mother tried to hide her relief. Although she didn't know everything that was going on in their relationship, she knew her daughter wasn't content with Brian and that she hadn't been for years. The look on Jewell's face at the mention of his name was enough to give it away. He had been a disrespectful young man that turned into a disrespectful son-in-law. He rarely attended any family functions, and if he did, Jewell would have to leave early because *he* felt like it. He carried ignorance everywhere he went and always seemed to have a snide remark. Brian was definitely not the kind of man she or her husband wanted to see their daughter with. As time passed, it became apparent to them that the relationship would just have to run its course. "What happened," she asked Jewell.

"I'll have to tell you more later, mama."

"Well, where are you going?" Jewell looked over at Xavier.

"Where am I going?" she whispered.

"Who are you with?" Jewell's mother yelled. "You have to tell me what's going on!"

"Umm... the Lumiere downtown," Xavier whispered.

"I'll be at the Lumiere, mama. Please don't tell Brian."

"I'm not stupid!" Jewell's mother yelled at her. "Alicia can stay here as long as you need her to, but sooner than later, you're gonna have to tell me what's going on young lady. And who are you with?"

"I'm with an old friend."

"You gone have to give me more information than that."

"Mama, can you just-"

"No, young lady, I can't *just*. You call here sounding scared as I don't know what, talking about don't tell Brian nothin', I'm staying at a hotel and I'm with some strange person. I know you grown, but you are *still* my child. And I need to know what's goin' on." Jewell was fighting back tears as she held the phone. She had no intentions of giving her mama any details over the phone. Xavier reached up and rubbed the back of her neck, giving her silent reassurance that he was there for her.

"It's over between me and Brian and I don't know what frame of mind he's in right now so I don't want Alicia with him. I'm gonna stay at a hotel at least for tonight, just to get my head together. I should know more by tomorrow. Kiss my baby for me."

"Ok, Jewell," her mama sighed. "I love you."

"Love you too, mama." Jewell exhaled after she hung up.

"You feel better?" Xavier asked her.

"A little." Jewell hesitated, unsure of what to say or what the future held for her and Alicia. She couldn't see herself going back to Brian, especially now that someone actually *knew*. It was easier to forgive bullshit when nobody was aware of what was going on. But *Xavier* of all people knew. He'd think so little of her if she went back to Brian, and would probably do his best to try and talk her out of it. But then what? What was his end game? "I know I'm not gonna answer my phone, but don't you have to?" Jewell tried not to sound salty. She left the dinner because Xavier had extended an olive branch. There would be no mending her marriage. It wasn't like some marriages where couples had to get used to not being together. She had long accepted the fact that she and Brian were on separate pages. Even Alicia was used to him being gone. Now it was just about making it official. Then she'd be a single woman still pining for a married man.

"I won't answer if you don't want me to," Xavier told her.

"That's not up to me, Zay. I decided to leave Brian tonight, and you helped me do that. But what I'm goin' through has nothing to do with your marriage. I can't tell you whether to answer or not." Xavier pulled in to the lot at the hotel and parked. He was about to speak, but the vibration of his phone threw him off and he jumped out of the car. Jewell followed him into the hotel as her heart started thumping double time. In less than an hour, she had ended her twelve year relationship, ran away with her married high school crush, and now she was walking into a hotel with him. What the hell was going on? She watched as he purchased a room and trailed him to the elevator where they rode to the fifth floor in silence. Jewell searched for something to say, but no words passed her lips. It was almost as if they were both scared of what might happen once they got into the room. They had been alone plenty of times, but the opportunity for anything serious had never presented itself the way they wanted.

Jewell admired Xavier as he walked a little ways in front of her. He had taken his suit jacket off and the white button down he had on underneath clung to his broad shoulders and muscular his arms. She wanted him to hold her and make her forget about each time she made the decision to go back to Brian after he hit her, make her forget that they didn't belong to each other.

"This is it.' Xavier slid the key card into the slot and opened the door for Jewell. She had to admit, it was a huge step up from the last hotel she had run away to. She ran her fingers along the crisp, white bedspread, then walked over to the window that peered out at the arch. The view was amazing. She turned to catch Xavier staring, looking like he was thinking the same thing about her. "You look gorgeous," he commented.

"Thank you." She smiled at him and took a seat on the bed.

"I'm not gonna go in to the shop tomorrow," Xavier told her. "Whatever you need to handle I'm free for you. I'll be back in the morning around-"

"Wait, you not gon' stay with me?"

~~~

Tori had tried to convince herself there was an explanation for Xavier leaving the party with a woman other than Deena. Maybe a cousin or something. She tailed them, constantly trying to peer in the rearview window to see how they were interacting. Her heart dropped when they pulled into the Lumiere hotel parking lot. She jumped out and followed them, making sure the floppy hat she had on covered her face. She was sure Xavier remembered her fine ass, and she didn't wanna blow her cover. She had to know though. She had to see if he'd stay with her. She waited until they got on the elevator and watched the numbers as they rode up. When the elevator stopped on five she hopped on the one next to it, praying she didn't have any stops. Luckily, she went straight up, and was just in time to see Xavier letting the woman in the room and following her in. She shrunk back into the elevator and slid down the side. *That muthafucka.* She rode the elevator back down and rushed out to her car, almost out of breath, feeling stupid as hell. "That's ok," Tori smiled to herself once she got in the car. "Payback is gon' be a bitch."

Ch. 21

*A*s soon as the words came out of her mouth, Jewell regretted them. Why would she ask Xavier to stay? Deena was either worried sick, ready to slash his tires, or both. He had snuck her out of the hall and purchased a room for her. What else did she want? As a married man, he was already doing much more than he should. It wasn't his job to save her.

"Jewell," Xavier started.

"No," she interrupted him. "I was outta line." Xavier walked over to where Jewell was standing.

"I would love nothing more than to stay here with you." He grabbed her wrists and slid his hands up her arms and over her bare shoulders where he paused. He stared into her soul, paralyzing her. He moved his hands behind her neck and pulled her to him. He had missed her, the taste of her lips, the feel of her body pressed against his, her scent... he kissed her like he'd never be able to again. Jewell grabbed hold of his shirt and kissed him back, relieved to finally be with him again. Xavier's hands caressed her back, and his heartbeat sped up when he felt the zipper of the dress. Slowly, he eased it down, making sure she wouldn't stop him.

She didn't.

When the dress dropped to the floor, Xavier picked Jewell up and laid her on the bed. He admired her for just a second before he climbed on top of her, kissing her neck, moving down to her breasts, sliding down to her belly button. Jewell moaned and arched her back at the feel of his mouth exploring her. She grabbed his head and bit her bottom lip. *This is happening, this is happening...*Jewell was trying not to hyperventilate by the time Xavier made his way back up to her face.

"You feel that?" He pulled Jewell's hand down and she felt his dick about to bust through his pants.

"Damn." She smiled, thinking about how he would feel inside of her. She had waited years for him.

"That's how bad I want you," he told her. He kissed her again, this time he took it slow. He wanted her to feel his love for her through that kiss. He leaned into her, sliding his arms under her and lifting her up to put her on his lap. She wrapped her arms and legs around him, ready to give in and let go. At that moment, nothing and no one else mattered.

BAM, BAM, BAM!!!
They both jumped at the pounding on the door. Jewell climbed off Xavier's lap and went to scurry back into her dress. Xavier walked to the door with his heart pounding. Was it Deena? If it was, how did she know where to find him? How would he explain to her that he was in love with another woman? He squinted through the peep hole, chest hurting like hell. All he could see was a big, country ass hat. That definitely wasn't Deena.

"Can I help you?" he asked.

"Nigga you can open the door! And you better have yo' pants on!" Xavier threw a confused look at Jewell who returned the look. She could tell by his reaction that it wasn't Deena. Who was it then? All the while, she had had this *knight-in-shining-armor* view of him, and here it was some other woman was pissed at him.

All of a sudden, a light went off in Xavier's head. He swung the hotel door open, ready to go off.

"Are you *stalkin'* me?" Xavier yelled.

"Damn right I am!" Victoria smiled and flashed her phone camera in his face. "That's what your wife is paying me for!" Xavier was temporarily blinded but his ears still worked. That bitch said Deena was paying to have him followed! "Where you at, heffa?!" she yelled into the room. He slammed the door in Tori's face and turned to see Jewell coming out of the bathroom.

"She's having you followed?" Jewell asked. Xavier

could only shrug his shoulders in disgust. Guilt hung heavy in the air like smoke. Jewell leaned against the wall, trying to sort through her feelings. She would never wish pain on Deena. The woman had never done anything to her, but the thought of she and Xavier being caught and the both of them getting a divorce had her on the verge of a smile. She quickly shook it away.

"I gotta figure out what to say to her." Xavier sat down on the bed and put his head in his hands. Jewell watched him, not sure what to say herself. She didn't know where his head was. Was he trying to figure out a lie to keep his marriage together, or was he trying to figure out how to tell Deena he was leaving her?

~~~

Brian sat in his living room fuming. It was obvious that Jewell wouldn't be answering his messages or taking his calls any time soon. He wanted to know where the hell she was. He knew she didn't get up and walk away from the hall by herself. It had to be that nigga she had been talking to. *Xavier Black.* It took a while, but Brian had put the name and face together. Jewell had been kickin' it with somebody years before they got married and he could swear that was him. Neeka was always talkin' shit, trying to keep him from Jewell, but it seemed like this time she was right. He looked around at the mess he made in the living room. He had yanked pictures off the walls and replaced them with holes made by his fists. He flipped the table and smashed all the lamps. He didn't stop until he got tired. Sitting on the couch, his hands started tingling, thinking about how bad he was gonna hurt Jewell when he got his hands on her.

~~~

Shaking her head, Tori looked at the pictures of Xavier in her phone. She didn't know who to be more mad at, him, herself, or the chick he was in the room with. She could tell, by the disheveled look of his clothes that he had been up to no good. She zoomed in on the female he had been walking with, but couldn't get a good look at her face. She had half a mind to bust into the room, but she was sure she wouldn't be able to get past Xavier.

"Damnit!" she yelled. She could've at least tried. She wanted to see the chick. She wanted to know what they were doing. That was why she couldn't stand just sitting in her car waiting and wondering. She had to make her way up to the room to at least see his face. He had recognized her voice. That was a plus, but he still wasn't budging. And with her blurting out the truth the way she did, she knew she'd have some making up to do. She was up for the challenge, though. She had never been one to back down. Sooner or later she was gonna get a piece of him.

~~~

"Thanks for bringing me home," Deena mumbled, still in disbelief.

"You're welcome, *boss lady*," Mason smiled.

"When are you gonna stop calling me that?" she asked, trying not to be irritated with him. Mason had dropped what he was doing to pick her up, no questions asked. She didn't feel like arguing.

"When you stop being scared and stop actin' like my *boss*."

"I'm not being scared, I'm being *married*."

"You weren't being married last month," Mason laughed.

"That was one time-"

"And that shit was good, right?" he asked. Deena rolled her eyes. *Damn right* it was good! Mason would flirt whenever he got the chance. Once he realized he could get away with it, he started in with the nasty comments, then came the quick slaps on the butt when nobody was looking. They began texting, then sexting and sending naked pictures and x-rated videos. One of Xavier's late nights at the shop, she let Mason talk her into meeting him at a hotel. He didn't waste time yanking her clothes off. He was tired of watching her switch her fine ass through the shop. Yea, her husband was his boss, but if she was willing, he was gon' get that shit.

"That doesn't matter. I said we wouldn't-" She stopped when Mason scooted right beside her. The old-school Cutlass seats went straight across from the driver's side to the passenger side, and he took full advantage of it.

"You sure?" he asked with his lips damn near on her neck.

"We can't, Mason."

"We can't?" he asked. He licked his fingers and slid his hand in the split of her dress. "You lookin' *damn* good." He kissed her neck as he moved her thong to the side and let his fingers dare her to say no. "I want it," he groaned. He yanked her breast out with his other hand and went to work on her nipple.

"Shit..." Deena moaned, grabbing the back of Mason's head. He moved his fingers faster, curving them up, tagging her G-spot over and over. She almost ripped her dress trying to get it up above her waist. Mason maneuvered her leg up onto the seat and positioned himself so he was just right to eat. She smelled so good he dug his face deep into her. Deena threw her head back against the window and licked her lips, grinding with every tongue thrust. Mason's head game was amazing! He was nasty and sloppy and she loved every minute of it. She had no doubt the seat was looking like somebody poured a cup of water on it. Before long, she was grabbing the back of Mason's head, jerking and yelling so loud she surprised herself. She glanced behind them and out of both of the side windows.

"All these trees in this yard, baby ain't nobody in our business like that." Mason took Deena's other breast out and went to work on her nipple. "Let 'em stay in they own yard." He went in the glove compartment and pulled out a box of condoms.

"Oh, you just keep 'em on hand, huh?" Deena asked.

"What, these? These new." Mason ripped the box open, eager to get in some wetness. He pulled his pants down and Deena sucked her fingers, ready to play. Mason was working with more than the average 22 year old, and his stroke was marvelous. Deena laughed. "What's funny?"

"We're in your *Cutlass*, in my *driveway*. I don't remember the last time I had sex outside, let alone in a car."

"Go ahead and lay back, baby. By the time I finish, you gon' be beggin' for this Cutlass."

Ch. 22

"So she just *left*?" Daisha asked in disbelief.

Neeka nodded and blew smoke rings above her head.

"Yep, and Brian was *pissed*."

"I bet he was. You ain't heard from her?" Daisha asked. Neeka shook her head. "Well I'mma call her."

"Go ahead and try. She ain't answerin' my calls." Neeka had tried a couple of times, just to make it seem like she cared. She knew Jewell had taken off with Xavier, and she was giddy on the inside. Hopefully Brian wouldn't be able to drag her ass back home this time.

"Well we know why she didn't answer for *you*!" Daisha rolled her eyes and dialed Jewell, getting the voicemail.

"I don't know what'chu talkin' about," Neeka shrugged her shoulders. Daisha hit her arm and she almost dropped her blunt. "Damn, heffa!"

"What's goin' on wit'chu and Jewell."

"*Man*," Neeka sat up straight and put her hands on her knees. "Look me in my eye and tell me you never felt like Jewell think she better than us?"

"No, I haven't." Daisha cocked her head at her.

"You lyin'." Neeka went back to her blunt.

"Whatever, cousin. You gon' have to talk this out wit' her one day." Daisha was getting real irritated. Neeka had a serious problem. The most specific she had gotten though was when she threw Jewell's marriage into the argument. It scared Daisha to think that there was anything even remotely going on between Neeka and Brian, but nine times outta ten when females were arguing, it had to do with a man. She watched as Neeka let the weed take her over, and decided to wait until she was good and high. She might be able to trick her into running her mouth.

~~~

Xavier looked at his phone shaking his head. Fifteen text messages, eight voice messages, and thirty-two missed calls, a couple from his parents. He knew Deena had more than likely called them. He looked back at Jewell asleep on the bed, still in her dress from the night before. He decided to step out into the hall and call his parents.

"Boy, where are you?! That woman got on me and ya mama's *last* nerve!"

"Hey to you too, pop," Xavier laughed.

"Hey my ass! Call ya wife before I hurt her feelings."

"Ok, pop, but I need some advice first."

"What is it, son?"

"A friend was in trouble and I had to help her-"

"What kinda friend made you leave ya wife at a party?!"

"A very special one. Honestly, Deena hasn't felt like my wife for a while," Xavier stated.

"That's understandable," his father answered. Xavier laughed at him. "I'm serious. You know yo' mama never liked her. Probably 'cause I thought she was fine. Whew-wee..."

"Really? I'm bein' serious right now."

"I'm bein' serious! Just because she's cute, son, don't mean she wife material."

"I spent the night wit' her," Xavier blurted out. There was silence on the other end before his father finally answered.

"It's one thing to not wanna be with Deena, but I highly suggest you wait until it's official before you go sleepin' wit' other women."

"We didn't even sleep together. Believe me, I wanted to. She just really made me realize what I been missing."

"The only advice I can give you is to discuss things with Deena before you go jump into bed with another woman. If you don't want her anymore then that's fine, but she at least needs to know that." Xavier nodded his head, already knowing what he had to do. He just needed some confirmation that he was making the right decision.

"Thanks pop."

"Anytime." Xavier hung up with his father and leaned against the wall wondering what would happen when he went back in the room. What would happen when Jewell woke up? Would she think that leaving with him was a mistake and decide to go back to what she knew, as messed up as it was? Would she wanna start a relationship with him? It seemed like she did, but he couldn't be sure. She had picked Brian over him before so how could this time be so different. He hadn't talked to her in almost two months. He knew his feelings for her, but he wasn't always so sure about hers. When he walked back into the room, she was sitting up in the bed.

"Morning." Jewell smiled at him. Being wrapped in his arms through the night had her waking up feeling rejuvenated.

"Good morning, beautiful." Xavier returned the smile. It was the moment of truth. He sat down on the bed beside her and grabbed her hands trying not to let the nervousness overtake him. His heart was pumping like he was about to ask for her hand in marriage or something. He looked at her and she was staring back at him with those eyes he had fell in love with years ago. "This would be simpler if I was texting you," he laughed. Jewell felt a little uneasy, wondering what he was about to say.

"What's wrong, Zay?" she asked him.

"Nothin'. Nothin' at all." He cleared his throat and kept going. "I can't ignore my feelings or push 'em away anymore. I can't just be your friend. I can't just be your lunch date. I can't just talk to you or see you when we both can sneak away." Jewell leaned in to grab Xavier's face and pull him to her. She wrapped her arms around him and kissed him. Xavier had to make himself pull her away. "Wait, baby."

"What?" Jewell was confused. She was finally hearing the words she had been waiting to hear, but Xavier was pushing her away.

"I want you to be sure I'm what you want."

"Really, Zay? For the past few months you have been *all* I want. I just didn't wanna cause problems where there were none."

"Oh we have *plenty* of problems."

"But were you planning on leaving her before we got back in touch?"

"Honestly, I was just settling. I was used to working hard, coming home to no dinner and a wife that didn't care that I was bustin' my ass for us. My marriage was doomed before it started."

"Is it possible that it could've worked, though?" The last thing Jewell wanted was for Xavier to make the decision to leave Deena because of what had happened the night before.

"Me and Deena have been together a long time, and I don't know her. I don't know what she likes to do, besides spend money. I don't know what kinds of movies she likes. I don't know who her friends are, or if she even has any besides her sisters. I stopped tryin' to learn her when I realized she didn't wanna be my wife. She likes the *idea* of family and likes to keep up appearances, but she has no idea how to be a wife or a mother." Jewell stared out the window, thinking about her own marriage.

"I thought you just got frustrated sometimes. I didn't know you were that unhappy," she replied.

"I didn't wanna waste our time together talkin' about that. And if that's the case, I don't think you even said Brian's name at all. When I didn't hear from you, I assumed you chose him again." Jewell wouldn't dare tell him about the things she had been through since she had spoken with him last.

"I made my choice last night when I left that hall with you." Xavier searched Jewell's eyes for certainty.

"And you won't go back to him?" he asked. He didn't think he could forgive her if she did. If she chose to try and work things out with Brian again, it would crush him. He wouldn't be able to handle it, especially knowing that he had been putting his hands on her.

"I won't go back to him," Jewell reassured. "Are we doin' this?" She smiled at him and he couldn't help but to smile back.

"We're doin' this."

~~~

"What is it, Neeka?" Brian had finally decided to answer the phone after the sixth call.

"I just wanted to check on you, dang! I'm sure Jewell ain't been checkin' on you-'

"That's the easiest way to get'cho ass hung up on."

"Don't you hang up on me!" Neeka yelled. She was so relieved that he had answered the phone. She had called countless times the night before, and he had ignored her. She tried to visit Daisha to get her mind off of him, but all she wanted to do was talk about him and Jewell's ass. *What do you think about them together? Do you think they gon' break up? Do you think one of 'em is cheating?* She was real close to chopping her in her throat to shut her up, but she left before she got that frustrated. Brian was the only thing on her mind. She wasn't gonna stop calling until he answered.

"Do you need somethin'?" Brian asked, irritated. Neeka took a deep breath.

"I need you." Brian huffed and rubbed his forehead. *Man, I gotta stop fuckin' these hoes so good,* he thought to himself.

"You don't need me, Neeka. And if you can't understand that, then we can't talk." Neeka felt the tears coming. Brian refused to cooperate and she had to figure something out.

"You thought I was sayin' I need you to be my man?" she laughed wiping her face. "Look, I ain't been done in right for a nice lil' minute. I'm sure you haven't either. I just thought we could make each other feel good." Brian put the phone in his lap for a minute, looking around at the bedroom he had trashed that morning. He had no idea where Jewell was, and was pretty sure she was done with him. His ego was bruised more than anything. He wasn't done with her, and she had the balls to leave him. Nobody fuckin' leaves him. He was getting mad all over again. He knew Neeka was lying, but oh well.

"Be naked when I get there," he told her, then hung up.

~~~

"I can't believe this muthafucka." Tori wanted to make sure she didn't miss Xavier and his mystery woman so she stayed awake in the parking lot. She'd rush into the hotel when she had to use the bathroom and even had a pizza delivery man meet her in the lobby. She was sleepy as hell, but she perked up when she saw Xavier exit with his arm around the woman. They looked much more relaxed than the night before, and it was obvious that they were together. He was all over her and she was smiling all in his face. *Bitch...*

She watched them, snapping pictures as they walked, lookin' all happy and shit. It gave her a migraine.

Maybe her mind was playing tricks on her. She could've sworn she knocked on the door and told him he was being followed. She had the power to blow all his shit out the water, so what was he so damn happy for?! She rolled her eyes at them, still looking like they were fresh and going out, even though the chick's hair was down now and their breath was probably funky. Tori laughed at the thought, but stopped when she saw them share a kiss before he opened the car door for her. She put her phone down and took a deep breath, thinking maybe she should just give up. The feeling only lasted a couple of seconds. As soon as Xavier started the car, Tori was right behind them, more determined than ever.

Ch. 23

"You wanna go wit' me to the reunion picnic?" Neeka asked Brian. He wanted to jump up and leave, but she still had a grip on his dick. She had it down to a science, stroking the head with her thumb, smiling when he jerked from the aftershocks.

"You crazy," he told her.

"Why you say that?"

"What the hell makes you think I'mma go anywhere wit'chu?" Neeka got up to wrap a sheet around her shoulders and straddled Brian.

"Look me in my eyes and tell me you don't have feelings for me." He couldn't look her in her eyes. He was too busy staring at her chocolate breasts hanging in his face. "Brian!"

"What?" He looked up at her and didn't like what he saw. Neediness and longing. He knew he shouldn't have taken his ass to her house, but he couldn't help it. It had been a while and he wanted to dig into her again.

"You don't feel anything except for when we fuck?" It took everything in Brian not to yell out *NO*! He had to pull it together if he wanted to keep that good head.

"Of course I do, Neeka." He spread his hands over her butt cheeks and she exhaled. "You know it'll be hard for us to be in a relationship, though. I don't wanna jump into anything not knowing where me and Jewell are." Neeka nodded and climbed off of him, finally coming to the reality that she couldn't compete with Jewell. Her cousin had done everything in her power to push this man away, yet she still had to beg for his time and attention.

"Ok," she said calmly. Brian sat up and looked at her with his head cocked. She didn't yell, she didn't curse, she didn't even look back at him. She simply slipped into her boy shorts and tank top and went into the living room. He followed suit, dressing quickly and going into the living room after her.

"Ok?" he asked. "That's all?" Neeka looked at him and shrugged her shoulders.

"That's all, Brian. I get it." She pulled her legs up in her chaise and flicked through the stations on the television.

"Ok then. I'm about to go." Neeka nodded at him nonchalantly and he zipped his shorts on his way out the door, shaking his head. He knew what she was doin', tryin' to act like she didn't care so he would be all up her ass. Well that shit wasn't gon' work. He had to repeat it to himself over and over again though, as he drove off.

~~~

Jewell and Xavier had looked like a couple of fools at McDonald's in their formal wear, but they didn't care. "So whats' the plan?" Jewell asked once they had finished their lunch. She was dreading coming back down to reality. She had to talk to Alicia and her parents, and eventually settle things with Brian. Xavier had to do the same.

"Well," Xavier started the car and rubbed his chin. "How do you feel about me dropping you off at your parent's while I take care of what I need to take care of. Later on, we can both talk to Brian." Jewell snapped her head towards Xavier and he cocked his head at her. "What? You think you goin' to see him alone? I don't think so." Xavier shook his head and pulled off. "The most space I'll give you is watching y'all from a couple feet away." Jewell tried to hide her smile. It felt good to be protected for a change.

"Now this place brings back memories," Xavier said with a smile when they pulled in front of Jewell's parent's house. She smiled right back, kissing him before she opened the door to get out.

"Good luck," she joked, wondering how things would go when he met up with Deena.

"Mmmhmm," He laughed and waited for her to get inside before he pulled off.

Jewell had trudged up the steps to her parent's house, not looking forward to the conversation she was about to have with them. Alicia rushed her as soon as she walked through the door. She picked her up and hugged her tight, thinking about the bombshell she was about to drop on her. She didn't spend much time with her father, but Jewell had to admit, Brian was a completely different person when he was with Alicia. He was a big teddy bear that she had wrapped around her finger... whenever he was around.

"Mommy, you look pretty!" Alicia yelled. Jewell laughed and kissed her cheek.

"Thank you, baby."

"Jewell!" Her mother came into the hall.

"Yea, it's me, mama." Her mother put her hands on her hips and poked out her lips.

"Well come on. Me and ya daddy been waitin for you to get here." Jewell sent Alicia out to play on the back and settled on the living room couch in front of her parents. She took a deep breath and began the story that started years before.

~~~

Xavier pulled up to his house and got knots in his stomach when he saw Deena's car was sitting in the driveway. Before he turned his car off, she was on the porch. He was almost scared to get out, but he could see by the way her arms were crossed that she didn't have any weapons in her hands. He grabbed his jacket and keys so slowly that Deena started tapping her foot impatiently. He didn't make it on the porch good before she was yelling.

"I don't know what the hell you think this is! But we don't stay out all night!" She flung her finger between the two of them. "We don't ignore our phone calls and texts! We don't leave each other stranded and make the other one scramble to find a ride home."

"I'm sorry, Deena. Can we go inside?"

"You're *sorry*!? That's all you got to say is you're sorry?!" Deena was on the verge of tears.

"Let's go inside," he said calmy. His soft tone only infuriated her more.

"Hell naw we can't go *inside*!" She started flailing around in front of him. "Where have you been all night?! Who were you with?! Why didn't you answer your phone?! Why didn't you answer your text messages?!" Xavier grabbed Deena around her waist and pulled her into the house. She had every reason to be pissed, but he wasn't about to stand on the porch and air their dirty laundry to the whole neighborhood.

"Get off me, Xavier!" Deena pushed away from him once they were in the foyer.

"Calm down," he held his hands out since she looked like she was about to rush him.

"Calm down, Xavier Black? Calm down and what? Forget you left me last night?!"

"Deena-"

"Forget that it's one in the afternoon and I'm just now hearing from you?!"

"Deena-"

"Forget that-"

"Deena!" Xavier grabbed her arms. "Stop for a minute and let me answer you!" She rolled her eyes and yanked away from him, stomping into the kitchen like she was Miranda. He followed, draped his jacket on the back of the chair across from her, and took a seat. "I'm not gon' beat around the bush. You know we been goin' downhill for a while-"

"Who did you fuck?" she blurted out, catching him off guard.

"I didn't *fuck* anybody, Deena." Xavier smiled to himself thinking about Victoria snapping the picture of him the night before. "Did your lil' snitch tell you that?"

"My snitch?" Deena seemed genuinely confused.

"It's scary to sit here and know you're lying to me so good."

"I don't know what you're-"

"Victoria," he said as calmly as he could. It wasn't like he hadn't been giving Deena any reason to suspect something was going on. He had been sneaking away and lying to her to be with Jewell. He wouldn't be surprised if she was sleeping with somebody herself.

"Victoria was an accident. I told her to stop weeks ago, the day she was at the shop." She reached out to grab Xavier's hand and he slid away, still thinking she was lying. "Xavier, whatever happened last night we can talk through it."

"But we can't, though." Deena leaned back in her chair and crossed her arms.

"What the hell happened last night?" she demanded.

"What happened last night is that I finally got sick of begging you and pleading with you to be my *wife*."

"Exactly what is that supposed to mean?!"

"*See*! As much as we argue about this, you act like you don't even know what I'm talkin' about. Deena lives for *Deena*. Not a day since we met was I more than just a win for you."

"A *win*?"

"Yes, a win! All the fightin' you did for me to choose you, and when you finally got me, the fight was over. You don't even try and put in work or impress me anymore."

"Put in work for *you*?! What about you working for *me*?!" Xavier wanted to smack some sense into her.

"Who held down *two* jobs so you could focus on school? Who keeps you walkin' around lookin' like you fuckin' made of money? Who keeps the bills paid in this bitch?"

"Ain't you my *husband*? That's what you *supposed* to do!"

"Ain't you my *wife*? So what the hell are *you* supposed to do? You don't cook, you don't support me, you don't clean, you don't take care of Miranda, I don't get ass or head on a regular, you don't even try and pay attention to me when you get home-"

"First off, who said the woman has to cook and clean and stay ready to have sex whenever-"

"*I* said, Deena. You don't do shit else. As hard as I work, a nigga stay havin' to stop and get somethin' to eat, or I gotta cook when I get home. When I'm off I still cook and clean. And when we have sex, why I gotta go in the bathroom and finish myself off?"

"Who the hell makes you finish yourself off?!"

"*You* when you go to sleep after you get yours!"

"Xavier, this is all bullshit!" Deena huffed, rolling her eyes.

"How is it bullshit if I been complaining about the same thing for years? Deena can you cook more? Deena can you straighten up more? Deena can you clean Miranda up? Deena can you give a fuck about me for a change?" Xavier felt his voice wavering. As much as he wanted to not care, it hurt that he had spent so long trying to be a good husband to her and she had yet to reciprocate it. Deena seemed to soften.

"I admit, I haven't been the perfect wife. But you're

far from perfect yourself."

"Nobody expects you to be perfect. And I sure hope you didn't expect that from me. At least I tried."

"Were you trying when you left me last night?"

"Honestly, Deena, I stopped trying a while ago." It was like he had punched her in the chest. The room might as well had been spinning.

"So what are you saying? You don't wanna be wit' me?" Deena laughed a little, knowing that couldn't possibly be what he was saying.

"No, I don't." Xavier was sure of it. He had made up his mind. Sure, Jewell had given him that push, but he had wanted the courage to give up on his marriage long before he crossed her path again. Deena shook her head at him.

"You're lying."

"I'm not lying." Xavier looked Deena right in her eyes, trying to help her realize that it wasn't a joke. Their marriage was over.

"You can't be serious." Deena jumped up from the table and Xavier kept his eyes on her just in case she decided to swing on him. "What will people say?!"

"Wow." Xavier got up from the table shaking his head. He grabbed his jacket and slid into it.

"What? Wait a minute!" Deena yelled, rushing over to him.

"Wait for what? We been together damn near ten years. We have a daughter together. And you ask me what will *people* say? I don't give a damn what your *sisters* are gonna say once they find out your husband isn't takin' care of you. I don't care what the people at your job are gonna say once they find out you actually do have to work and pay your own bills. I don't care what your old classmates will say when they find out you don't have a husband to show off like a trained puppy."

"That came out wrong." Deena grabbed Xavier's arm and he yanked away.

"No it didn't," he told her. "Bye, Deena." He turned away from her and felt relief as he walked out to his car. Deena, on the other hand, was livid. Who the hell did he think he was? She ran to the living room and looked out the window, waiting until Xavier pulled off to make a call.

Tori jumped at the notification beep of her phone. She wiped her eyes and squinted, trying to get a feel of her surroundings.

"Fuck!" she yelled once she realized what had happened. The beautiful, tree-lined street was Xavier and Deena's. The lack of sleep had caught up with her and she passed out. She had followed Xavier to take his lil' chick to McDonald's, of all places, and then to drop her off. She trailed him until she saw Deena standing on their porch. She decided to pass them up, circle the block , and park a little ways up the street. She'd wait until he was alone to talk to him. Unfortunately, she wasn't able to hang, and she fell asleep. She picked up her phone, still groggy, and saw that she had a missed call and a message from Deena. Groaning and still half sleep, she listened to the message.

"I don't know what the hell you did, but when I catch you bitch, I'mma beat yo ass!"

Ch. 24

"Hi, Brian." Jewell's voice was timid. It took her a while to calm her parents down after she talked to them. Her mother couldn't stop crying and her father wanted to pull out his shotgun. She had to convince them that she was handling things. Then she had to focus and center herself to call Brian.

"Oh you callin' anonymous? That's what we doin' now? Where are you so I can come get you?"

"No, Brian. We need to talk."

"About yo' lil' disappearin' act last night? I don't even wanna hear the excuse. Just have yo' ass home in the next ten minutes." Brian's hands were itching to get a hold of her.

"I'm not coming home." Jewell heard that familiar tone in his voice. Even if Xavier stood between the two of them while they talked, it wouldn't be pretty. She had left him alone and stayed out all night. There wouldn't be any calm conversation. She knew she'd have to keep her distance.

"The fuck you mean you ain't comin' home?!" Brian yelled. He looked around his living room for something to break, but there was nothing left. He had damn near demolished the house.

"I mean it's over, Brian."

"You mean *what's* over?!" Brian yelled so loud that Jewell had to take the phone away from her ear.

"Us. I can't do it anymore." Instead of a response, Jewell heard smashing in the background. "*Brian*!" She yelled his name over and over again, thinking he was tearing up the house, not knowing the house was beyond torn up already. She listened for a few more seconds until her line clicked.

"Hello?" she answered in a panic.

"What's wrong?" Xavier asked.

"I told Brian it was over and he started flippin' out. It sounded like he was breakin' everything in the house!"

"You need me to take you over there? You still gotta get your car and clothes and stuff." Jewell slapped her forehead. "Jewell?" Xavier asked.

"I probably don't even have anything left," she whispered.

"What?"

"Brian is *crazy*, Xavier! By the time we get there everything I have will be trashed, my clothes, my car-"

"Ok, just calm down, baby. Whatever steps you wanna take, we can do that. You want me to come get you and take you over there, that's fine. You wanna call the police and have them take you over there, then I'll meet you, we can do that too."

"I have a headache." The weight of everything was falling on her. She was ending her marriage. Her *marriage*. When she was pregnant, she had envisioned a life of happiness. Brian had quickly, and efficiently, shattered that vision. It had been broken for years, Jewell just kept blinders on. She kept trying to make it work, kept telling herself that it was for Alicia, that she needed her father. Even though he was great to his daughter, Brian was a part-time father at best. Would she legally be able to put Brian out of the house? What would the divorce be like? It wasn't like they had any for real money, but would he fight her for what little she had? Would he fight her for *Alicia*?! "I just need to lay down," she told Xavier. She honestly felt sick. Her life had been flipped on its head in a matter of hours.

"Ok." Xavier felt defeated. He wanted to do more. He knew hopping out of a marriage and into a relationship wouldn't be a cakewalk, especially for Jewell. He just wanted her to know that she could count on him. "You go ahead and rest. Just call me when you get up."

~~~

"I don't know what the hell his problem is!" Deena cried to her sisters as they laid around comforting her.

"Fuck him!" Trina yelled. She was the oldest, then came Deena, then the youngest sister, Lena. "Give him a minute and he'll realize what he lost." Trina liked Xavier as long as he provided for her sister, but he was about to cut off the money train.

"What did he say?" Lena asked.

"Girl that I wasn't supportive and didn't give him enough head or some shit."

"Ugh, his ignorant ass," Trina chimed in. Lena rolled her eyes. She knew Xavier had to have said more than that. Sadly, when it came to relationships, she had more sense than both of her sisters put together. She got bored with their constant complaining about how men never lived up to women's ridiculous expectations. Deena expected Xavier to spoil her to no end, and when she felt like he fell short, she decided to slack on her wifely duties, which was every day all day. She was scared to say what she genuinely felt, which was that her sister had messed up big time. Her brother-in-law was a good man who had always been there for her, and she loved him. Deena had seriously messed up and it was irritating as hell to Lena that her sister didn't see it.

"Ain't he stupid," Deena agreed. "He'll be back, though. He can't resist all this." She started grinding in the middle of the floor and she and Trina started laughing and giving each other high fives. "What's wrong wit'chu?" Deena asked Lena who was sitting with her arms crossed.

"You just lost your family and you don't even seem a little sad," she responded.

"First off, I didn't lose my *family*. My husband is actin' like an ass right now. Secondly, who are you to tell me how I feel?" Deena walked towards her and she straightened up in her chair a little. "I can feel however the hell I wanna feel about my situation." Lena had half a mind to back down like she always did, but the way Deena was walking up on her made her rethink it.

"You are the one who messed up, and if you don't fight to win Xavier back then somebody else is gonna snatch him up."

"Oh, somebody like who? Like you, Lena? You jealous? You want my husband?"

"*What*? No, Deena," Lena closed her eyes to try and stop the headache that was brewing. "Why do I have to be jealous and want him just because I told you *you* were the one in the wrong?"

"You are *my* sister, not *his*! You're supposed to have my back!"

"Have your back how? By lying to you, or telling you the truth?"

"Bitch you do whatever you have to do to have my damn back!" Deena yelled. Lena snapped her head towards Trina, who threw her hands up.

"What'chu want me to do?" Trina asked. "You in *her* house." Lena exhaled and braced herself, turning back to face Deena.

"Your 'fuck everybody and everything' attitude is why you're in this situation in the first place. The saddest part about it is that I know you know you're wrong, but for whatever twisted reason in your mind, you want everybody to believe you're right and praise and kiss your ass in the process. You know what, forget I said fight for him! Just leave him alone, he's better off without you!" Lena screamed.

"Get the hell outta my house." Deena waved her off.

"Gladly." Lena grabbed her purse and stormed out to her car. She looked back up to the window of Deena's bedroom where she was sure her sisters were talking trash about her. She was only hurt for a little bit. She smiled before she pulled off, proud that she finally spoke her mind.

"Her lil' ass was way outta line," Deena told Trina as she settled down on her bed.

"Right," Trina popped her gum.

"Oh, I meant to tell you, I'mma have to beat somebody ass."

"Who ass we gotta beat?" Trina was amped, always ready for a fight.

"I had this lil' trick following Xavier for me, just to see if he was messin' around. I think she had the nerve to start likin' him. I told her to back off a couple weeks ago and last night she had the balls to *snitch* on me."

"The bitch told on you?!"

"Yes! While Xavier was talkin' all that shit, he said he knew about my snitch. I called and you know her scary ass didn't answer. I had to leave a message. That's ok though. I'mma catch that heffa."

"Naw, we gone catch her scary behind." Trina slapped hands with her sister, eager for a fight.

Tori lounged on her couch, twiddling her fingers, and decided to finally return Deena's sixth call. She figured she might as well get it over with. There was no need for anybody to be embarrassed at work. There was only half a ring before Deena answered. Tori laughed and thought to herself she must have her phone in her hand waiting.

"I want a damn explanation!" Deena had called Xavier and Tori numerous times getting more and more aggravated each time she was sent to voicemail.

"Well hello, Deena. How are you?" Tori smiled.

"Bitch are you serious?" Deena was fuming. "*What- happened- last night*?"

"Last night while you were wondering where yo' man was, Deena, I was on the job."

"I told you there was no more job!" Deena screamed.

"Anyway," Tori ignored her, "I followed Xavier and some female to the Lumiere hotel where they stayed the night." Deena slumped down on her chaise. She had suspected there was someone else, but Tori had never found anything. She knew she had done her dirt, but hell, she and Mason had only happened twice. There was no telling how many late nights Xavier had spent doing God knows what.

"Who was it? Did she have on a dress?" Deena was fuming thinking about Xavier leaving with any one of the dusty hoes from their class.

"I didn't get a picture of her," Tori lied, "but she had on a red dress."

"Why the hell didn't you call me?" Deena yelled.

"Wait, I'm confused. Am I on the case, or off the case?" Tori joked.

"That's what the hell I wanna know! You know damn well I told you I wanted you to stop. And I haven't been paying you. So why the hell were you still following my husband?" Deena was pissed that she had made the decision to ask Tori to help her in the first place. She should've known the heffa was looney by the way she talked about her own man. There was no doubt in her mind that she had a thing for Xavier. Who wouldn't? Her husband had been perfect, up until the past few months. She couldn't put her finger on what had happened, but she knew she had been the same spoiled brat that she had always been. She hadn't changed. As much as he complained, he had always put up with her.

"I was doin' you a favor-"

"A favor my ass. I had to threaten you for you to call me!"

"Well anyway, now that you know, what are you gonna do about the chick in the red dress?" Deena ran through all the dresses she could the night before and a bulb went off in her head. Only one stood out.

"Jewell..."

"Jewell is her name?" Tori asked, sitting straight up.

"Ugh." Deena hung up, irritated. That crazy heffa had actually given her something she could use. She could think of three red dresses that she had seen, but the other two were nobodies. She had heard Jewell's name way too many times when she and Xavier were younger. Deena never did believe his claims that they were just good friends and had never messed around. She made it her business to knock her ass out of the box, and she had. But was it only to lose him to her years later?

Tori wasted no time at all hopping on Facebook. She had found that people were so sloppy when it came to their business, whether they knew it or not. All she needed was a few minor details and she could take off. She wasn't a pro by far, but she was nosy as hell and had mastered the art of lurking. Now that she had a name, she went to Xavier's page and searched his friends. There were a couple named Jewell, but she quickly recognized one brown-skinned beauty and eagerly clicked her profile. It was only semi open, but that was all Tori needed. "Well hello Ms.-" she stopped as she scrolled down the page. "*Misses* Jewell Palmer." A big smile spread across Tori's face. "You just made this so much easier, boo." She threw her phone in her purse, slipped into her tennis shoes and was out the door.

<div align="center">~~~</div>

"Mommy!" Jewell jumped up at the sound of Alicia's voice. She sat up and wiped slob from her cheek. As soon as her daughter popped into view, Jewell remembered why she needed a nap in the first place. She looked at her phone and it read 7:59 p.m. That was more than a nap. She had been out of it all day. Xavier had texted her a couple of times.

from Zay:
HEY BABY, HOW ARE YOU FEELING?
from Zay:
I JUST WANT YOU TO KNOW THAT IM WILLING TO DO WHATEVER IT TAKES TO HELP YOU THROUGH THIS.

Before she could respond, her phone was ringing. It was a number she didn't recognize and, with everything that was going on, she let it go to voicemail. She started to text Xavier when the same number called her back. Irritated, she answered.

"Hello?"

"Hello, yes, I'm looking for Mrs. Palmer?" Jewell rolled her eyes. The woman on the other end sounded professional, but she didn't put anything past Brian.

"Who's asking?" she asked with an attitude.

"This is Dr. Solsa in the Barnes-Jewish Hospital emergency room. Is Mrs. Palmer available?" Every bit of tired vanished, and Jewell popped straight up in the middle of the bed.

"This is she. What's going on?"

"Yes ma'am, your husband is Brian Palmer?" Jewell paused for a second before she answered.

"Yes he is."

"Ma'am we need you to please come to the E.R. Your husband had been involved in a shooting."

Ch. 25

Jewell barely mumbled thank you to her father as she hopped out of the car. Her mind was racing so fast that she almost ran dead smack into the E.R. doors. *What the hell happened?!* Rushing to the desk, she pulled out her I.D. and plopped it down.

"My name is Jewell Palmer. Dr Solsa called me and told me my husband, Brian Palmer, was here." Jewell was out of breath for no reason at all, other than the fact that she was scared. She surely wasn't in love with Brian anymore, but the thought of him being hurt hit her hard.

"Have a seat, Mrs. Palmer, and I'll get her out here to speak with you," the nurse assured her. The couple of minutes she was sitting felt like an eternity. What's even worse was that she had called Xavier three times and he hadn't answered. She didn't wanna send a text saying Brian had been shot.

"Mrs. Palmer?" Jewell looked up and there was a doctor standing with two police officers. "I'm Dr. Solsa." She held her hand out to shake Jewell's. "These are officers Canter and Montgomery. They have some questions for you."

"Can I at least *see* him first?" Jewell blurted out. She felt like they were being rude as hell. Dr. Solsa stared at the officers until they moved over, signaling that it was ok for Jewell to go ahead. She followed the doctor to a room where Brian lay in a medicated sleep. He seemed so small and helpless that tears immediately stung Jewell's eyes.

"I apologize Mrs. Palmer," Dr. Solsa said as Jewell stared on in disbelief. "The police can be so pushy," she whispered.

"That's okay. What happened?" she asked, afraid to get too close to him.

"That's what we want to know," Officer Canter chimed in sneaking up from behind. "At approximately 6:15 this evening your husband was at the stop light at Jefferson and Cherokee where witnesses say the Taurus was fired upon." Jewell's knees got weak and Officer Montgomery caught her under her arms.

"I'm sorry," she apologized.

"No need to apologize," Dr. Solsa said, moving between Jewell and Brian. "He was hit twice in his left side. The bullets were removed easily and no major organs were compromised. He's doing as well as can be expected. Right now he's being given morphine and he's able to sleep so hopefully he isn't feeling much pain." Jewell nodded, wiping the tears from her face and peering past the doctor to get a glimpse of Brian.

"You said, Taurus?" Jewell asked. Then she shook her head. Why was she tripping off of Brian driving her car when he was laid up in the hospital unconscious. None of that mattered. "Who- who would -" Jewell whispered, barely getting the words out.

"We're in the very early stages of our questioning process. We do want to ask you if you can think of anybody who would want to hurt your husband?" Jewell closed her eyes and shook her head, not wanting to think of the answer that was burning in the back of her mind... *Xavier*...

"Why am I not surprised?" Xavier mumbled from his office landing. He looked down to the main floor at his younger sister-in-law, Lena. When Mason told him there was someone there for him, he hoped it would have been Jewell, but he quickly realized that he was her ride. He had called and text her a few times from the office but he figured she was still asleep, so he let her be.

"Hey, Xavier, can I come up?" Lena called out to him.

"Sure," he groaned. "Why not?" It was almost time for the shop to close, and if she started in on him, he could easily brush her off. He really wasn't in the mood.

"No need to beat around the bush," Lena started once Xavier closed the door behind her. "I'm sure you know I talked to Deena."

"Yep." He crossed his arms.

"I tried to call and you didn't answer, so I decided to just stop by."

"Mmmhmm..." He normally didn't have a problem with Lena, but, given the circumstances, he was automatically on the defensive.

"Well, I just wanted to make sure we'd still be cool." Xavier stood from where he was leaning on his desk and uncrossed his arms. He tilted his head at her, confused. "I love my sisters, but I don't have anybody to give me any brotherly advice or help me out when I need it. You know how they are." Lena was almost pleading with him. She loved her brother-in-law dearly. It could've been the fact that he actually had some sense and she could relate to him. Deena and Trina, though older than her, gave her a constant headache.

"Or course, you can call me whenever." They stood there in silence for a few seconds.

"I feel like a traitor, but I need to get this off my chest," Lena shook her head. "Deena is a spoiled brat and I honestly always felt like you were too good to her. Whatever you did, I'm sure she deserves it."

"Whatever I did, huh?" Xavier laughed. "Well I appreciate that, Lena. Just know that I'm your brother no matter what, ok? You can always call me, ok." Lena nodded and moved in for a hug. Xavier returned her embrace and led her out of the office. Half way down the stairs, the shop door flung open, causing Xavier, Lena, and the couple of the shop workers to jump.

"Xavier!" Jewell screamed. All eyes were on him as he rushed down the steps to her.

"What's wrong, baby?" he asked, concerned. It looked like she had been crying and hadn't had any sleep at all. Her eyes darted behind him and he turned to see Lena approaching them.

"Jewell, this is Deena's sister, Lena. Lena, this Jewell, a very good friend of mine."

"Hi." Lena smiled and extended her hand. Jewell looked at it, then went back in on Xavier.

"Are you really that crazy?!" she screamed. Xavier squinted at Jewell and Lena eased her way past them. She wanted to stick around and find out who this supposed 'good friend' was that he had called baby, but when Xavier practically dragged the woman up the steps and closed the door behind them, she left. The workers looked around at each other, wondering what was going on. Before either of them had a chance to speak, Xavier was out of his office.

"Aye, y'all go ahead and close up for the night and head home." Then he ducked back in. His staff didn't waste any time packing up. Mason waited just up until he had closed and locked the front door to pull out his phone.

"What is it? I have a stupid headache and I really don't feel like talking right now." Deena rolled her eyes.

"What you been up to, Boss Lady? Why you got a headache?"

"None of your business, Mason. What is it?"

"I was callin' to give you a lil' insight on what's goin' on at the shop wit' yo husband, but-"

"What is it?" Deena was all ears.

"Oh, you listenin' to tha kid now, huh?"

"What, Mason?!"

"How important is it to you?" he asked, grinning. She wasn't surprised at all. She knew exactly why he was dangling the information above her head.

"What do you want?" she asked, already knowing the answer.

"What I *need* is a lil' taste of that sweetness again. Can you make that happen?"

"I guess so," Deena sighed, not in the mood.

"I mean damn, you not excited about this dick, I'll just take it somewhere else."

"That sounds like hoe shit."

"Look, can I fuck, or not? You know and I know how we get down, so wassup?" Deena held the phone. She wanted Mason. He was damn good at what he did, and he did *everything*. His ass was a freak and she loved it, but she wanted her husband back. She wanted to keep her family. She wanted to know what was going on at the shop.

"Yes, Mason," she gave in. "Are you gonna tell me now?"

"Don't be messin' wit' me. Can I get that or not?"

"Yes! You can get it!" she yelled. Mason laughed.

"Yo' lil sister came by and they was in his office for a couple minutes, then some chick named Jewell came and was screamin' at him askin' if he was crazy and he took her upstairs and told everybody to leave." Deena was breathing so hard her chest was hurting. She gripped the phone until her palm started to hurt.

"So when you comin' over here to put it down?"

~~~

"First thing you need to do is calm down, 'cause by the look on your face, you about ready to beat my ass." Xavier said, utterly confused.

"How could you?" Jewell yelled.

"How could I *what*?" Xavier was extremely lost, and was close to losing his patience.

"You shot Brian!" Jewell blurted. Xavier recoiled, dumbfounded. "My daughter's *father*! I know you don't like him. I don't like him either, but-"

"Hold on-"

"I just came from the hospital-"

"Is he alive?"

"Yes- *Xavier*- he'll *live*," she spat." Xavier grabbed her arms to calm her down. She yanked away and he held his hands up in defense.

"I'm so sorry that happened, ok, and you're right, I *can't* stand his ass. But I would *never* do that to your daughter." He and Jewell stared at each other. He waited until her expression softened before he moved in. He slowly pulled her to him and held her, making her give in to him. She wrapped her arms around him, and breathed a sigh of relief as he stroked her head.

"I kept tryin' to call you. Why didn't you answer your phone?" she asked.

"Something must be wrong with it. Lena couldn't get me either."

"Mmhmm..." Jewell mumbled. Xavier backed up.

"What was that about?" he asked.

"Your sister-in-law came to go off on you?"

"Actually, she came to give me her blessing." Jewell's eyes got big.

"I'm sorry," she sighed. "You said you'd do anything, and when I couldn't get in touch with you I assumed the worst"

"I understand, baby. You don't have to apologize. But just so you know, that's some real bitch nigga shit, and that ain't me." Jewell looked up at him, still unable to grasp everything that was going on.

"Can you take me back to the hospital? I took a cab here."

"Damn you were on a mission, huh?" Xavier shook his head.

"I'm about to stay on a mission, now that I don't have a car."

"We can go get it, don't worry about that," Xavier commented, locking his office door.

"No, Brian was in *my* car," Jewell explained. Xavier stopped in the middle of the staircase and Jewell turned to look at him.

"He was in *your* car?" Jewell nodded and his chest got tight. "Baby," he looked her dead in her face.

"What's wrong?" The terror on his face made her heart beat faster. He was scaring her.

"What if they weren't trying to hit him? What if they were trying to hit *you*?"

Ch. 26

*J*ewell stared at Xavier in disbelief. She huffed and laughed a little. "I take it Deena wasn't exactly *happy*?" she stated, making Xavier cross his arms.

"I hear what you're implying, and of course she wasn't happy, but I never mentioned your name to her."

"Well, the only people I can think who wanna hurt me are Brian and Deena, and I'm kinda sure Brian didn't shoot himself."

"Deena doesn't know-"

"She has a *spy*, remember?" Jewell stomped down the steps with Xavier following close behind, reaching out to grab her arm.

"It didn't even seem like she had talked to her, baby-"

"Don't baby me." Jewell yanked away, confused and hurt. "What made us think that we could just jump out of marriage and into this- whatever it is?" Xavier stared at her and rubbed his chin in deep thought.

"Are you scared of *whatever* this is?" he mocked her sarcastically.

"What?" Jewell balked.

"One minute you're all over me, the next minute this is a mistake." Xavier was trying not to get upset. Of course, he sympathized for Jewell. A man she had spent the majority of her life with, however bad those years seemed to have been, was hurt. He could feel her trying to use that to pull away from him again. As selfish as he felt, he had to call her out on it.

"Xavier, this is hardly the time to discuss what's going on with us. My husband is-"

"Oh, your *husband*?" he glared at her. Jewell could feel his eyes burning into her, questioning her, cursing her. She couldn't change what was going on, no matter how bad she wanted to.

"Legally-"

"Yea, ok." Xavier cut her off, walking straight past her to the door. He opened it and stood looking at the wall. When she didn't follow, he sucked his teeth and shook his head. "You need a ride back to the hospital, right?" Jewell swallowed the lump in her throat and walked quietly out. Xavier opened the car door, even though he was irritated to high hell. Once she got in, he slammed the door behind her. He hopped in and refused to even turn the radio on. He wanted Jewell to think about what was going on, about how she was trying to push him away again. He was only going to beg so much. He wasn't up for kissing ass, and there was no way he was trying to compete with Brian being shot.

Jewell wanted to say something so bad, but she was stuck and at a loss. Her mind had fractured into a million pieces, and it was giving her a headache. She sincerely wanted to start a life with Xavier and she was certain that she did *not* want to be Brian's woman, but she couldn't leave him in the condition he was in. She wasn't sure where that would leave her and Xavier.

Before long, they pulled up in front of the emergency room. Jewell didn't have any idea how to explain what she was feeling, so she reached for the door handle.

"You wanna know what I think?" Xavier started. Jewell looked in his direction, but he wasn't looking at her. He was staring out of the front window. "I think Brian knows he's losing you, and is obviously desperate. I wouldn't be surprised if this was all a ploy to get you back."

"Xavier, that's crazy."

"No, Jewell, *he's* crazy. You said it yourself. I don't put anything past him, and you're playin' right into his hands."

"He wouldn't go this far, Xavier."

"Oh, but I would shoot him? That's why you came in my shop showin' out, right? You can think the worst of me?"

"I don't know you!" Jewell blurted out. Xavier couldn't believe his ears. The hurt in his eyes rocked Jewell to the core. She hadn't meant for it to come out as harsh as it had. He turned his gaze back out the front window without uttering a word. "Xavier, I-"

CLICK

The sound of the doors unlocking surprised her. It was like she was being dismissed. "You say Brian, I say Deena." Xavier didn't blink, flinch, or even acknowledge that Jewell had said anything. She nodded and quietly got out. As soon as she closed the door, he pulled off. She closed her eyes and took a few deep breaths to keep the tears at bay. *What the hell had she just done?*

Xavier turned the radio up sky high, rapping along with Dr. Dre.

Now it's time for me to make my impression felt.
So sit back, relax, and strap on ya seatbelts.
You never been on a ride like this before...

No matter how loud he was, or how hard the bass was pumpin' through the speakers, he couldn't get Jewell's words out of his head. *I don't know you!* She hadn't just said it to him, she had screamed it. She had insinuated more than once that Deena had targeted her. It was a very good possibility that Brian was just playing a sick ass game, but the thought of anybody, especially Deena, wanting to hurt Jewell so bad was making his blood boil.

**It's the capital S, oh yes I'm fresh, N double O-P
D-O double G-Y, D-O double G ya see...**

He banged the beat against the steering wheel with his fists, not realizing where he was headed until he got on the highway. Subconsciously, he had decided to confront Deena. She'd gone as far as paying a woman to spy on him. The thought had never crossed his mind that she would do something like that, but it had certainly worked out in her favor. He couldn't help but wonder how much information Victoria had on him and Jewell, and if Deena would actually take things that damn far.

~~~

"Damn, slow down Boss Lady." Mason grabbed Deena's hands and held them behind her back. "Why you in such a rush?"

"Because you're in my *house*." Deena spat, trying to free her hands.

"Black ain't comin' home. He wit' his other chick, remember?" Deena's expression got dark. "Ok," he smiled. "My bad." He let her arms go and she went to work on his jeans. Her attitude was on ten. Fuck Xavier. Fuck Jewell.

Fuck Victoria. What she wanted right then at that moment, was for Mason to shut up and fuck *her*. She needed help to clear her mind before all hell broke loose. She knew from experience that Mason's dick could knock more than a few things free.

"I want you to make me scream," she told him.

"You know that's not a problem at all." Mason stepped out of his pants and yanked Deena's capris down. "You should've been naked and ready when I got here," he scolded her.

"Next time," she answered before she thought about it.

"Oh, next time?" he asked, perking up. She huffed and he spun her around and bent her over the back of the couch. He stooped down and dug his face between her cheeks, enjoying every lick. Deena bucked at him, moaning and gripping the pillows, trying not to fall.

"I'm cummin'..." she moaned after a few minutes, causing Mason to speed up. "I'm cummin'!" she yelled. Mason got a grip on her hips as her body started to vibrate.

"Stop runnin'," he told her as he stood and slapped her butt. She jumped and spun around, grinning in Mason's face. He stooped down and picked her up, sliding her down on his dick. He moaned as she tightened around him, watching her throw her head back in ecstasy. Before they could enjoy it good, the beeping of the front door alarm cut the sex short.

"Shit," Deena whispered, trying to grab her capris. "Oh my God, move." She pushed Mason who tried to stoop behind the couch. There wasn't much floor between the front door and the living room. While Deena was scrambling around, Mason already knew what time it was. He tried to slide in his pants anyway, even if only to save a little of his dignity.

"I knew I recognized that damn Cutlass," Xavier stood in the doorway of the living room watching Deena and Mason fumbling with their clothes behind the couch.

"Baby-"

"Save it, Deena." Xavier's voice was flat, like he didn't give a damn, and that scared her. He walked over to the couch and Deena and Mason froze, until he stuck his hand out. Mason stood up straight, his pants still unbuttoned, and stuck his hand out too. "Wassup, my dude?" He took Mason's hand and yanked him close to pound his fist into his back. "You're fired." Mason backed up abruptly.

"Man, how you gon' fire me for somethin' personal?! I work my ass off for you!" Xavier laughed out loud.

"Nigga who you think you work for? You ain't at Firestone. You at *Black's*. That's my shit and I say yo' ass is gone." Mason looked from Xavier to Deena, who had her eyes glued to the floor.

"You ain't even gon' say nothin'?" he asked her.

"Naw she ain't gon' say shit," Xavier answered for her. "Now get the fuck outta my house." Mason, fuming, snatched his keys off the table and stormed out, muttering to himself about how it was bullshit. Xavier kept his ears towards the door until he heard Mason's car start up and pull off, then he turned to face Deena.

"Xavier," she came from behind the couch and walked towards him, pleading. "It's not what it looks like!"

"Oh, really? So you weren't just fuckin' one of my employees in my living room?" To say Xavier was tired would be an understatement. He was mentally and physically drained. He hadn't had much sleep, a couple of hours in the hotel with Jewell and a little at the shop. His head was banging at the sight of Deena with Mason's dumb ass.

"I can explain," Deena started with tears in her eyes. She hadn't been thinking straight and she needed him to know that.

"I'm not interested."

"How can you not be interested?!" Deena yelled. His whole *I-don't-give-a-damn* act was getting old. She knew he had to be falling apart inside, just like she was.

"What's surprising was Mason disrespecting me as a man and as his manager. But you? I always assumed you were cheating."

"Well ain't that the pot callin' the kettle black! Like you ain't been havin' sex wit' Jewell?"

"Oh, so you do know?" Xavier's eyebrows furrowed at the thought of what she'd do for revenge.

"Damn right I knew, lyin' ass. Y'all were havin' sex back then too, huh?"

"I didn't have sex with Jewell then, and I haven't had sex with her now. I've had opportunities to, but it hasn't happened." Deena rolled her eyes. "You can believe me or not, I don't really care. What I wanna know is, did you do anything about it?"

"What opportunities did you have?"

"You think we havin' sex, right? Me and Jewell?" Xavier yelled. Deena crossed her arms. "So what did you do about it?" Xavier's chest was heaving with each breath. He didn't want to believe that Deena was capable of something so horrible. Then again, he had never expected to catch her having sex with somebody in his house.

"What do you mean what did I do about it? I fucked Mason." Deena caught what seemed like a relieved look on Xavier's face and became livid. "What? Did something bad happen to your little *Jewell*?" she asked. Xavier shook his head and turned to leave. He was positive she had spent her afternoon running her mouth to her sisters.

Mason had been at the shop when Jewell stopped by, trying to chew him out, and it was evident that he couldn't wait to spill the beans. "Where do you think you're going?" Deena asked, hurrying to block the door.

"Move." Xavier said nonchalantly. He accomplished what he had come for, to look Deena in the face and find out if she had tried to hurt Jewell. He had his answer and was ready to go.

"No, Xavier, I need you here," Deena pleaded. Xavier closed his eyes and put his face in his hands. "Please, I can't live without you." She was grasping at straws. He grabbed her by the waist and pulled her away from the door. "If you leave, I have nothing to live for!" At that, Xavier spun around and yanked Deena to him. For a split second, she thought she had him, until she noticed the look in his eyes.

"There's a little girl at your mom's house who goes by the name of *Miranda*." Deena was quiet, ashamed even. "You may not act like you give a damn half the time, but she *adores* you. And all that shit you talkin', it's not cute, and it's definitely not gonna make me wanna stay." He gave her a gentle push away from him, causing her to stumble a little. Without waiting for her to think of a response, he was out the door.

Ch. 27

Jewell made her way through the hospital doors in a daze, trying to keep her thoughts on Brian. Even as she made it to the desk, she couldn't get Xavier off her mind. Before she could speak to the nurse, she was bombarded.

"Where the hell you been?! And why didn't you call us?" Neeka screamed. Daisha was right behind her. "Yo' mama had to call us and tell us to come up here for moral support because they have Alicia, but the nurses here won't even tell us shit!" Neeka was in panic mode. The man she loved could be somewhere dead for all she knew, but since she wasn't his damn *wife*, she had to wait for Jewell.

"The better question is why didn't she call us?" Jewell spun around at the woman's voice and was met with the glaring eyes of Brian's parents. The two of them and Neeka started talking a mile a minute and Jewell grabbed her temples, trying to suppress the headache that had been growing since she got the call from the E.R. Daisha felt sorry for her. She was obviously stressed out. She had seen which hall Brian's parents came out of, and took the opportunity to slip away. She didn't know what to expect as she peeked in each room. When she finally found Brian, he was propped up staring at the ceiling. She glanced up and down the hall, making sure no one was paying attention, before she eased the door open.

"Brian?" she whispered, being careful not to scare him or cause him to make any sudden movements. She didn't know where he'd been shot or how serious it was.

Brian turned his head slowly towards the door. The doctor told him he had been hit twice, once in his side, and once in his hip. The pain had been so incredibly excruciating, and even after surgery and all the medication he had been pumped with, he wasn't feeling much relief. It was all a blur from the moment he stopped at the light. There had been loud noises, pain, and commotion. He had been in and out of consciousness. The next thing he remembered was his parents fussing over him. They were asking question after question, messing with machines, cursing Jewell, wondering where she was and why they had to hear the news from her parents instead of her. He wouldn't dare tell anybody what was going on between them. And make himself look weak? *Hell* naw! He couldn't deny the fact that he wanted her by his side to help him get through the pain. He had allowed his hopes to get up when he heard the door open, but he groaned when he heard Daisha's voice. By the time he was able to focus on her, she was at his bedside.

"What'chu doin' here?" he asked. She started to talk, but he cut her off. "Where is my *wife*?!" he yelled with an attitude. Daisha shook her head.

"Jewell is up the hall gettin' chewed out by your parents," she stated matter-of-factly. Brian looked back up at the ceiling. "I just wanted to check on you. We didn't know if you were half dead or what."

"Well, as you can see, I'm still kickin'." He tried to scoot up and groaned. Daisha dropped her head.

"Still in a lot of pain, huh?" she asked.

"I got *shot*, Daisha. What the fuck you think?" She was working on his last nerve.

"Oh, God," Daisha broke down.

"Man, get on wit' that shit. I ain't dyin' or nothin'. Stop that damn cryin'."

"I'm so *sorry*," she sobbed.

"What'chu sorry for? You ain't-" Brian stopped short, looked over at Daisha and squinted at her. "This was *you*?" he asked in disbelief. Daisha nodded, crying and shaking. "Are you fuckin' kiddin' me?!" Daisha slumped down in the chair next to the bed. "Stop that fuckin' cryin! If I could get outta this bed I swear to God I'd beat the shit outta you!"

"I was just doin' what you asked!" Daisha blurted out.

"I didn't ask you to shoot *me*! Shit I *didn't* ask you to shoot *Jewell*! I wanted yo' ass to try and scare her, not *kill* her. And what happened to waiting for the okay from me? Did I give you a gotdamn green light?!"

"I saw the opportunity and I took it!"

"And look where thinkin' for yourself got you!"

"I'm sorry, baby," Daisha mumbled through sobs. Brian groaned and turned away. Hearing her call him baby made him regret givin' her the D. He had been so mad when he found out Jewell had left Alicia at her house a few months back that he was willing to do whatever to get his anger out. Daisha had always been so quiet and had never paid him any mind, unlike Neeka. He thought he'd have to lay it on thick, but after a few compliments and a couple rubs on her neck, it was smooth sailing. He had talked her through her guilt easily. It was obvious to him that both of Jewell's closest cousins, the chicks she called her best friends, were jealous of her and shady enough to give in to him. He knew that if he played his cards right, he could get whatever he wanted. After he got the feeling that Jewell was moving reckless, he wanted her to pay. He had wanted her to be scared shitless and run to him, but he knew Neeka was too damn crazy to even ask. He was starting to think that shit ran in the family.

"All I said was that I wanted to teach her a lesson and you took that as you needed to shoot at her?"

"*Please* forgive me," Daisha begged. Brian glared at her. He had to suppress the urge to grin. He was proud of his dick. A few fucks and some good ol' school game and he had her ass goin'. He prided himself at how easy it was for him to get into any woman's head, and he definitely knew how to pick 'em.

"This is a hell of a thing to try and make up for, Daisha." He spoke softly and grabbed her hand. "Where would you even start?"

"Wherever you want me to start." Daisha bent her head down, thankful that Brian seemed to be coming around.

"Daisha?" they both jumped at Jewell's voice. "I was wondering where you slipped off to." She moved slowly towards the bed, slightly confused as to what she had walked in on.

"Everybody was arguing. I just came in to pray wit' him a little. Figured he needed it."

"Thanks, Daisha," Brian said, sliding his hand away. Jewell gave her a half smile, happy there was at least one person who wasn't trying to go off on her. She had felt like she was being jumped by Brian's parents and by Neeka. She had tried to explain to them that her first reaction after she got to the E.R. was to try and figure out what happened. She practically had to beg them to let her go to the room. "It's good to see you up." She smiled at Brian and it was so warm and genuine that it made him second guess all the foul things he had done to her. He smiled back and glanced at Daisha who squeezed Jewell's shoulder and made her way out the door. He couldn't help but think that maybe her fuck up had done a little good. "How are you feeling?" Jewell asked, settling in the chair beside the bed.

"Better, now that you're here," he responded. Jewell smiled again and looked down at her hands. Her wedding ring still shimmered on her finger. She twiddled it around and around with her emotions tangled. She loved Brian for the daughter they had together, and in no means did she want to see him in pain the way he was, despite all the hurt he had inflicted on her. In no way, shape, or form was she still in love with him, she just wasn't cold-hearted like he was. If the tables were turned, she wasn't sure he'd be sitting with her while she was laid up. So why, she wondered, had she pushed Xavier away? What was she afraid of? "Jewell?" Brian called. She had been on a daze.

"Yeah, I'm sorry."

"Oh," Brian exclaimed. "Just a heads up, we gotta try and get somebody over to clean the house before we get discharged."

"We?" Jewell asked in surprise.

"You don't expect me to go home like this alone do you?" He asked, feeling himself getting angry.

"Brian," Jewell shook her head. "We already talked about this-"

"Fuck that, Jewell. You comin' home wit' me!" Brian jerked his arm and caught Jewell's shirt. She yanked away, causing him to groan in pain. Jewell stood and shook her head, laughing a little.

"Wow. This is amazing. Even while you're laid up in a hospital bed with bullet holes in you, you are still able to be an ass."

"Jewell," Brian tried to calm himself. "I need your help when I get outta here."

"That's not my problem anymore, Brian." She turned towards the door feeling empowered.

"Jewell!" Brian yelled, but she kept walking. "*Jewell*!!" he screamed at the top of his lungs as the door closed softly behind her.

Ch. 28

*D*aisha sat hidden in a bathroom stall, rocking back and forth. The severity of what she had done was hitting her hard and she was cursing herself in her head. When Brian had called her a few months earlier looking for his daughter, she hadn't thought anything of it. He had stopped by to get Alicia and then sent her in the basement to play.

"Wassup?" Daisha had asked him. He looked her up and down, making her feel naked. She blushed and turned away. "Um, is something wrong?" she asked nervously.

"Did I ever tell you how attractive you are?" he asked.

"No," Daisha responded glaring at him. "Why are you telling me now?"

"Sexy women should know they're sexy, right?" he asked. Daisha frowned at him. Brian started walking towards her and she scooted away until her back was against the living room wall.

"What are you *doing*?" Daisha asked, holding her hand out to keep Brian from getting any closer. She was scolding herself for the way her body was reacting to him. Her pulse was racing and she could feel that all too familiar heartbeat between her legs that she hadn't felt in God knows how long. The excitement that a flesh and blood man gave her was much different than a toy, no matter what anybody said.

"Come on now. Don't act like you ain't never thought about it." Brian inched closer, daring Daisha to move her hand from his chest. She honestly hadn't thought about it at all. Who in their right mind would think about having sex with their cousin's husband?! But there she was, wet as hell, anticipating what was about to happen. Brian stopped an inch away from Daisha's face, paralyzing her. She wanted to slap him. How dare he?! But he smelled *so* good. She kept telling herself to move... *MOVE*! She pushed against his chest.

"Brian, I-" Before Daisha could finish, he grabbed her hand and pinned her arm above her head. She stared at him, startled, and he smiled at her. It was a sexy, horny smile that she of course had never seen from him before. For a moment, she was speechless. Brian took a good look in Daisha's eyes and could see the longing wavering behind them. He laughed inside, initially thinking she'd be more of a challenge. Then he smiled even harder, convincing himself that she wasn't easy at all, he was just *that* good. He went in for the kill before she could protest, grabbing her breasts, kissing her neck, making sure he held her ass up good against the wall just in case she tried to stop him. If she was serious about him stopping then he would, but he could tell by the moans and the grip she had on his head, that stopping him was far from her mind.

What the hell am I doing?! We need to stop!! Despite what Brian thought, Daisha's mind was going crazy. It had been over a year since she felt a man's touch, and Brian had her head in the clouds. She *knew* she needed to stop him. She *knew* it was wrong. She *knew* Jewell would kill her.

"Brian," she managed to moan. "We need to-" He stopped her with his lips on hers, actually surprised at how soft they were. When he felt her sink into the kiss, he began lifting her shirt. She started to panic, not wanting him to see her naked. He moved back so he could look into her eyes.

"You ain't got nothin' to be worried about," he whispered, slowly easing her shirt up. He didn't break his gaze as he slipped it up over her head. "Let me make you feel the way you deserve to feel." He reached behind her and unhooked her bra, freeing her huge breasts. His eyes danced at the sight of her chocolate nipples, and he stooped to give each one a lick. Daisha threw her head back, biting her bottom lip, and Brian dipped a hand into her pants. She tried to grab his wrist, but he was too quick. Once he found that dripping sweet spot, it was over.

"What are you doin' to me?" Daisha asked, unable to believe she was half-naked with her cousin's husband in her living room.

"Do you want me to stop?" he asked hitting her G-spot with expertise.

"Oh...God..." Brian took that as a no. Suddenly aware that Alicia was still playing in the basement, he decided to go ahead and get it over with. He turned Daisha around and yanked her jogging pants and panties down before she had a chance to comprehend what was going on. He gave her a soft bite on her thick, bubble butt. Like second nature, he retrieved a condom from his pocket, ripped it open, and slid it on his dick, surprised that Daisha had him rock hard so soon after he'd been with Neeka. He pulled her back some and bent her towards the wall. He stooped and rubbed the head of his dick against her clit, trying to get her ready. She was already wet as hell, but he knew he was packin'. What he hadn't expected was for her to be so tight. Her shit felt like virgin pussy. She gasped when he worked himself into her, slapping her hand against the wall.

"Damn," Brian found himself enjoying her. Once she got in her groove, she started throwing it back at him and

forbidden distractions   *t.c.flenoid*

he had to hold on tight. She had a lot more body than he was used to, and had him wondering why he had shied away from big girls all those years. She was rollin' that ass like she had been waiting for him. They grinded, grunting quietly, until Brian finally came. "You got a lil' magic in that thang, huh?" he asked, staggering back away from her. Daisha blushed, momentarily forgetting that it was her cousin's husband standing in front of her.

"That ain't the half of it," she responded.

"Oh, is that right?" He leaned around the wall and dropped the used condom in the hall trash. "You gon' let me find out about that other half?" He zipped his pants as Daisha pulled hers back up.

"We'll see," she told him, knowing she was fronting. He had hit that spot that had her hooked already. She felt the trouble she was getting herself into, but also felt powerless to stop it. Brian was slick as hell and had her eating out of the palm of his hand so fast that Daisha didn't even know it had happened. She'd listen to him talk about thinking Jewell was cheating and try not to let it get to her. It was a stroke of luck, running into her at Wal-Mart, shopping like she hadn't just beat her man with a skillet. She tailed her to the hotel, and when she told Brian, he was more than grateful. He had no problem showing her just how grateful he was. When they were together, he made her feel like the most important, most beautiful woman ever. Granted, they never did anything other than have sex, but he had awakened a fire in her she had all but forgotten about. She knew it was a fantasy that could all come crashing down at any minute, but when he told her he wanted Jewell to learn a lesson, she felt obligated to pay him back. She wondered how Jewell could always seem so unhappy, and wanted to help her see that she needed him. Twisted as it sounded, she wanted to help the both of them. Brian had planted the seed and that was all it took.

    Being a short, big woman living in the city alone, Daisha kept her gun and taser by her side at all times. When she saw Jewell, or who she thought was Jewell, she reacted and sped off, figuring she'd scare her back into Brian's arms. It happened so fast that it seemed she blinked and it was over. She spotted the car going the opposite direction, pulled her gun, floored the gas, and fired as she sped past. She barely took a breath until she made it safely to her garage. She sat there for a moment in shock, thinking about the argument Jewell and Neeka had had at her house, wondering if she felt the same and just never realized it.

    Thinking she had shot Jewell's tires was enough to make her have a panic attack. After a while, she started to think about how Brian would thank her for what she had done. She got chills thinking about the things he did to her, the way he manipulated her body to do things she had no idea she could do. Her phone rang before she had built up the nerve to call and tell him. She glanced at the caller I.D., seeing that it was her aunt. She panicked wondering how Jewell's mom knew it was her, then snapped out of it, knowing there was no way she could. Daisha would never forget the sinking feeling when she heard the news.

"Daisha! Baby, Brian was shot and I have Alicia so I need you to go meet Jewell at the hospital!" Daisha drove like a maniac, realizing the horrible mistake she made. There was no way it could be a coincidence. She had fucked up... *bad!* How could she have been so incredibly stupid?! She knew she'd never be Brian's woman. She was just a filler while Jewell did whatever it was she was doing. She knew that eventually the affair would have to stop, but she never would've guessed that it would have this ending! She had taken the opportunity to ease away before Jewell started questioning her real reason for being in Brian's room. Now alone in the bathroom stall, she had a few quiet moments to contemplate the past three months, her horrible decisions, and even her sanity.

"Daisha?" She jumped at Neeka's voice.

"Yea, I'm here," she moaned, opening the stall door.

"Damn, girl, where you been? I been lookin' all over for you." Neeka stopped when she saw Daisha's face. "You been cryin' that hard?" she asked. Daisha broke down and Neeka put her arms around her. "Calm down. Jewell said that nigga gon' be ok." She tried to soothe her cousin, but she was getting irritated. What was *she* so damn upset for?

"You don't understand, Neeka."

"What don't I understand?" Neeka asked with her head cocked.

"It was me. I did it," Daisha mumbled. Neeka took a step back and looked at her.

"What did you say?" she asked, positive she had to have heard her wrong.

"I shot Brian," Daisha sobbed. Neeka huffed and grabbed her head, feeling the room start spinning. She blinked a few times and her breathing fell short. She cocked her hand back and swung, knocking Daisha into the bathroom wall.

Ch. 29

"What the hell, Neeka!" Daisha cried, grabbing her eye.

"What the hell, *Neeka*?" Neeka yelled back. "You *shot* him!" Her blood was boiling.

"You *hit* me-"

"What the fuck happened?" Neeka grabbed Daisha's shoulders and started shaking her like the answers would fall free. Daisha yanked away and leaned against the wall, watching Neeka pace back and forth, wide-eyed and swinging her arms back and forth like a mad woman. At first, she was confused as to why Neeka lashed out the way she had, but it quickly started making sense. The sudden hatred for Jewell, the arguing, the fakeness, the damn sucker punch to the eye... She walked over and put her hand on Neeka's shoulder causing her to jerk away. "Get away from me. You don't wanna be touchin' me right now," she growled. Daisha nodded, backing up a few inches, and the two stared each other down.

"How long you been fuckin' him?" Daisha asked. Neeka laughed nervously, and folded her arms, wondering how she made the assumption.

"What are you talkin' about?" she rolled her eyes. No way was she about to tell the truth and have Brian mad at her. The last thing he needed was to find out she was confiding in the bitch who shot him. Daisha was lucky all she was gonna have would be a black eye.

"I know you fuckin' him, Neeka." Daisha shook her head. She knew first-hand how Brian got down. His dick was so dangerous he had them doing stupid shit and turning against each other and Jewell. Neeka glared at her.

"What make you think that?"

"Just admit it. I am." Daisha was frustrated that Neeka wouldn't say it, like her secret was a precious diamond that needed protection.

"You are *what*?" Neeka laughed. She knew damn well Brian couldn't possibly be hittin' that when she satisfied him front, back, and side to side.

"He used us-"

"Aw naw, see he ain't usin' me. Brian loves me." Neeka was fuming. There was no way in hell Brian had been with Daisha. "You know you lyin'!" Daisha was about to go off, figuring Neeka was trying to take jabs at her weight. Little did she know that Brian had licked every inch of her with no complaints, and loved it. That was beside the point at the moment, though.

"You know what's sad, I can't even call you delusional without sayin' the same thing about myself."

"Shut up, Daisha!" Neeka yelled and kicked at the stall door. She couldn't be telling the truth, could she? There had been a point when Brian wouldn't give Neeka the time of day, no matter how much she begged. Had he been ignoring her to spend time with *Daisha*?! It hurt enough to think that he been putting her off for Jewell, but that could be explained away. Technically, Jewell *was* his wife, but Neeka knew in her heart that *she* was the one he loved, married or not.

"Why do you think you did it?" Daisha asked. She, herself, was quiet and private and didn't put herself out there are all. Neeka was opposite in every way. She demanded attention everywhere she went, and men seemed to flock to her. She could quite possibly get whoever she wanted. So why Brian? Why her cousin's husband? Daisha knew exactly what her problem was. She hadn't been looking for a man, and they weren't exactly breaking down her door. It had been forever, she was horny, Brian was persuasive, and he was damn good- addictive. It was a hypocritical question, but she still wanted to know.

"I don't know what you think this is, but it ain't a fuckin' therapy session! He don't want you and y'all ain't fuckin'-"

"I don't know what the hell your problem is!" Daisha had had enough. "You act like I can't get a man."

"Nobody who wants me would touch you!"

"Fuck you, Neeka!"

"Fuck you!"

"What is goin' on?!" Neeka and Daisha turned and saw that Jewell had burst into the bathroom. "People are all outside the door listenin'. I walk up tryin' to be nosey and hear y'all cursin' each other out." They both stared at Jewell with their mouths hanging open. "*Somebody* start talkin'. Wassup?"

Daisha turned her eyes towards the wall. She had never planned on saying anything to Jewell about sleeping with Brian. It was what it was- sex. Furthermore, it was over. She definitely wasn't about to say she shot him. That would be crazy on her part. She was sure Neeka wouldn't rat on her because she had secrets of her own.

"We're arguing because Daisha shot Brian." Neeka blurted. Without warning, Daisha pulled her fist back and slammed it into Neeka's face, sending her stumbling back into a stall.

"Really, bitch?!" she yelled, watching Neeka try and pull herself up. Jewell shook her head, confused by what she had heard. Before she had a chance to say anything,

Neeka had bounced out of the stall, still trying to focus, and swung back, missing completely. "That's all you got?" Daisha asked. "Big, bad Neeka who think she better than everybody else and all she is is a hoe." Jewell couldn't believe what was going on. *Daisha* shot Brian? Her head was banging.

"I'm a hoe? What does that make you? That's *if* you tellin' the truth. I still think you lyin'."

"Ok both of y'all shut up!" Jewell was irritated out of her mind. Neeka and Daisha looked at her, both heaving and out of breath. "*Daisha*! Is she telling the truth?" The silence in the air said it all. Daisha didn't want to tell her the truth, but she hadn't had time to come up with a lie. She didn't think she'd have to, but Neeka's snake ass had thrown her under the bus the first chance she got. There was no telling what else she'd say. Jewell stared at Daisha, unsure of what she was feeling. As much pain as Brian had caused her over the years, she felt like she should be praising whoever put him out of his misery. It was petty, but it was the first thing that came to mind.

Daisha didn't know whether to be loyal, or to be ignorant. She glared at Neeka, realizing she couldn't do it. The weight of everything began to crush her, how weak she had been, how badly she had betrayed her cousin, her *blood*, the fact she possibly could have ended a man's life, and because of what? Some *dick*? She broke down again just as a random woman walked in.

"Just a minute!" Jewell yelled and turned back to Daisha.

"I'm sorry- I- I didn't..." Daisha sobbed, unable to get her words out. Neeka rolled her eyes and folded her arms. Jewell softened, walked over to Daisha, and wrapped her arms around her.

"How did you know?" Jewell asked, assuming Daisha had shot Brian in her defense. What other reason could there be? Daisha tried not to stiffen in Jewell's embrace, wondering what she was talking about. After a long pause, Jewell backed away, causing Neeka to speak up.

"I told her," she said. Daisha was utterly confused, but Neeka knew exactly what Jewell was referring to, and she couldn't wait to tell Brian. First she'd go off on him for fuckin' Daisha. She knew her cousin didn't have a reason to lie, and it hurt like hell. And she still needed to know the real reason Daisha shot him. It damn sure wasn't because he put his hands on Jewell, since she obviously had no idea about that. She knew she wouldn't get any answers with Jewell around, so she'd just have to be patient. As soon as she found out though, Brian would hear it from her first. He'd never wanna touch Daisha again. When Jewell leaned in and gave Daisha a hug, Neeka was outdone. She gawked at them in horror. Daisha had shot Brian, and Jewell was actually *comforting* her! When the truth came out, she was sure he'd leave Jewell.

"You told her what exactly?" Jewell needed to know what her cousins knew, or *thought* they knew.

"I told her Brian was puttin' his hands on you." Neeka said. Daisha fought to keep her composure, surprised and disgusted at the accusation. "I didn't think she'd *shoot* him though." Jewell exhaled and dropped her head.

"I tried to hide it for so long." Jewell took a few deep breaths, relieved that her secret was out. Daisha didn't know what to say, so she leaned in and hugged her again. Now that she knew Brian wasn't just a cheating husband, but an abusive one also, her views on him changed drastically. She looked past Jewell to Neeka as she stood mugging them. She didn't know how Neeka knew the truth, or what her angle was, but she knew she wouldn't get off that easy.

Ch. 30

Xavier had his lounge chair pulled to the middle of his office so it could recline all the way back. He lay there staring at the ceiling trying not to laugh, but it was a shame he designed his office like a mini man cave just in case he needed to crash there. It was more than just office comfortable, it was *home* comfortable. He even had a shower. He told his workers it was just for rare instances when he had to work on a car, but that had never been the case.

He clasped his hands together to put them behind his head and realized he still had on his wedding band. Thinking back, he was surprised he hadn't flung it at Mason. He took it off to sit it down and the soft clank it made on the table in the silence of the office seemed so final. The rollercoaster with Deena was far from over, though. He had made sure he stopped by Deena's parent's house to see Miranda. She seemed chipper, and his soon to be ex in-laws weren't acting any differently towards him. He was positive Deena hadn't spoken a word of what happened to them. She was much too focused on keeping up appearances, and was way too proud to admit that she had done anything wrong. He prayed he wasn't in for a fight when it came to their daughter. He didn't have the patience to go through a custody battle, and he didn't have the stomach to expose Deena for the half-ass mother that she was. That would really weigh heavy on his conscience.

He glanced at his watch. It was almost midnight and what a day it had been! He hadn't heard back from Jewell. He wanted so badly to just say forget it and call her. She was seriously messing with his mind, and his ego. He had tried his best to understand why. Why couldn't she see that the shooting wasn't random? He felt in his gut that in some way, that Brian was behind it. He had always been an asshole, so why did Jewell act like she didn't know? If Brian treated her like gold and for whatever reason, Jewell just wasn't feeling him, then he could see her being hesitant to end things. But she had so many reasons to leave, so why had she continued to go back?

It crushed Xavier's heart to hear the pain in Jewell's voice, to read her letters about how much she wanted a new life, and to have Brian still standing in the way of her happiness. He laughed a little thinking of the way she had stormed in the shop with her accusations. It was a logical assumption, and he could see how she'd be upset. It was surprising and hurtful though to have her kick him to the curb while she defended her relationship with Brian- yet again. He was a much better man, of that he was 100% sure. So why wouldn't Jewell choose *him*?

Xavier looked at his watch again and huffed. It was late, but he decided he needed to get out. His circle of friends had been having fun without him for the past few months while he had immersed himself into his shop expansion. He'd been out to celebrate with them once, but Deena had insisted on coming and clung to his hip. He couldn't really be his reckless talk shit with my friends self. He needed to throw back a few and let loose.

He let the chair up and that's when he heard it. He thought he was trippin', but he could've sworn he heard knocking. He grabbed the glock from his desk and pulled the office door open. He stood there for a minute before he heard the knocking again. He took the steps down two at a time, eager to get in somebody's ass. It was late, much too late for anybody to be there looking for service. Once he reached the ground floor, the thought occurred to him that it may be Jewell. He tried his best to calm his heartbeat on his way to the window. He looked out of the blinds and groaned.

"What do you want, Victoria?!" he yelled through the glass.

"I heard you were single!" she yelled back. The way Deena had called and chewed her out, she knew it was over.

"How did you even know I was here?" he asked.

"Slits in the side door, baby." Xavier shook his head. Victoria was far past crazy. He had purposely parked in the car bay so no one would know he was there. Deena or Jewell may have actually looked into the doors off the side street looking for him, but what the hell did this random chick want?

"You got paid for a job. You did it. It's over."

"Can we have a conversation as friends?" Victoria leaned against the door eagerly listening to the silence.

"We aren't friends. Go home!" Xavier was done going back and forth with himself, because Victoria was obviously not listening to a word he was saying. He turned and climbed the steps to his office, irritated. *Why couldn't it have been Jewell?*

"We can be though," Victoria responded. She smiled and bit her bottom lip, waiting for him to finally give in. "Xavier?" she called out. She stood, feeling foolish, and waited a few more seconds before she knocked again. "I know you hear me!" She banged on the door, hurting her fist in the process. Pissed, she stormed back to her car. For a quick moment, Xavier had her second guessing herself, then she laughed it off. Naw- she was sexy as hell, and what man didn't like to be chased? She wondered if he was actually in love with that other chick. To Victoria, Jewell was a basic bitch. She could blow her out of the water on her worst day. She flipped down her visor, reapplied gloss to her full lips, and blew herself a kiss. Jewell didn't have shit on her. The night was still young and she wasn't about to let her freak'em dress go to waste. She put her jeep in drive and peeled off.

~~~

    Deena had barely gotten any rest. She had Miranda sleep in the bed with her because she couldn't bare sleeping alone. She had never felt so weak. Going over everything that had happened, everything Xavier had said, him catching her with Mason... she put her face in her hands and shook her head. For the first time in her life, she had no idea how to come out on top. She lay in her lounge chair staring at Miranda while she slept. Xavier had been right about a few things. He *had* been a prize for her. It seemed like every female in school wanted him. So many people had laughed at her and dogged her in high school, but *she* was the one who finally won him over. *She* was the one who got pregnant and made him put a ring on *her* finger. She was an ugly duckling turned swan, and she wanted to be treated like a queen. She hated to admit it, but at times she *was* a spoiled brat. Xavier gave her whatever her heart desired, but it was never enough for her. She always wanted more. More money, more time, more freedom, but what had she given him, besides his daughter? She had been a shitty wife. It took him to walk out on her for her to see it. She wrapped her fingers in and out of the belt of her satin robe, deep in thought. As much as she messed up, and it had been a lot, she couldn't stop thinking about Jewell. The more she thought, the harder she wrung that belt around her hands. They had her fucked up.

She got up with a new attitude and took a nice, long, hot shower, soothing some of her stress. She got Miranda ready, made her a bowl of cereal and sat her in front of the television. She pulled her hair up off of her face, the way Xavier liked it, and put on a flowing blue halter top, capris that hugged her ass, and black flats. She threw on a little eye-liner and lipstick and she and Miranda were out the door.

From the moment she realized that Xavier was back in touch with Jewell, she had been all over her Facebook, and Instagram. She'd googled her and even looked to see if she could find anything on Case Net. There was barely any activity. From what Deena could see, Jewell didn't post much besides pictures of her and her daughter- who she inspected thoroughly to make sure looked nothing like Xavier. She shared empowering woman posts and memes, which, to Deena, meant she needed empowerment her damn self. There was one picture of her husband, a family photo from when their kid was still an arm baby. They weren't friends on Facebook, but people had started tagging the two of them together the night before saying they were praying for them. It didn't take much lurking to find out that her husband had been shot. She wanted to feel bad, but she really didn't feel anything at all. She wondered if Jewell felt anything either. From the looks of it, she barely claimed the man and had commented dry 'thank you's' under all the prayers and well wishes. Deena figured that since they had a kid together, Jewell had to go to the hospital at some point. Hopefully she wasn't crawled up in Xavier's ass somewhere. Deena groaned at the thought and kissed Miranda on her forehead.

"Have fun with Granny, ok baby," she told her as she dropped her off at her parent's house. Whenever Jewell decided to show her face at the hospital, Deena would be ready for her. She didn't care how long it took.

Ch. 31

"Daisha, stop worrying. I told you I'm not gonna say anything." Jewell had been bouncing between her cousin's guilt and Alicia's questions about her daddy all morning. Tired of the calls, texts, and Facebook alerts, she had decided to turn her phone off the night before so she could get some sleep. That only made things worse with Daisha.

"I thought you were pissed and ignoring me! Why didn't you answer?!" she screamed at her.

"I didn't answer anybody, cousin! I just wanted to get some rest!" They had all hugged it out and decided to end their conversation then and there before they left the bathroom. There was no telling what nosey people in the hallway had overheard already. Jewell told her cousins they'd have to continue in private and that was that, or so she thought. She turned her phone on when she woke up and all the notifications she had missed started pouring in. She rolled her eyes at Daisha's voicemails and texts, but she knew she needed to call her back before she did or said anything stupid. The last thing she needed was for Daisha to get locked up for protecting her.

"What are you doing?" Daisha asked. "Can we talk now?" She was so paranoid that everything would blow up in her face. Brian knew, and she wanted to be sure he wouldn't tell anybody. She had been so sure that Neeka would keep her secret, but she ratted her out the first chance she got. She hadn't completely spilled the beans, so Daisha knew she hadn't heard the end of it.

"I'm on my way to the hospital-"

"The *hospital*?!" Daisha yelled.

"I'mma need you to calm down." Jewell whispered, like her parents were really paying attention. She almost wished she didn't know. She gave herself a once-over and nodded in approval. She didn't have any extra clothes there and her mom's striped summer dress didn't look half bad on her. "I have to keep tabs on him for Alicia. What do you think I'm going for, to snitch on you?" Daisha was quiet. "Look, go get a massage. Go get your nails done. Didn't you tell me you got a lil' boo? Go get some dick." Daisha cringed. "However you need to do it, you *have* to chill out."

"Mommy, can I sleep in my own bed tonight?" Alicia was tugging at Jewell's dress. "Daisha, I'm sorry, I have to go." She hated to do it, but she hung up on her before she could respond. She felt like she was coddling Daisha like a child. She had *one* daughter, not two. Daisha did what she did and yes, they still needed to have a conversation about it, but in a weird way, she didn't even care. Brian was out of the woods. The initial shock of him having been shot had worn off, and a feeling of freedom was seeping in. She needed to face him. She needed to tell Brian how he had made her feel like less of a woman, wife, and mother for years. He may have thought he had broken her all the way down, but she was slowly building herself back up. Confronting him was her first task of the day. Her second would be to take her house back. She had no idea what shape the house was in, but she figured she could have Neeka and Daisha come over and help clean up while they talked. There were tons of details missing, and hopefully they'd be filled in by the time they finished.

"Remember, mommy told you we were taking a little vacation with Granny and Papa?"

"Yes, but I miss my toys," Alicia pouted.

"You have toys here." Jewell reminded her. She hurried around, grabbing her purse and her mom's car keys. "I might be able to bring a couple more things from home today, okay?" she told her, frowning at the disappointed look in her eyes. All she had told Alicia about her daddy was that he was sick and had to get better in the hospital. Brian's mother had left a message wanting to pick Alicia up, but Jewell was hesitant about calling her back. All the accusations and yelling at the hospital the day before had her feeling some type of way. They *were* her grandparents, but she had to put that on hold for the time being. She kissed Alicia's forehead, thanked her mom for letting her use the car, and was on her way.

    Of all the messages and texts she had, none had been from Xavier. She hoped there would be, but honestly, how much pushing and pulling could she expect him to put up with before he cut ties. She had done it plenty of times and she was sure he had to be tired of her. Her burning question was, if she called would he talk to her? She thought that he would, but she couldn't be positive. As much as she'd rather think about Xavier, she had to shut that down. She'd be pulling up at the hospital soon, and she needed a clear head to confront Brian.

~~~

    Deena's butt had fallen asleep from sitting so long. Her feet were tingling and she had to pee. She'd been there a couple of hours already, and she was getting antsy. She assumed Jewell hadn't spent the night at the hospital and prayed she wasn't with Xavier. The thought made her chest tighten. It was only a few minutes later when Deena saw the familiar face coming her way. She had gotten so tired of hearing Jewell's name when she and Xavier were just starting out. She would remember that face anywhere. It dawned on her that maybe it was a little ignorant to confront a woman at the hospital while her husband was recovering from being shot, but desperate times called for desperate measures. She waited until Jewell was close enough, then stood with her heart pounding, to block her path.

"Well, would you look here," she said plainly, trying her best to keep a straight face and not focus on Jewell's perfect, caramel complexion, thick, curly hair, or the way her hips and chest popped out of her dress. *Pretty bitch...*

Jewell stopped dead in her tracks at the sight of Deena. She was gorgeous, a drastic improvement since high school. She could feel the intimidation rumbling in her gut. She hadn't really thought about what Deena would do if she ever got wind of what was going on. The only thing she could think was *oh shit.*

"Don't look so confused. I'm sure you know who I am." Deena was proud her voice didn't waver, even though she was on the verge of tears. She couldn't help but think about everything Xavier told her she didn't do, all the times he said she didn't listen to him, how she didn't satisfy him, and every opportunity she ignored to say or do something supportive. Had Jewell done any of those things? Had she done *all* of those things?

"Yea, Deena-"

"Xavier's *wife*." She cut Jewell off and watched her fidget. "Does it make you uncomfortable to hear that? That I'm his *wife*?"

"Why would that make me uncomfortable?" Jewell bluffed. Staring into the face of the wife of the man she had tried so desperately not to love since she was a teenager was about as far from comfortable as she could be. She'd much rather be yelling at Brian.

"Oh it bothers you." Deena folded her arms and sneered. "I can see it in your eyes." There were so many things Jewell wanted to say, so many things that could shut Deena up, but she wasn't that type of person. Plus, she didn't have a leg to stand on. Xavier was married, and she *knew* it. All the late night conversations, the secret lunches and meetings, the kisses... through all of it, it was never a secret that he was married. True, he had given Jewell the impression that he was unhappy, but there was absolutely no way for her to be certain of what he was telling Deena- his *wife*- who had no problem flashing her huge wedding ring. She was nothing to Xavier, a friend at best. After their last conversation, she wasn't even sure of that. If Deena clocked her upside her head with that ring, Jewell figured she just as well deserved it. How was she supposed to fight for someone who didn't even belong to her?

"Like I said, Deena, I'm not uncomfortable at all," Jewell lied. "Xavier and I are old friends and that's it-"

"I'mma say this one time," Deena cut Jewell off and walked up until their noses were almost touching. "I have no problem fuckin' you up Jewell," she whispered. "Stay the hell away from my husband and take care of yo' own shit." Deena purposely knocked shoulders with Jewell as she stormed past on her way out.

Jewell was fuming and embarrassed, even though there was probably no one paying attention to them. She didn't want to believe that Xavier had lied to her all this time and that he and Deena were perfectly fine. She huffed on her way to Brian's room, wondering what business it was of hers. At that point, he probably didn't have anything else to say to her anyway. After Deena had made it a point to confront her, at the *hospital* no less, she'd have to be a real bitch to reach out to him. There was no reason for the 'tell your wife to leave me alone' text, or the 'are you still with her because she sure acts like it' text. She had pushed him away again, and whatever he did after that she couldn't bother herself with. The only thing she knew for certain was that her own marriage was over. If nothing else had come of her time with Xavier, she appreciated that he had helped her see that she deserved better than what Brian had given her over the years.

Ch. 32

"You need to tell me what the fuck is goin' on, babe." Neeka paced back and forth in her living room. She had been trying to get in touch with Brian since the night before, blowing his phone up with calls, voicemails and texts until he finally decided to answer. Brian sighed and switched his phone to his other ear. It was always something with Neeka. That's why he hadn't bothered answering. He was the one shot, so how was he the one getting yelled at?

"Tell you what's goin' on wit' what, Neeka?"

"Wit' you and my damn cousin!" she yelled.

"Why do we have to keep goin' over this? Your *cousin* is my *wife*-"

"Not that cousin, asshole!" Neeka yelled making Brian pause. "Yea nigga, cat got'cha tongue?"

"What are you even talkin' about?"

"Admit it, Brian! Daisha already did! Who the fuck do you think you fuckin' over? I'm tryin' to deal wit' you and Jewell, but you expect me to have to try and deal wit' you and Daisha too?"

"*Deal* wit' Jewell? How the hell does yo' crazy ass think I have you *dealin'* wit' my wife?"

"Bet you didn't know yo' lil' side bitch was the one who shot you!"

"*What*?!" Brian yelled in a panic. His whole body hurt and he couldn't tell if it was from being shot, or pure anger at Daisha for running her damn mouth. What did she say to Neeka? He thought about the way she had broken down the day before, wondering if she'd been spilling her fat ass, retarded guts to Jewell since she had obviously told Neeka everything.

"Did I stutter, nigga?" Brian closed his eyes and slammed his head back onto his pillow. "Oh and you should've seen the look on your wife's face when Daisha told her." Brian's heart dropped. He squeezed his phone so hard his fingers started to hurt. His mind focused on wrapping his hands around Daisha's neck. Never had he wished so bad that he hadn't fucked somebody. At least Neeka had kept her mouth shut. Just as he was fantasizing about hurting Daisha, his room door creaked open. At the sight of Jewell, Brian ended the call with ease, sliding his phone away from his ear and stuffing it under his sheet.

"Hey, baby," he smiled at her trying to judge her demeanor, but he couldn't.

"Hi, Brian." Jewell gave a half grin as she moved to the chair beside the bed. Once she sat down, she glared at her husband. All of the years spent with him flashed through her head. The bad definitely outweighed the good. Alicia was the single solitary bright moment that came out of their twelve years.

"Hopefully they won't hold me that much longer and I can be back home in no time," Brian told her. The sound of his voice made her want to reach out and slap him. The sight of him disgusted her, and not because being in a hospital bed made him look any worse, but because she had let this man make her feel like less of a woman, wife, and mother. He had belittled her, abused her mind and body whenever he felt like it, and exposed their daughter to it. Sure, she had played her part by staying, however big or small that had weighed into the equation, but no more. She took a deep breath before she started.

"Brian, I need you to hear me, okay?" Jewell made sure to keep her distance. He may have been shot, but he had already proved he was still the same old Brian. "I'm not sure if you thought I'd change my mind about us because of this-"

"What'chu mean?" Brian asked, seemingly confused. Jewell shook her head in disgust.

"This is one of the things that drives me crazy, Brian. You can't act like I didn't tell you it was over two days ago. I hate seeing you laid up like this, but it doesn't mean I'm gonna go soft on you. It doesn't mean I want you back, or that I'm gonna help you recover. You need to find somewhere else to go when you get discharged."

"What the fuck you mean?" Brian sat up, attempting to get out of his bed. Jewell hopped out of the chair and backed up towards the door. Brian grabbed his side, but was determined to get to Jewell. She had lost her damn mind.

"This is one of the reasons we are where we are! It's your attitude! You act like you don't remember me telling you it was over. You don't remember me leaving you at the party?" For a moment, Jewell's thoughts drifted to Xavier, but she quickly got herself back on track. "I refuse to get on this rollercoaster with you again."

"If this is about Daisha..." Brian started, causing Jewell to snap her head back. He paused, studying her reaction. *She doesn't know anything...* He was gonna ring Neeka's neck. Between those three women, him getting shot, and Jewell threatening to leave him, he had let himself slip up. That was something he did *not* do!

"What about Daisha?" Jewell asked, squinting. She waited impatiently for him to answer. There was no way Daisha would've told him she was the one who shot him. She had to wonder again, why she was in his room the day before. What had they been talking about, and why had she been so upset? There had to be more to the story. Brian blinked twice, trying to come up with a lie.

"You mad 'cause she was in here yesterday."

"I'm really not, but I'm sure that ain't why you brought her up."

"Why else would I bring her up?"

"I don't know, Brian. You tell me." Jewell folded her arms and watched him closely as his jaw tensed up.

"What the hell you got all these questions for? You come in here tryin' to tell me I can't go back to a house where I pay the damn bills, then you wanna accuse me of shit."

"I'm not accusing you of anything," Jewell said with a slight laugh.

"I don't see shit funny," Brian growled, trying to unhook himself from the machines he was plugged up to. Jewell turned on her heels and headed out the door with him calling after her. She practically ran down the hall and out of the hospital doors. The thoughts swimming through her head had her feeling like she was about to pass out. What the *hell* was going on?! She thought about how upset Daisha had been, how she'd caught her and Neeka arguing, and how Neeka had jumped to her defense. She thought about how much shade Neeka had been throwing lately, especially when it came to Brian. And she had been mad as shit when she hadn't called her to let her know he was in the hospital. She text both Neeka and Daisha asking them to meet her at her house later. She felt like she had so many pieces of a puzzle but didn't quite know what the picture was. She was sure in the hell gonna find out though.

Ch. 33

"You went off on her while she was on her way to see her husband in the *hospital*?! Damn sis, you ruthless!" Deena laughed at Trena. Of course she had embellished a little, added more curse words and down played how pretty she thought Jewell was. She had definitely left out the part where Xavier caught her and Mason ass out and told her it was over. Nobody needed to know she went to see Jewell out of desperation instead of anger. She was trying to keep the tiny ounce of dignity she had left until she figured out how to get her man back, and she was determined to get him back.

~~~

"Do you think she knows?" Daisha paced back and forth on the phone with Neeka. She had answered Jewell's text to meet at her place with no problem, but the thought of being confronted about anything had her frantic. She had no idea what she was gonna say once Jewell started in on her with questions. Neeka had thrown her under the bus, then covered her butt in the same breath. She had a bug up her ass about Brian and wouldn't let it rest. It crossed Daisha's mind to not show up to Jewell's at all, but she knew she couldn't hide forever.

"Calm the hell down," Neeka scolded on the other end. "And stop frontin'! If you gave a damn about Jewell's feeling then you wouldn't have been fuckin' Brian."

"You are too!" Daisha yelled. Neeka sucked her teeth.

"Who said I gave a damn about her feelings?" Daisha rolled her eyes. At least she felt some guilt. "What I'm dyin' to know is why you did it in the first place. I know damn well it wasn't because he was beatin' on her. I wonder if *Jewell* even still believes that. I covered for yo' ass and I could've easily snitched on you so you owe me the truth and I wanna know!" Neeka listened intently, until she realized she had been hung up on. "Oh hell no she didn't," she yelled. She called Daisha back four times before giving up. She tried calling Brian back, knowing she wouldn't get an answer. She had been calling on and off since he had hung up on her earlier. She couldn't understand why he was so mad at her when Daisha was the one who hurt him, and Jewell was the one who didn't give a damn. The only woman who truly cared about him was her. She shook her head, knowing that eventually he'd come around. She started getting ready, even though Jewell was the last person she wanted to see. A meeting between the three of them was drama that Neeka couldn't pass up though.

      She decided to try Brian's phone again. Yea, he'd been shot and probably needed to rest, but he had another thing comin' if he thought she was gonna continue to let him ignore her. She needed answers. What possessed him to have sex with *Daisha*? Why hadn't he hit the roof when she told him Daisha was the one who shot him? Had he been putting her off to spend time with *her* ass? When was he finally gonna stop bein' a punk and leave Jewell? She smiled to herself, wondering if Jewell was gonna tell them that she was leaving Brian. She had been acting like it for God knows how long. She couldn't wait for Jewell to finally let Brian go so there'd be nothing keeping them apart.

<p align="center">~~~</p>

    "Mason won't be coming back," Xavier finally told his staff after he got tired of the questions. He wondered if a few of them knew, or even assumed that something was going on with Mason and Deena. He tried his best to put it out of his mind. The last thing he wanted to think about was more disloyal employees. He knew he'd have no problem replacing Mason, he was just upset because the boy was damn good. He couldn't have anyone working for him that didn't respect him though. He started going through the numerous applications he had, needing to replace Mason sooner than later. Before he could get settled in good, there was a knock at his office door. "Yea," he called, looking up from his computer screen. He groaned when Deena walked in, staring at her with a flat expression, uninterested in whatever it was she had to say.

"Hey," she said quietly, closing the door and sitting across from him. He nodded at her and folded his arms. Deena closed her eyes to keep from rolling them. She knew he wouldn't make a scene at work, but by the way he was acting, she could tell he wasn't in the mood. "I want you to know I listened to every word you said, and I *heard* you." Xavier answered with the same blank stare and Deena cleared her throat. She wasn't used to this side of him. She was used to getting her way and he was acting like a butthole. "I don't believe in divorce, Xavier, and I'm willing to do whatever you need me to do-"

"Deena," Xavier shook his head.

"No, you got to talk yesterday. Now it's my turn." Xavier leaned back and put his hands in his lap. "I don't believe in divorce, or breaking up families, or any of that. I want us to work. I'm able to look past anything that happened with Jewell and just get us back on track." Deena stopped and the two of them stared at each other in silence. It finally dawned on Xavier that Deena was done talking.

"That's it?" he asked, smiling.

"What do you mean *that's it*? And what are you smiling for?" Deena had had about enough of Xavier's bullshit. He'd had his fun and so had she. They both had a lapse in judgement, but it was over and it was time to get back to normal.

"You didn't listen to *anything*, Deena." Xavier shook his head. "You never have."

"How can you say that?" she yelled at him. "I'm here! I'm trying-"

"Trying to what? Piss me off?"

"Piss you off *how* exactly?"

"You come in here like you're really tryin' to turn a new leaf, which woulda been hard to believe anyway, but you still don't take the blame for anything! You're gonna forgive *me* and look past what *I* did?! I keep tellin' you nothin' happened, but obviously your mind is made up."

"Xa-" He held his hand up before she could finish his name.

"You came in here and said what you had to say now it's my turn. I suppose since *you're* bein' kind enough to look past *my* shortcomings that the least I can do is look past yours, right?" Xavier popped up from his chair and Deena jumped. "I guess I can look past the years of feelin' like I was beggin' for attention from my own wife." He rounded his desk to get closer to her. "I guess I should just get over you bein' so damn selfish and treatin' me like a bank instead of a husband." He grabbed the arms of the chair and bent down in Deena's face. "I guess I'm supposed to act like I didn't catch you fuckin' my employee *in my house*," he growled and gave the seat a little shove. Deena was caught off guard with her mouth hanging open, staring up at him. He turned away and leaned against the door. "You *paid* a crazy bitch to follow me around-"

"That's not fair, Xavier!"

"What's not fair?"

"The only reason I did that was because I knew somethin' was goin' on."

"And exactly what was goin' on, huh? What did you make up in that mind of yours?"

"I know what I *didn't* make up." Deena caught her second wind, and got up from the seat. She stopped arms-length from Xavier. "I didn't make up you bein' in a hotel with that bitch!" Xavier grinned and nodded, crossing his arms.

"At that point, Deena, I was done. And at least I had the decency to take her to a hotel instead of fuckin' her in the house. That's flat out blatant-"

"Oh, so you admit you *did* fuck her!" Xavier closed his eyes and rubbed his temples.

"I can't do this, Deena. I don't *wanna* do this."

"Do this *what*, get caught up in your lies."

"I don't wanna argue and give myself a headache for no reason. It doesn't matter what you say. I'm just tired. I'm done." Xavier felt like a weight was lifted off his shoulders. He loved Deena for giving him the most amazing daughter, but he couldn't remember ever feeling like he was deeply in love with her. From the time they were just messing around, to getting her pregnant and basically being forced into marriage, and then treating him like a trophy husband- he hadn't had time to fall in love, as horrible as that sounded. Deena had taken advantage of his kindness for much too long. She was a beautiful woman. He was sure it wouldn't be hard for her to find another man to spoil her rotten.

"You let that bitch get to you," Deena snapped. Xavier sighed and dropped his head. It was pointless. "We'll see if she still feelin' you when her *own* husband get out the hospital." Xavier huffed, not surprised at all that she knew about Brian. "See if she still want you after I got done goin' off on her ass." Xavier looked up and glared at Deena, wondering what the hell she had said to Jewell. "Oh, that got a rise outta you, huh? You know what, I'm too good for you anyway! It's a million niggas out there dyin' to have me!" Xavier nodded and twisted his lip up, ready for Deena to leave. "Fuck her. You and that bitch can have each other." Deena grabbed her purse. "And fuck you too!" She stormed out the door and slammed it as hard as she could, putting a crack in the frosted glass.

Ch. 34

Jewell pulled up to the house she had shared with Brian, regretting asking her cousins to come over. She had no idea what she was about to walk into, but it was time to start putting her life in order. Her morning definitely hadn't gone as planned, but she'd said what she had to say to Brian. She'd been trying to shake off her encounter with Deena all day so she could have a clear head to talk to her cousins. Hopefully she could get to the bottom of whatever was going on with them.

Jewell was nervous as hell, putting her key in the lock like she was walking into somebody else's house. Nothing could've prepared her for what she saw. She almost broke down when she turned the light on. Her living room was in shambles! The couch cushions had been ripped open, pictures were knocked off the walls and thrown across the room, there was glass all over the place, a lamp was broken, and there was a hole in the wall where she assumed Brian had put his fist through. Of course, the television was still intact. She had to scoot the coffee table out of the way to get down the hall. Their bedroom was littered with clothes and shoes, the bathroom mirror was shattered, and the kitchen floor was covered with broken dishes with the table upside down against the refrigerator.

Jewell was speechless. What she knew as her life had been shattered in two days. She had half a mind to call her cousins and tell them to forget about coming over, but she was much too curious about what they had to say. She closed her eyes and took a few breaths, trying to calm herself down. When she finally did, she grabbed the trash can from the bathroom and went to the living room to start getting the glass up. Not five minutes later, there was a knock at the door. She looked out the window and saw Neeka on the porch. Pushing away her embarrassment, she pulled the door open and stood aside, letting her in.

"Hey-" Neeka stopped mid-sentence. "Damn it look like y'all asses got raided by the feds. What the hell happened in here?!"

"*Brian* happened." Jewell closed the door and put her hands on her hips.

"*Brian* did this?" Neeka looked around and scrunched up her face. *No way.* "You sure?"

"What'chu mean, am I sure? I didn't do it and Alicia sure as hell didn't." Jewell grabbed the trash can with an attitude while Neeka stared around with her mouth hanging open.

"What for?" she asked, looking for a place to sit her purse. The house looked like shit, but she couldn't help thinking about when Brian made love to her in the bedroom.

"I told him I was leaving him," Jewell said without looking up from the glass. Neeka almost choked on her spit.

"You *what*?" she asked. Did she hear her right? She held her hand over her mouth to hide her smile, hoping she looked surprised.

"I'm getting a divorce. I can't do it anymore." Before Neeka could say anything, there was a knock at the door. She breathed a sigh of relief, knowing she was about to say something stupid. She needed to have something else to focus on before she spilled her own beans.

"Cousin!" Daisha yelled once Jewell let her in. She and Neeka shot a glance at each other, then stared at Daisha as she stumbled through the living room. "Oh damn, look like a tornado hit this bitch!"

"Daisha, are you drunk?" Jewell asked, already knowing the answer.

"You damn right!" Daisha laughed and Neeka laughed right alongside her. Jewell rolled her eyes.

"You don't drink like this. What's wrong?" Jewell scooted Daisha back against the wall to keep her steady.

"I'm a grown ass woman, *Jewell*!" she yelled. "I needed to be drunk to come to this bitch anyway."

"Ok, what is the problem?" Jewell was irritated. Daisha only drank socially, and clearly, she'd gone far past her limit.

"I didn't mean to fuck him. Well, that first time I didn't. But *shiiiit*, once you pop." Daisha started laughing and bouncing her butt and Neeka gawked at her in horror. Jewell leaned back, putting all her weight on one foot, and crossed her arms.

"You didn't mean to fuck *who*?" Even as she asked, Jewell felt like she knew the truth, no matter how foul and unthinkable it was. She'd been trying to ignore the intuition she had, but the anxiety was building up in her chest, making it feel like she was about to explode.

"At least I don't love him. She the one all in love and shit." Daisha pointed in Neeka's direction and Jewell swiveled her head. Neeka held her hands up in the air.

"I ain't in love!" she lied, fighting the urge to tackle Daisha. She had wanted things to go her way, but that drunk bitch was spoiling it. Jewell let out a low laugh.

"Who y'all fuckin'?" she asked, staring Neeka dead in her face. Neeka wanted to say it. Everything in her wanted to admit it. She'd waited for years to get it off her chest, but for the life of her, his name wouldn't leave her lips.

"I always knew yo' ass was a punk." Daisha cut in. Jewell spun around to face her. She knew the answer, but she needed to *hear* it. She needed to hear them *say* it. "Cousin, yo' husband fucked everybody in this room."

"*This* bitch," Neeka flung her arms and spun around dramatically. Jewell couldn't take her eyes off Daisha. She couldn't move. It felt like if she did, her head would explode.

"This bitch *what*?" Daisha yelled at Neeka. "You so mad Brian wanted a big girl and got tired of yo' skinny ass?"

"Please, he love this thick ass!" Jewell smashed her hands on her temples, unable to believe what she was hearing. They were talking like she wasn't even there. Her *cousins*. Her *blood*!

"If he loved it so much, why was he grippin' all on this?" Daisha squeezed her titties and Jewell squeezed her eyes shut. "You desperate and wantin' to fight me because I was puttin' it down like you couldn't."

"*Desperate*? Bitch you the one who shot him because he was done wit'cho ass."

"*What*? Naw, he *wanted* me to do that! I was tryin' to help y'all!" Daisha told Jewell, who was finally able to convince her feet to move.

"Who the hell is believin' that bullshit?" Neeka laughed as Jewell made her way to the kitchen. She grabbed the mop and headed back to the living room

where her two trifling cousins were still arguing...
over *her* husband. She flipped the mop up and swung the stick twice, first catching Neeka in her back, then on the back of her thigh.

"What the *fuck*, Jewell!" she screamed out in pain. Daisha started laughing and Jewell caught her in the chest. Immediately, Daisha's laughs turned into crying as she doubled over in pain.

"Ok, I guess we deserve-" Jewell swung again, hitting Neeka's right knee, before she could finish her sentence.

"*Cousin-*" Jewell swung again and hit Daisha's thigh, shutting her up.

"Y'all bitches need to get the fuck outta my house before I lose my damn mind." The two of them stared at her like she already had. Daisha took a step forward, but Jewell cocked the mop back, ready to swing again. "Get-the *fuck*- outta my house-*now*!!" Daisha and Neeka eased out of the house quietly, and Jewell slammed the door behind them. She leaned against the wall and slid down it, flinging the mop out in front of her. Unable to do anything else, she curled up in a ball in the living room and cried herself to sleep.

Ch. 35

"Aw damn, dissolution of marriage, huh?" Tori had snuck up behind Deena sitting in the cafeteria at work.

"Don't you know how to mind your own business?" Deena asked, flipping her papers over.

"Nope, that's why you were paying me, remember?" Tori quipped. "You messed around and lost all that man." She shook her head at Deena. She'd given up on Xavier, knowing that if he'd given her the chance, she would've made his toes curl.

"For your information, I felt it was best if-"

"Girl! Why are you lying? I've been looking over your shoulder long enough to see that Xavier filed those papers." Deena hopped up, grabbing her belongings, and stormed away, trying not to pay attention to Tori laughing after her. Feeling like she was about to have a panic attack, she hurried out to her car so no one would see her break down. Once inside, she really let go. When Xavier dropped the papers off at the house a week earlier, Deena thought she'd lose her mind. She got home from work and they were sitting smack dab in the middle of the coffee table. She ripped the envelope open and called Xavier as fast as her fingers could move. He, of course, tried to convince her that it was a long time coming and that it was for the best. To her, that was a crock of bullshit. She'd done an amazing job lying to her family, pretending like things were as perfect as they had always been, but how the hell was she supposed to hide a divorce?

~~~

"Oooh *shit*. Yes- yes- yeeesss..." Neeka pulled her locs out of her face and slid her hands between her legs to play with her clit. She sucked her teeth as she was being dug into from behind. Not wanting to cum just yet, she spun around and stroked the dick in her face. "You shole don't fuck like somebody who was laid up in the hospital less than a month ago."

"Why you keep bringin' that shit up?" Brian slapped Neeka's hand away and turned to find his clothes. Just that quick she had messed up the mood.

"Damn, you leavin' because of somethin' I said?" She sat up on the edge of the bed and crossed her arms, wondering if she'd ever finally get tired of him. "I thought once you moved in here you'd stop actin' like yo' shit don't stink. No wonder Jewell put yo' ass out," she griped.

"What?" Brian laughed at her. "Jewell put me out because you and yo' cousin stupid asses couldn't keep y'all mouths shut!"

"Naw, nigga she was done wit' you a long time before she even knew about us. I don't know why yo' dumb ass entertained Daisha anyway when this is really where you wanna be."

"You think *this* is where I wanna be? In here wit' yo' crazy ass?" He pulled his shirt down over his head. "I'm here because I know you won't tell me no. I can come, go, shit, eat, and fuck when I want for free, and I know you down for that because you down for *me*. You want the best for me, but you know I'd rather be with my daughter."

"You know I'mma always be down for you, baby." Neeka eased over to Brian, wrapping her arms around him. He laughed to himself wondering how that was the only thing she paid attention to.

"I got a work meeting I gotta get to, though." He kissed her forehead and headed out the door, eager to get away. As soon as he got in his car, he started scrolling through his contacts, looking for any other bitch that would let him crash. He had a few he could call on for pussy, but none for a place to lay his head. What he had told Neeka was the truth. She was truly down for him, but she irritated the shit outta him at the same time. He was so tired of her, and he didn't want to burden his parents. He wasn't trying to pay for a room, but he'd have to.

He scrolled past Jewell's number, still listed under 'Wife', and wondered how he had managed to fuck up so bad. She hadn't spoken more than five words to him since the day she left the hospital telling him it was over. He hadn't even known about the blowup between her, Neeka and Daisha until he answered Neeka's sixth call. He had only answered that one because she text him saying 'she knows!' He had wanted to get up and break everything in the hospital room listening to Neeka telling him what had happened. He had cursed her out and hung up. He called Daisha to curse her out, but she didn't answer, and hadn't answered since. He texted her threatening to tell Jewell the truth, but that didn't work either. Probably because she knew as well as he did that there was no way he was admitting fault for anything ever.

Brian pulled over and thought long and hard about what he was about to do, then said fuck it and sent Jewell a text.

to Wife:
**I MISS YOU. YOU ARE STILL MY WIFE.
I KNOW THINGS HAVE BEEN ROUGH
BUT I BELIEVE WE CAN GET THROUGH
THEM. I NEED YOU AND ALICIA.
THE TWO OF YOU KEEP ME SANE.
I WANT MY FAMILY BACK.**

He sat for only a couple of minutes before his phone beeped in response.

from Wife:
YOU HAVENT LOST ALICIA. BUT
I FILED FOR DIVORCE. THE PAPERS
SHOULD BE AT UR PARENTS HOUSE
ANY DAY NOW.

Jewell relaxed on a park bench, keeping an eye on Alicia as she bounced all over the playground. She took a deep breath and smiled, enjoying the sun, and the freedom. It had been a hectic couple of months fighting with Brian, who had done everything in his power to stop the divorce. In the end, there was absolutely nothing he could say or do that would change her mind. To add insult to injury, she knew he'd been shacking up with Neeka while he had the nerve to be begging her to come back to him. She was at a place though where she could really care less. Once Neeka and Daisha walked out of her house that day, they were nothing to her. Daisha called repeatedly, sometimes once a day, sometimes numerous times. Jewell never answered though. She was so far removed from it that she didn't even want the details about the shooting. She didn't care. Maybe she could find it somewhere deep in the depths of her heart to forgive Daisha. It wouldn't be any time soon, but at least *she* showed remorse.

Neeka, on the other hand, was much too far gone. Brian had her head in the clouds. Jewell had no idea how long they'd been messing around, and she had no interest in finding out. Just knowing that it happened, and had continued to happen, was more than enough. Even though she knew she wouldn't answer, she thought Neeka would at least call or text an apology or something. There was no regret in her cousin's soul at all, but it was cool. Jewell wouldn't wish what Brian did to her on anybody, but she was sure that Neeka had at least gotten a little taste.

Explaining things to Alicia hadn't been as tricky as she thought it would be. She'd probably have plenty of questions down the line, but for the time being, daddy had moved out because they couldn't get along. Of course they made it known that it had nothing to do with her and that they both still loved her. She was still able to see her dad and it was understood that he'd forfeit that right if he brought any of his hoes around her, including Neeka. It had been a long road, but the divorce was finally final, and Jewell could think of no other way to celebrate that with Alicia. She let her mind wander for a moment to Xavier. She wondered what he'd been up to. She had long removed him as a friend on Facebook and scolded herself every time she thought about contacting him, which had been every single day. She shook her head and sighed, pushing the thought from her mind, knowing that ship was long gone.

Ch. 36

"*I* don't care what lil' work thing you got. I can't keep Miranda this afternoon." Deena yelled into the speakerphone while she concentrated on her make-up.

"It's not a little business thing," Xavier groaned, closing his office door. "It's the grand opening of my new shop."

"If I was still your wife, maybe I'd care."

"We know *that's* a lie," Xavier mumbled.

"Anyway, *baby daddy,* you are just gonna have to find somewhere for her to go, seeing as though it's *your* weekend."

"This had been planned for *weeks,* Deena. We had an agreement."

"Come get your daughter, Xavier Black!" Deena hung up and Xavier rubbed his temples. His ex-wife worked every nerve in his body. He looked at his watch and saw that he had two hours to get from his first shop in the Central West End, to St. Charles to pick up Miranda, find somewhere to drop her off, then get back to his new shop in University City. It was doable, if he left right then, but he shouldn't have to do it. Deena found every angle to irritate him, from flaking on plans with their daughter to posting bad reviews about his shop online. If it weren't for shared custody of Miranda, he'd have cut her completely off, but they were connected for years to come.

    Xavier snatched his suit jacket from the back of his chair and headed to his old house. He had since found a place in South City, much closer to his shops. He had only stayed in St. Charles because it was what Deena wanted. Now, he had just enough space for him and Miranda and he was fine with that. He didn't need all that extra space that Deena had wanted. That was her though, extra. When he walked up and rang the doorbell, he sighed, knowing it was about to be some bullshit. It always was.

    "Hey baby daddy." Deena eased the door open, making sure to stay behind it. Xavier crept in, staring at her suspiciously.

    "Are you hidin' from somebody?" he asked, looking out into the yard. Deena laughed and slammed the door, revealing her half nakedness. Her hair was in burgundy curls halfway down her back, her make-up was done to perfection, and her body was glistening. The red, lace bra

forbidden distractions   *t.c.flenoid*

popped against her light complexion, and it had her titties sitting up *right*. She spun around showing the matching panties that hugged her round cheeks. Xavier mistakenly let his eyes linger.

    "Oh, does somebody miss me?" Deena grinned, licking her fiery, red lips.

    "Put some clothes on." Xavier kept his eyes on her face. No doubt she was beautiful- on the outside, but he *knew* her, better than she knew herself. His ex-wife was a selfish, conniving, arrogant, cynical woman who patronized him, ignored their daughter, and left his manhood to question despite everything he'd done and had tried to do for her. He wasn't perfect, but he for damn sure wasn't as bad as her. And there she stood, thinking she could use her body to get to him.

    "Now you know you don't want me to put any clothes on." Deena reached her arms out and Xavier backed away and shook his head.

    "I'm out. I know Miranda's not here." Xavier went for the door and Deena hopped in front of it.

    "She's at my parent's house, but don't waste gas for nothin'. You're already here. You don't have to leave empty handed." Deena had put in too much time. She'd been working out, she had her teeth whitened, she'd waxed everywhere, her face was *beat*, and she paid way too much for those burgundy bundles. She was ready to win her husband back. Yes, she had signed the divorce papers, but it was under duress. She figured she had to give in a little, let him know she cared about what he wanted, and when the time was right, she'd win him back. The time had come.

"It's sad that you don't even see what you're doing."

"Sad?" Deena ran her hands down the front of her body. "Baby *nothin'* over here is sad."

"You thought you could use sex to get to me. You lied about Miranda and had me waste time drivin' all the way out here *today* of all days! This is a *big* day for me, Deena, and you still don't get it."

"I do get it. I was just playin' when I called it a little work thing. You know I care-"

"If you gave a damn about anything besides whatever is goin' on in your head, you wouldn't have pulled this shit today." He scooted Deena away from the door and opened it. "Don't try this again because it's not gonna work. Honestly you just seem desperate." He walked out and closed the door behind him, leaving Deena dumbfounded.

~~~

It seemed like the whole city showed up for Xavier's grand opening. He was looking like a million bucks in his grey, tailored, three-piece suit. He had made sure his new employees were dressed to impress too, letting them know it was definitely their time to shine. There was food and drinks of course, and Alli Mays blessed the event with her pipes. There were raffles and games, and he introduced his new crew. Even Channel 5 news and the St. Louis American paper showed up. According to them, he was the most eligible bachelor in the city. He laughed them off, though he was definitely feeling like a hood celebrity. His family showed up, and even Deena's parents and her sister, Lena, came with Miranda for a while to congratulate him. Xavier was on cloud nine. All his dreams were finally coming into fruition. Well, most of them.

~~~

"Man, I don't need nothin' else to drink." Xavier waved off the next round of shots his friends had ordered.

"Come on! We celebratin' ain't we?" another one yelled, laughing. Xavier couldn't help but laugh too. He had only had a couple of drinks at the grand opening. He wanted to seem like he could be laid back, but still keep a level head. The impromptu after party with his friends was completely different.

They'd been there almost an hour before he saw her. The Mexican restaurant, El Burro Loco, sat directly across the street from the Vodka Bar where he and his friends were. He could see Jewell through the glass that surrounded one side. He admired her as she laughed with the ladies she was sitting with. He could hear that laugh clear as day in his head, and he smiled to himself thinking about it.

It had been three months since Xavier had heard from Jewell, but he had thought about her every day. He always believed their paths would cross again, and wondered what he would say to her when they did, if anything. The last time they were together, she had yelled at him and claimed she didn't know him. He wanted to curse her clean out. She had cut him deep, but seeing her stirred up so much emotion. He couldn't take his eyes off of her.

"Wassup, man?" one of his friends asked, noticing he was zoned out. Xavier waved him off and took out his phone. He scrolled until he reached Jewell's name, something he had done numerous times over the past few months. This time, however, he wasn't planning on changing his mind.

to Jewell:
YOU LOOK ABSOLUTELY AMAZING TONIGHT

He sat, watching her intently, waiting for her reaction. He felt like a stalker but he didn't care. He wasn't about to pass up the opportunity. When she picked up her phone from the table, his heart started beating fast, praying she didn't sit it back down and ignore him. Instead, she snapped her head towards the window, confused, scanning the crowd outside. Xavier stood up, drowning out his friends, and walked out into the valet parking lane in front of the bar. When he and Jewell locked eyes, Xavier felt the same way he had that first time she showed up at his shop. He couldn't wait to be in her presence. He opened his arms, hoping she would take that as an invitation. When she got up from her seat, he told his friends he'd be right back, and crossed the street to meet her.

    Jewell was nervous as hell and way too excited at the same time. She tried, unsuccessfully, to calm herself down on her way outside. She was positive Xavier had gotten tired of her pushing and pulling him. She had no idea which way was up and which way was down the last time they had spoken. So much was going on then, and so much had happened since. She rounded the corner and there he was at the bottom of the steps, handsome as ever, waiting for her. As if by reflex, her heart skipped. She wanted to take the steps down two at a time to get to him and jump in his arms, but she kept it cool.

    "How you been?" Jewell asked. Xavier shoved his hands in his pockets, admiring her- the way her smile lit up her face and the cute, nervous expression he could tell she was trying to hide. Not to mention how delicious her jeans and heels had her hips looking.

    "You were right," he said.

    "I'm sorry?" Jewell asked, confused.

    "The last time I saw you, you told me you didn't know me." Jewell lowered her head. "I admit I was pissed and hurt." Xavier laughed a little, thinking back to that day.

"I didn't realize it then, but you were right." Jewell shook her head, unsure of what to say. "The Xavier you know is twenty and carefree. He hasn't lived or experienced life really. He's still a boy. This man," he took a hand out of his pocket and held it over his chest. "This man, you *don't* know." Jewell stared at him for what felt like the longest time, breathing heavy, taking in what he had said. "I see you're with some friends and I don't wanna impose, I just-" he stopped mid-sentence and grinned at her, making her melt. All of a sudden, he stuck his hand out. "Xavier Black." Jewell cocked her head, but reached out and grabbed his hand nonetheless.

"Jewell Rodgers," she stated. She felt his grip tighten a little.

"Rodgers, huh?" He couldn't hide how pleased he was at the sound of her maiden name.

"Newly divorced," she smiled, flashing her bare ring finger. Xavier wanted to do cartwheels up and down the street. Instead, he held up his own naked left hand. Jewell dropped her head and bit her bottom lip, trying to hide her relief.

"Well, I'm hoping we can get to know each other, Miss Rodgers." Jewell looked in his eyes and saw everything she felt herself- excitement, lust, sincerity...love... She took a deep breath before she answered, knowing there was finally nothing and no one standing in their way.

"Yea," she grinned, blushing at his gaze. "I'd like that."

The End